DEAD MAN'S WHARF

An Andy Horton Marine Mystery

Pauline Rowson

severn House

This first world edition published 2009
in Great Britain and in the USA by
SEVERN HOUSE PUBLISHERS LTD of
9–15 High Street, Sutton, Surrey, England, SM1 1DF.
Trade paperback edition published
in Great Britain and the USA 2009 by
SEVERN HOUSE PUBLISHERS LTD

British Library Cataloguing in Publication Data

Rowson, Pauline
  Dead man's wharf
  1. Horton, Detective Inspector (Fictitious character) -
  Fiction 2. Murder - Investigation - England - Portsmouth -
  Fiction 3. Police - England - Portsmouth - Fiction
  4. Detective and mystery stories
  I. Title
  823.9'2[F]

  ISBN-13: 978-0-7278-6769-8   (cased)
  ISBN-13: 978-1-84751-132-4   (trade paper)

All Severn House titles are printed on acid-free paper.

Typeset by Palimpsest Book Production Ltd.,
Grangemouth, Stirlingshire, Scotland.
Printed and bound in Great Britain by
MPG Books Ltd., Bodmin, Cornwall.

To Harry

ACKNOWLEDGEMENTS

My grateful thanks to Ian Barefoot, Project Officer, Diving into History of the Nautical Archaeological Society; to English Heritage at Fort Cumberland; and to Andy Luxton of the Kendalls Group, Portsmouth.

ONE

Monday 5 January

'Has Mr Jackson received death threats before?' Inspector Horton tried to contain the anger in his voice. Usually he took such matters seriously, but not this time.

'No, Inspector, and neither has Nick.' The woman opposite him dropped her eyes as soon as they connected with Horton's. Was that from guilt, he wondered, at wasting police time?

She was perched nervously on the large leather chair opposite him. The woman dressed from head to toe in black looked more like a nun without the wimple than a television director to Horton. But then he guessed his views of directors were coloured by newspaper and magazine articles where they were usually men of presence and power. *Wrecks Around Britain*, though, was hardly *Titanic* and Perry Jackson wasn't exactly Leonardo DiCaprio. Not that Horton had met Jackson yet as Corinna Denton had waylaid him and Sergeant Cantelli the moment they had entered the plush reception of the Queen's Hotel on the Southsea seafront.

On their way there, Sergeant Barney Cantelli had told him that the programme always contained an element of danger, which had convinced Horton that the anonymous threatening telephone calls were a publicity stunt designed to attract media coverage. He had bet Cantelli a month of free canteen lunches they were.

'Television personalities do get stalked, you know, Andy,' Cantelli had replied. 'There are some seriously weird people out there.'

'I know, I've met them.'

'Then why so sure these calls are fakes?'

'Let's just say I can feel it in my gut.'

Did he? Or was he simply angry that he'd been ordered here by his boss, DCI Lorraine Bliss, because of the status of Perry Jackson and his television partner, Nicholas Farnsworth. Horton had never heard of either of them, but that was hardly surprising when he didn't own a television on the boat where he lived.

'Where is Mr Jackson now?' he asked Corinna Denton.

'Having breakfast with Nick.'

The threats obviously hadn't affected his appetite then! Horton had missed breakfast. Not that he could have eaten a thing anyway. Since he had decided, in the middle of the night, to meet Emma at Heathrow Airport earlier that morning, food had become of periphery interest.

His mind slewed back to the arrivals lounge and Catherine's incensed expression as their eight-year-old daughter had run into his arms. He had promised Emma that she could stay with him on the boat. She was overjoyed. Catherine was outraged. A state she seemed to be permanently in regarding matters relating to him gaining access to Emma. He didn't know why. He guessed that Catherine was already on to her solicitor complaining. Well, let her.

He brought his attention sharply back to the matter in hand. The sooner he got this out of the way, the quicker he could return to the station and get on with solving real crimes.

'Where are your film crew?'

'Jason, our camera and sound man, is probably still in bed.'

Horton noted the slight shift in her tone that told him she didn't approve of this. Or perhaps she didn't approve of Jason.

'We work on a very tight budget, Inspector. If we need any extra lighting or cameras then we hire it in wherever we're shooting. We're only here for a few days, doing some external shots, meeting with the diving contractors, working out a schedule. And Perry's doing some additional research. He's writing a book.' Corinna said it as if it was the only book in the world, and maybe it was to her and Mr Jackson. 'The dive is being filmed in May,' she added, running a hand through her short dark hair. 'We'll call up anyone else we need then.'

So why the anonymous calls now if this was a publicity stunt? Surely it would have been better to have staged them when the programme was being filmed. But because Horton was a cynical copper, he asked, 'Are they showing the programme on television now?'

There was a slight hesitation and lowering of eyes before she answered. 'I think they're repeating the *Diving off Devon* series.'

You think! You bloody know. And the media attention this stunt would attract would draw in additional viewers. Not bothering to hide his contempt, he said, 'Have you mentioned these calls to the press?'

She looked surprised. 'Of course not. Perry didn't even want me to phone you. I wouldn't have bothered, only Nick insisted. If it had been just the one call, but three—'

'I'd like to speak to Mr Jackson.'

'I'll call him.'

'He's having breakfast, you said.'

Before she could stop him, Horton was marching across the reception area and heading for the restaurant, his eyes scouring the room for any likely looking media types. He wouldn't mind betting he was being filmed or that Corinna Denton had a Dictaphone stashed in her handbag. He had a deep mistrust of journalists and it wouldn't surprise him if his voice, and Cantelli's, rang out on the programme when it was aired. Something along the lines of: *Perry Jackson continued diving despite the threats to his life*. Well, bollocks to them, he thought, scanning the restaurant. No more than half a dozen tables were occupied and none of them with journos unless they had suddenly got a hell of a lot older.

There was only one table with two men sitting together. He didn't need to be a detective inspector to work out they must be Jackson and Farnsworth. They seemed to be arguing. Their heads were bent low over the table, their expressions serious. One of them definitely looked out of sorts. A deep frown showing on his receding hairline and a faint flush on his swarthy skin.

They both looked up as Horton drew level.

The man with the frown paused mid-sentence. 'Yes?' he snapped.

'Mr Jackson?'

'What is it? Can't you see I'm having breakfast?'

Corinna Denton, who had scurried up behind him, hastily made the introductions.

Jackson's frown didn't automatically vanish, but it rested on Corinna for a moment, before he forced his round features into an expression he obviously considered to be welcoming.

If that was welcoming, Horton thought he'd rather meet Dracula on a cold dark night in a cemetery.

Horton pulled up a chair. His first impressions of Jackson as a pompous prick were confirmed when the man said, 'I really don't know what you are doing here, Inspector. It's not at my behest.'

Who the hell used words like that these days? Prime Minister John Major had come close, but then even he was history.

Jackson was stockily built, with dark hair and hot, angry brown eyes that had a way of looking both through you and into you. Horton guessed he was in his early forties. He was the complete opposite of the fair man sitting across the table from him, who Corinna had introduced as Nicholas Farnsworth.

Farnsworth's expression assumed one of concern. 'Corinna is worried, Perry, and so am I. We have to take these calls seriously. Coffee, Inspector?'

'Thanks.' He might as well get something from this farce. He was even more convinced now that it was one after seeing the fake expression of concern on Farnsworth's face.

Catching the waiter's eye, Farnsworth commanded another cup and more coffee with an ease that Horton both resented and secretly admired. He had those rugged good looks combined with sophistication that made Horton instantly think of James Bond. Though the character rather than any of the actors who had played Bond over the years. He would have said that Farnsworth was a little younger than Jackson, but he could have been mistaken. He was taller with a leaner, more athletic frame. Horton wondered if Jackson was Farnsworth's plain man against the handsome and if he'd been cast because of it.

Horton addressed himself to Perry Jackson. 'Tell us about these calls, sir.' He thought that now that he was here, he might as well go through the motions.

Cantelli pulled his notebook from his jacket pocket and removed the small stubby pen from behind his ear while Horton shrugged off his sailing jacket.

'It's just some prank.' Jackson dismissed it with a wave of his hand. 'I told Corinna not to bother you. I hate fuss.'

'When did you receive the first call?' Horton ignored his protest.

Jackson frowned, and then obviously seeing he wasn't going to get rid of Horton easily, resigned himself to answering.

'Six p.m. yesterday. We'd only just checked into the hotel. The caller said, "Watch your back."'

That suggested to Horton that the mystery caller, *if* there had been one, had either seen them arrive or knew what time they had been scheduled to check in.

Cantelli said, 'Nothing else?'

Jackson swivelled his gaze. 'No. I said, "Hello, who is this?" and the line went dead. I hung up and didn't think anything of it. Then last night after dinner, I returned to my room and the phone rang. It was the same caller. This time he said, "You've been warned."'

'It was a man then?' Horton said.

Jackson looked surprised, as if Horton should have known that. 'Yes.'

'What time was this?'

'Midnight.'

'And this morning?'

'Just on eight.'

On the hour again. Horton wondered if that was significant. But if these two had organized the bogus calls between them, perhaps they thought it sounded more dramatic that way.

'This time the caller said, "You'll pay for what you've done."'

'Have you any idea what he meant by that?' Horton didn't really expect a sensible or an honest answer, and he didn't get one.

'If I had, I would tell you,' Jackson snapped.

I bet you wouldn't, Horton decided, wondering what Jackson had done to upset someone *if* these calls were genuine. He still had his doubts about that.

'It's just some weirdo,' Jackson added, echoing Cantelli's words earlier.

'You get them, Inspector,' Farnsworth intervened. 'Especially when you're famous.'

Hardly that, thought Horton, looking at Farnsworth to check he wasn't kidding. No, the man was deadly earnest.

He swivelled his eyes back to the scowling Jackson. 'Can you describe the voice?'

'I've already told you. It was a man.'

'Was there any accent?' Cantelli interceded.

Jackson frowned. 'No.'

'Posh voice or common?' pressed Cantelli, his pencil poised over his notebook.

'For heaven's sake, I've no idea.'

'Young or old?'

'Voices can be deceptive when heard on the telephone, Sergeant,' Farnsworth said pleasantly.

Horton bristled at his tone, or rather at the patronizing smile that went with it, but Cantelli simply nodded as though he'd just learnt something. Horton knew he was playing dumb cop. Cantelli was looking thinner than before his Christmas leave, Horton thought, and his dark eyes were sunk just a little deeper in his gaunt face. A shadow seemed to have fallen on his usually cheerful countenance and Horton knew the reason for it. On Thursday his father's funeral was being held.

'Sometimes you can get an impression, sir,' Cantelli said.

'Young rather than old then,' Jackson capitulated with exasperation. 'I mean his voice didn't quaver like some old people's do.'

Cantelli seemed to take a long time writing this down in his notebook, which Horton knew was a deliberate ploy. He noted Jackson's impatience and Farnsworth's disdain.

Horton asked, 'Who knows you're staying in the hotel?'

It was Corinna who answered. 'No one except us. I made the reservations myself.'

'What about family, friends, business acquaintances?'

'Oh, yes, sorry. I didn't think you meant them. It can't be anyone we know.'

'Perhaps you could give Sergeant Cantelli a list of names.'

Jackson exhaled noisily. 'It's a waste of time.'

'If you wouldn't mind, sir,' Horton said firmly, eyeing Jackson coldly. The man flushed angrily, but he pressed his lips together tightly. To Horton he seemed a man with a short fuse. 'Has anyone threatened you in the past?'

'Look, I'm sure you've got far more important crimes to solve than bothering with this.' He scraped back his chair, preparatory to rising, but neither Horton nor Cantelli moved.

'The call was on the hotel phone not your mobile?' Horton enquired.

'Yes.'

'Then it must have come through the switchboard. We'll check it out and ask them to screen all further calls to your room.' Now, Horton rose and gathered up his jacket. 'How long will you be in Portsmouth, Ms Denton?'

'Until Saturday.'

'You'll let me know if there are any further calls, Mr Jackson?' Horton extracted a business card and handed it over. 'Or if anything unusual happens?'

'If I must.' Jackson looked pointedly at his watch. 'Now, I've got a meeting for which I'm already late. I'll see you later, Nick.' Why did Horton get the feeling it sounded more like a threat than a friendly farewell?

Farnsworth addressed Horton. 'He's not usually that grumpy. These calls have unnerved him more than he wants to let on. You did the right thing by calling the police, Corinna, but as I said, Inspector, it's probably just some nutcase.'

Farnsworth now also glanced at his watch. Horton noted that it, like his clothes, came with a designer label and an expensive price tag, whereas Jackson's had been of the High Street chain-store variety.

'Time we were making a move, Corinna,' Farnsworth announced, pushing back his chair. 'Aren't we meeting the dive boat owner?'

She scrambled up, grappling for her phone in the depths of her capacious handbag. 'I'll call them to tell them we're on our way. Where the devil is Jason?' She was punching a number into her mobile as they left the restaurant.

Horton's gaze followed them. He was even more convinced it was a publicity stunt, but he said, 'I'll check with the hotel staff, just to show willing. Get a list of the people who know they're staying here, Barney.'

The duty manager confirmed that no calls had been put through to Mr Jackson's room at any of the times mentioned and there were no telephones available in the public areas that could connect directly to a guest's room, which meant that the threatening calls, if they had occurred at all, must have come from another hotel bedroom.

Horton asked for a printout of the guest list for the previous night and that morning. His request was greeted with as much enthusiasm as a health and hygiene inspector. He told them he would send an officer along to collect it later. He'd get DC Walters to run the names through the computer to check for any previous convictions. Of course, even if there was someone staying in the hotel with a criminal record, that didn't mean that he was the mysterious caller. It could be a member of staff. Until Jackson received another call – if he did – then Horton wasn't going to waste too much time on it. His desk was groaning with paperwork and not all of it crime related. This morning he'd found an email from DCI Bliss announcing yet another crap initiative called C.A.S.E. = R. He had no idea what it stood for because he hadn't bothered to read it.

'Farnsworth gave me a signed photograph for Marie,' Cantelli said, as Horton climbed into the car. 'She'll be chuffed to pieces.'

Marie was one of Cantelli's five children. The ten-year-old, Cantelli had explained to him earlier, was an avid fan of the programme.

'And the list of people who know they're staying here?'

'Corinna says she'll give it to us later. You should have heard Farnsworth rip into the poor sod of a cameraman,' Cantelli added, starting up. 'He made Superintendent Uckfield sound like a Sunday school teacher.'

Across the wet and windswept car park, Horton watched Farnsworth climb into a new Range Rover whilst Corinna pushed a large holdall into the back of an old Ford and made an impatient gesture to a thin, scruffily dressed scraggy man to get in. He wondered why they hadn't all gone together in Farnsworth's car.

The radio crackled into life and Cantelli stretched across to answer it.

It was Sergeant Stride. 'PC Somerfield and PC Seaton are at the Rest Haven Nursing Home in Whitaker Road, Southsea. They've got a bit of trouble and want assistance.'

'What kind of trouble?' asked Cantelli warily.

'Well, it's not armed response. I don't think the old dears are going to shoot their way to freedom.'

'Ha bloody ha.'

'There's a relative kicking up a fuss. Claims his mother's been assaulted.'

'By a member of staff?' asked Cantelli, concerned.

'No, by an intruder. There's no sign of a break-in though, and the manager swears blind no one's assaulted Mrs Kingsway. Somerfield says they've done their best to calm her son, but he won't have it. He insists on speaking to someone from CID, and DC Walters is still at Oldham's Wharf.'

Where Horton knew the detective constable was investigating a suspected break-in. He said, 'Tell them we're on our way.'

He was getting the impression it was going to be one of those days, full of frustrations and frayed tempers, and on top of the list was his. As they headed along the blustery, deserted seafront he wondered if he should call his solicitor, Frances Greywell.

He doubted, though, if she'd achieve the miracle of getting permission for Emma to spend some time with him next week, when he was on holiday. After this morning's debacle, Catherine would probably ensure he was prevented from seeing his daughter for at least another six months. Maybe it hadn't been such a good idea to go tearing up to Heathrow Airport. But it was too late for that now. Just like it was too late for many things – his divorce was progressing slowly and painfully, and his initial enquiries into the disappearance of his mother over thirty years ago had come to a stumbling halt.

Over Christmas he'd reread her missing person's file. It hadn't got him any further forward with fathoming out why she had walked out of their council flat one November day in 1978 and had never returned. He had thought about trying to track down some of the people who had known her, such as Irene Ebury, who had worked with his mother at the casino. Thoughts weren't action though and he knew his unusual indecisiveness was because a small part of him was telling him to let the dead past bury its dead and to get on with living.

His thoughts had taken him to the nursing home, where he could hear a man bellowing as soon as PC Somerfield answered the door to them. She hastily introduced Cantelli and Horton to the manager, Mrs Angela Northwood.

'He's upsetting all our residents. I've tried to pacify him, but it's impossible,' Mrs Northwood said.

Horton noted the Irish accent and the fact that Mrs Northwood – a large-boned woman with untidy bleached-blonde short hair and a tired expression – looked fit to drop. He wondered how many hours she'd been on duty. He nodded Cantelli towards the direction of the booming voice, where he guessed PC Seaton was trying to calm Kingsway, obviously without success.

'I've never seen him like this before. He's usually such a calm, quiet man,' she continued. 'I tried to tell him that with his mother's condition – she's got vascular dementia – this sort of confusion is common, but he just won't have it.'

'Where is Mrs Kingsway now?'

'In the residents' lounge, staring at the television.'

Which Horton could now hear because Mr Kingsway had stopped shouting. Cantelli was working his magic. 'Can you show me her room?'

'It's on the first floor.'

She led the way. Squeezing past the stairlift, Horton noted that the decoration in the hall of this sprawling, detached Edwardian house looked as tired as Mrs Northwood. The paintwork was scuffed and the carpet on the stairs was wearing thin in places. At least the smell of urine and sickness had been blotted out by the reek of disinfectant.

There was a small turning halfway up the stairs and Horton glanced out of the window to look down on a flat-roofed extension and a small garden, which gave a view on to the gardens and the backs of houses on the adjoining road.

Mrs Northwood said, 'Mrs Kingsway shared a room with another lady who passed away on New Year's Eve. The doctor visited her in the early morning of New Year's Day to certify death, and I'm convinced this is where Mrs Kingsway has got her story from. She's simply got the night muddled up in her head. Dementia patients have very little or no concept of time. Here's her room.'

It was directly opposite the staircase with a bay window that faced north on to the street. Horton took in the two single beds with mauve floral counterpanes, each with a bedside cabinet. On top of one was a box of tissues, a glass jug and beaker, and a lamp. There was a white painted wardrobe facing each bed astride a chimney breast and in the bay, under the window, a matching chest of drawers. In the corner, behind the door, was a commode and a sink basin and beside it a cabinet with towels and toiletries. Horton noted that there were no curtains around the beds to screen them off and provide privacy. The room felt cold even though it was centrally heated. It smelt of old age and death and made him shudder.

'This is Mrs Kingsway's bed.' Mrs Northwood indicated the one nearest the door. Horton had already guessed as much. 'I'm sorry to be wasting your time, Inspector, when you must have so much else to do. I can understand Mr Kingsway being upset. It is terribly heartbreaking for the family when they see someone they love suffering.'

He crossed to the window, thinking that this didn't feel like a waste of his time, unlike his interview with the television divers. He thought of the puffed-up egos of Jackson and Farnsworth, who obviously considered they were doing something of vital importance by filling the public's television screens with their diving antics, when the really valuable jobs, like Mrs Northwood's, went relatively unseen and unrecognized. The contrast between the splendour of the Queen's Hotel and the shabbiness of this nursing home also struck him. But then, that was the nature of his job. It took him into all walks of life.

He lifted the net curtain and peered out. There was a burly, dark-haired man in a green waxed jacket on the opposite side of the road, walking away from the nursing home towards the junction. Other than that, the street was deserted. All the houses in the road were of a similar period as the Rest Haven, but most, as he'd noted on arrival, had been converted into flats, except for the bed-and-breakfast hotel opposite. The curtain twitched as he turned away. Probably someone being nosy like him. There was nothing to see here and Mrs Northwood's explanation of the circumstances seemed logical enough. Now they just had to convince Mr Kingsway that his mother was mistaken about this mystery night visitor.

'Who was the lady who died?' Horton asked casually, as they headed down the stairs.

'Irene Ebury.'

Horton started with shock. It was as though thinking about her not ten minutes ago had suddenly conjured her up. He could hardly believe what he'd just heard. Surely it couldn't be the same Irene Ebury – the woman who had worked with his mother? Could there be more than one Irene Ebury in Portsmouth? It was possible. But with spine-creeping certainty he just *knew* it was her.

Angela Northwood had said that Irene had died on New Year's Eve, so who had collected her belongings? A son or daughter? Perhaps a husband. Would Irene have spoken to them about Jennifer Horton? Why should she though? It was over thirty years ago and they had only worked together for a year between 1977 and 1978. But what if Irene *had* spoken about his mother? And what if she had kept diaries? Chance had brought him here. Wasn't it silly not to go that little bit further and check? He knew he was clutching at straws, but now that the idea had entered his head, he couldn't ignore it.

'No one's collected her things. They're still in storage here,' Mrs Northwood said in answer to his question. 'Her son Peter is her next of kin and he's in Kingston prison.'

Horton hid his surprise. That was a Category B lifer, and Category C prison, which meant that Peter Ebury must have committed a very serious crime to be there.

He told himself not to raise his hopes. There would probably be nothing in the old lady's belongings that was useful. But still, he needed to be certain.

Angela Northwood looked surprised at his request to see them. She made as if to protest, then must have thought better of it, because she said, 'They're in the cellar. I'll fetch the keys.'

Perhaps she was too tired to argue, he thought, following her into an office about the size of a broom cupboard, where she took a set of keys from a board behind the door. Locking it again, she said, 'I suppose you're interested because of that son of hers?'

She'd given him a reason. Good. Let her think that. He contrived to look both secretive and knowledgeable. He wasn't sure it convinced her, but she led him to a door under the stairs, which she unlocked.

Horton peered into the gloom and his heart leapt into overdrive. Suddenly the memories of being locked in a cellar in that God-awful children's home rushed in to torment him. He could feel the walls closing in as he followed her down the stairs. His heart was racing and the sweat was pricking his back. He struggled to fight away terror and panic and to ignore the smell of dust, damp and decay. *Think of Irene Ebury, think of Emma. Think of anything but that bloody cellar twenty-seven years ago.*

'There's not much, just a . . . that's strange.'

Her voice jolted him back to the present, and swiftly he came up behind her seeing instantly that the drawer had been forcibly opened. Frowning, he scanned the rest of the cellar, his heart gradually settling down as he considered this new puzzle. In the far left-hand corner, stacks of incontinence pads were piled high and beside them were a couple of commodes, some walking frames and other medical appliances. He brought his eyes back to rest on the filing cabinet and busted drawer. None of the others had been touched.

He tried to tell himself this was probably a case of petty theft, but in his heart he knew it was more. How much more though? Did Irene Ebury's death and her missing belongings have anything to do with this alleged intruder? But who would want an old lady dead? And what did she have worth stealing? Even more crucial, though, was did it have anything to do with his mother?

For a moment the small voice inside him urged him to walk

away and forget he had seen this, to leave it to uniform, but when had he ever listened to reason? He guessed he wasn't about to start now. This was one puzzle that he knew, without any doubt, he had to solve. It might come to nothing, but he couldn't leave that to chance. And neither could he leave it to others to discover something that might just have a connection with his past.

TWO

'Would a member of staff have taken them?' he asked, pulling on a pair of latex gloves.
'If they had, they would have signed them out.'
'Can you check? And send Sergeant Cantelli down here, please.'
Angela Northwood looked about to object, then had second thoughts. As she clattered up the stairs, with enough noise to tell him she disapproved of all this fuss, Horton examined the lock. It was flimsy and wouldn't have taken much to force open. A wrench or other similar tool would have done the job.
Who had keys to this room? He recalled that Mrs Northwood had taken them from the board in her office. She had locked her office door behind her with another set of keys, so whoever had taken Irene Ebury's belongings must have had a key to this basement. The lock on the door hadn't been forced, which meant it must be a member of staff. Or had the cellar door been left open for the thief – this intruder that Mrs Kingsway claimed to have seen?
Hearing footsteps, he turned to see Cantelli descending. 'Any joy?'
'He's quiet enough now and apologetic. What are you doing down here?'
'The cupboard was bare,' Horton said, stepping aside.
Cantelli looked puzzled. Horton quickly explained leaving out the connection between Irene Ebury and his mother.
Cantelli frowned. 'Peter Ebury rings a bell, but I can't recall why.' He peered into the empty drawer. 'Inside job?'
Before Horton couldn't comment, Mrs Northwood returned.

'No one's signed out for Mrs Ebury's belongings.' She looked understandably concerned.

Had someone taken them and forgotten to sign the book? No. That didn't explain why the drawer had been forced open.

'Are the keys to this basement and these cabinets always hanging on that board in your office?' Horton asked.

'Yes.'

'And do all the staff have access to them?'

'Only when my office is open and either I, my relief or the night manager is there. Otherwise the office is locked and if staff want something they have to ask.'

'But you don't accompany them.'

She looked at him as if he were mad. 'Of course not. I'd be up and down these stairs every five minutes. But they don't get the keys to these cabinets without explaining why they want them.'

So, although the staff wouldn't have keys to this cabinet, they could easily have broken into it whilst fetching incontinence pads or a surgical appliance. Horton said, 'Do you have a list of Irene's belongings?'

'In my office.'

'I'd like to see it. In a moment,' he added, preventing her from leaving. 'You mentioned the night manager. Was she on duty when Irene Ebury died?'

'Marion Keynes. Yes. She comes on at six thirty along with the other night staff. But I had to stand in for her last night. She's off sick. And I'm a care assistant down. Wretched woman didn't show up for work yesterday or today, and there's no word from her. It happens in this job, all too often I'm sad to say. I've got an agency nurse in tonight, thank goodness.'

Horton saw Cantelli note this. 'How long had Mrs Ebury been a resident?' he asked.

'Just over two years.'

So, why steal her things now, Horton wondered, when whoever it was must have had ample opportunity to do so over the years? And it must have been recent otherwise that busted lock would either have been reported or repaired.

'When was the last time you checked these drawers?' he asked.

Her fair face creased up in thought. 'A week ago on Sunday, the twenty-eighth of December, when Mrs Jenkins passed away. Mrs Ebury's drawer was locked then.'

Horton made no attempt to hide his surprise or his disapproval at the time lag. 'Mrs Ebury died five days ago—'

She flushed. 'Look, we're short-staffed. I'm rushed off my feet, there was no need to hurry down here and bundle her things up. Her son is hardly coming to claim them.'

No. And how bloody convenient. Horton had a bad feeling about this.

'What was the cause of death?'

'Heart disease. She had high blood pressure and was on medication for that, as well as having Alzheimer's.'

'Who certified death?'

'Our GP: Dr Eastwood.'

'What time did she die?' Horton held her hostile stare.

'I wasn't on duty, remember,' she snapped. 'You'll have to ask Marion, though I doubt she'll know exactly. According to her report, she found Mrs Ebury dead at five thirty a.m. on New Year's Day. She called the doctor straight away. He issued the death certificate.'

No autopsy then. Horton definitely didn't like the smell of this. Would he have cared though, if there hadn't been that connection with his mother? Would he simply have accepted the burglary as an inside job and sent a constable or DC Walters to investigate? The tightening in his gut gave him his answer.

Because of the holiday period, Horton knew it was unlikely that Irene Ebury would have been buried yet. 'Who's organizing her funeral?'

'I am, when I get round to it,' she answered defensively. 'Her son can't do anything, can he?'

By Cantelli's expression, Horton could see he was still trawling his memory to pinpoint exactly what Ebury had done. He wondered if Cantelli would recall Irene Ebury.

He said, 'Did Mrs Ebury have any visitors?'

'No.'

'Never?'

'Not one. I doubt if anyone will be at her funeral except me.'

Unless they let Peter out for it, accompanied by a couple of prison officers, thought Horton. He asked if she had put an announcement in the deaths' column of the local newspaper and got an incredulous look. His suggestion that she should do so earned him a deep frown and a heavy sigh of exasperation.

He excused her grumpiness on grounds of lack of sleep, noting at the same time that his own disgruntled mood had slipped away.

'I would like you to lock the door to the basement and not let anyone down here until the fingerprint bureau has been, and . . .' Turning to Cantelli, he added, 'I also want someone from the photographic unit here.' Cantelli, reaching for his mobile phone, climbed the stairs.

'Surely there's a simple explanation for this,' Mrs Northwood cried in exasperation, locking the door behind her.

'Then we'll find it,' he answered, wondering if she was right, but feeling uneasy nevertheless. 'I'll take a look at Mrs Ebury's room again while you get me a list of her belongings.'

He wasn't sure what he would gain from seeing the room a second time, but on the first occasion it had simply been a bedroom where an anonymous elderly resident had died. Now he was looking at it with a very different set of eyes, though initially he couldn't see anything more revealing than on his first visit. Had Irene died of natural causes or was there something suspicious about her death? Maybe he was looking to complicate things unnecessarily.

Standing beside Mrs Kingsway's bed, he could see it would have been easy for her to have witnessed an intruder looming over Irene Ebury. Or, as Mrs Northwood had suggested, it could have been the doctor bending over to examine the body. But, no, that wouldn't wash. If it had been the doctor, then he or Marion Keynes, the night manager, would have switched on the light. The doctor could hardly examine the body in the dark. Marion Keynes had discovered Irene Ebury's body at 5.30 a.m. and even if the GP hadn't arrived until 6 or 7 a.m. it would still have been dark. And surely they would have taken Mrs Kingsway out of the room whilst the doctor was examining the body. As Horton had noted earlier, there were no curtains around these beds to give any degree of privacy. If Mrs Kingsway was right, and she had seen an intruder, perhaps that intruder had frightened Irene Ebury into having a heart attack and had then stolen her belongings. Mrs Northwood had said that dementia patients got the days and times muddled up. He felt a frisson of excitement that told him he could be on to something.

Hearing footsteps on the stairs, he turned.

'Someone from the fingerprinting and photographic bureaus will be over within the hour,' Cantelli announced, gazing round the room.

Horton could tell by his expression that he didn't approve of it.

'I want Seaton and Somerfield to take statements from all the staff. And if Walters has returned from Oldham's Wharf get him over here too. I want to know who had those keys to the basement, and when and what they were all doing on New Year's Eve. We'll talk to Marion Keynes later.'

Horton found Mrs Northwood in her office. She gave him Marion Keynes' address and then handed him a list of Irene Ebury's belongings. There was a small amount of jewellery listed: a wedding ring, a dress ring, a gold charm bracelet, some bead necklaces and earrings. There were also some letters and a small photograph album noted. No diary. The photograph album and letters might have been interesting though. It didn't seem much to show for a life or worth killing for. *If* she had been killed.

He asked, 'Do you know who the letters were from?'

'No. I never read them. She might have got one of the staff to read them to her though.'

That was a question Seaton, Somerfield and Walters could ask later. He guessed they could have been from her son.

'Who told Peter about his mother's death?'

'Marion Keynes informed the governor.'

Was it worth a visit to Kingston Prison? Definitely. He'd like to know if Peter Ebury had ever written to his mother. He was also curious to know how he felt about his mother's death.

Mrs Northwood said, 'Irene's toiletries were given to the other ladies, and we kept some of her more decent clothes. We get through quite a lot here. The rest went to a charity shop. I've got her pension details, birth and death certificates, but I can't hand those over to you until I have permission from her next of kin.'

'You can at least give me her date and place of birth.' He would be able to get access to her pension details and previous employment records from the various government department computers.

She unlocked her filing cabinet and withdrew a folder. Flicking through it, she handed Horton the birth certificate. Irene Ebury had been born on 4 January 1939 in Portsmouth to Gladys and William Ebury. Had she never married? Unless she had reverted to her maiden name on divorce.

'Where's her marriage certificate?'

'I've never been given one.'

There was a wedding ring in her personal belongings and she had adopted the title of Mrs. Maybe it was just for show. He jotted down the details and then, handing back the certificate, asked, 'Are those her medical records?'

'Since she's been in our care, yes, but you can't see them,' Mrs Northwood said quickly, clutching them close to her as though he was going to steal them. 'They're confidential.'

'Irene Ebury is dead,' he said evenly.

A quick glimpse might be all he needed, though Horton didn't really know what they could tell him.

'She may be, but until her son says you can see them, or you have a warrant, they stay with me.'

Pity, but if that was how she wanted to play it, then so be it. He'd get Peter Ebury's permission to access those medical records. It would be quicker than getting a warrant.

He explained about his officers taking statements from the staff, which drew a scowl from her.

'Why all this interest, Inspector? I know there's the case of her missing belongings, but that hardly warrants so much police activity.'

'We'll try to be as quick and discreet as possible,' he answered evasively.

She wasn't happy with his answer. That was too bad, Horton thought. In the corridor, he asked Cantelli if Mr Kingsway was still on the premises.

'He's in the staffroom having a coffee. I asked him to hang around for a moment. I thought you'd like to talk to him.'

Kingsway looked up as they entered, and Horton felt some sympathy for him. The poor man seemed to be on the edge of a nervous breakdown. Fatigue was etched on his weather-roughened face. His grey eyes were red-rimmed, whether through crying or tiredness Horton didn't know. He was wiry, like Cantelli, but shorter than the sergeant and his close-cropped hair made it difficult to put an age on him. Horton would have said late forties possibly early fifties.

'I visit my mother every Monday,' he said in answer to Horton's question. 'So today was the first time I'd seen her since Mrs Ebury died. She knew who I was this morning, which is unusual, and she seemed more like her old self. She told me that she didn't like it here, there were things going on. When I pressed her, she said she'd seen a man standing over the bed next to her. She was scared. She pretended to be asleep. But he turned and saw her and grabbed hold of her.'

'Did she scream?' asked Horton.

'She says she was too scared to cry out. The man shook her and let her go.'

'Did she give a description?'

'Sorry, no. I don't even know if it is true. She seemed so certain this morning, but now it's like it never happened and Mrs Northwood explained how she can get dates and times muddled up. I'm sorry for putting you and your officers to so much trouble,' he said sheepishly, rising.

'It's no trouble, sir.' And it wasn't. Horton was glad the son had called them, because he might never have bothered to find Irene Ebury, or if he had done then he might never have known about her missing belongings. He had a feeling that Mrs Northwood wouldn't have reported it. He asked Mr Kingsway if he'd known Irene.

'I'd met her a couple of times, but I didn't really know her. Thanks for taking me seriously anyway.' He stretched out a hand. Horton took it, noting its firmness.

Horton watched him head down the corridor, where he entered the lounge, presumably to say goodbye to his mother.

'Must be tough,' Cantelli said, shaking his head.

Horton knew he was thinking of his own mother, who had been widowed just before Christmas. Fortunately, from what Horton had seen of Mrs Cantelli senior, her mind was still firing on all cylinders.

'Make sure Seaton and Somerfield know what questions to ask.'

Cantelli went off to brief them, while Horton stepped into the damp, windy morning and called the mortuary.

'Have you performed an autopsy on Irene Ebury?' he asked when Dr Clayton came on the line. 'She died on New Year's Eve.'

'You must be kidding – we've got them piled up. What with the holiday and this vomiting bug, I don't expect we'll get around to her until next Christmas. Is it urgent?'

Horton didn't much relish the vision of corpses piled sky-high. 'Possible suspicious death . . .'

'Hold on, did you say Ebury?'

'Yes, why?'

'I've just had another Ebury brought in for an urgent PM. Any relation?'

'Don't know yet. You haven't told me who it is.' Horton suddenly felt very cold. There had to be several Eburys in Portsmouth, but he'd wager a million pounds on who this dead one was. 'Is it Peter Ebury?'

'Yes! How did you know?'

He pulled up the collar of his sailing jacket as an icy blast of fear wrapped itself round his heart.

'How did he die?' He hoped his voice sounded normal.

'That's what the post-mortem will tell me,' she said pointedly.

'What did the doctor say?' he rephrased.

'Respiratory failure.'

Brought on how? Mother and son dead within five days of each other – wasn't that strange? OK, so it might not be unique and perhaps Peter Ebury, wracked with guilt, had given up and died. Or perhaps he'd suffered from asthma and had had an attack. It was pointless for him to read too much into this. But he did.

'When will you have the results?'

'The autopsy's scheduled for tomorrow morning. It's the earliest I can do it.'

Damn. He noted her unusually defensive and slightly aggressive tone and thought that someone must have been getting at her. The prison authorities probably. They'd want this sorted out, and a verdict of death by natural causes, as quickly as possible.

'Was there any mention of suicide?'

'You mean he killed himself because he couldn't face the guilt of being in prison when his mother died? No, and he wasn't on suicide watch. I suppose you want me to do Irene Ebury's autopsy tomorrow too?'

'Please. Call me as soon as you've got the results on them both.'

Cantelli joined him in the car. 'Walters is on his way over.'

'Good. How's your claustrophobia?'

Cantelli raised an enquiring eyebrow. 'Mine's fine, how's yours?'

'You know me and closed-in spaces. But when duty calls . . .'

'We're going to prison.'

'Got it in one.'

THREE

Geoff Welton was ill, Horton could see that instantly. The prison governor was a balding man in his mid-fifties with a gaunt face and an excess of ear and nostril hair. His suit hung off his scrawny body. And whilst he might have developed the sallow hue from having spent a lifetime working in prisons, the bags under his sunken eyes and the strain around his wide mouth told Horton a different story.

'What was Ebury like?' Horton asked. He'd told Welton that they were investigating some irregularities concerning Irene Ebury's death and had been surprised to learn that her son had now also died. He'd said nothing about Irene's missing belongings, and Cantelli had been dispatched to talk to Ken Staunton, Ebury's personal case officer.

On the way to the prison Cantelli had remembered the case and a quick phone call to the station had confirmed it by checking the computer. Peter Ebury had been convicted of an armed robbery carried out in 2001, when he'd been twenty-seven. That had been the year of Horton's promotion to inspector and a spell on secondment to Basingstoke, which was why he hadn't recalled the name.

Ebury had shot and killed a security guard called Arthur Buckland in a hold-up on an armoured van, which had just collected the weekend's takings from a superstore in Havant. Ebury and his accomplice Derrick Mayfield had been caught with the money on the A3 to London. Cantelli didn't remember Ebury's mother and Horton again said nothing about her connection with his own mother.

Welton said, 'Ebury was surly, arrogant, crude, bullying and manipulative. He never earned any privileges and was often in trouble.'

Clearly not a model prisoner then or one of Welton's favourites.

'Who was the last person to see Peter Ebury alive?' Horton asked.

'Ken Staunton. He was on duty on Ebury's wing. He unlocked the cell this morning and Ebury went about his usual routine before going to work in the kitchen. He was a cleaner. He returned to his cell at nine thirty a.m. when Staunton locked him in.

'When Colin Anston, my deputy, went to the cell half an hour later, he found Ebury dead. He never said he felt unwell.'

'Why was he locked in?'

Welton frowned and shifted a little uncomfortably. 'He attacked one of the men in the kitchen this morning; nothing came of it. He wasn't injured.'

'You had him medically examined?'

'Of course not,' Welton bristled. 'There was no physical sign of the attack on Ebury, or Ludlow, the other man. And the prison officers separated the two men before the fight even got started.'

'Do you know what it was about?'

'No. Neither man would say.'

Horton wondered if Ludlow would tell him. He doubted whether Welton would allow him to speak to the prisoner. Horton wasn't here in an official capacity to investigate Ebury's death. Ebury might not have been ill, but Welton was looking sicklier by the minute.

'Did Ebury have any visitors?'

'No.'

Peter Ebury had been too young to have known Jennifer Horton; he would only have been four when she disappeared. Yet his death and Irene's bugged Horton.

'Peter was very young to die of respiratory failure. Did he suffer from asthma?'

Horton could see the strain on Welton's face, but the man called up his reserves. 'A death in prison is always awkward, as you are no doubt aware, Inspector. Questions get asked. I shouldn't speak ill of the dead, but Ebury was an evil man and a troublemaker. I'm not that sorry to see the back of him.'

And, Horton thought, Welton looked ever keener to see the back of him. But Welton hadn't answered his question, which made Horton even more suspicious. 'Could I talk to Mr Anston?'

Welton hesitated. He seemed about to deny the request, then thought better of it. Or perhaps, Horton thought, he simply didn't have the energy to protest.

'I don't see how that will help you with your inquiries into Mrs Ebury's death, but, if you must, ask Richard to take you to Mr Anston's office.'

Dismissed, Horton found Richard, Welton's administration

officer, in the outer office. As Richard led him down the corridor, Horton commented on Welton's health.

'I've told him to see the doctor,' Richard replied, with a worried look on his lean face, 'but he won't.'

'What's wrong with him?'

'Stress, I expect.'

It looked more than stress to Horton. He guessed a liver problem, judging by the man's colour. And would a sick governor have enough of a hold on a prison like this? Maybe, but Horton wondered nevertheless. He halted just outside Anston's office. 'Take a look at him when you return. Make sure he's all right.'

Richard nodded, knocked on the door and pushed it open after a loud and brisk, 'Come in.'

Horton found himself facing a broad, muscular man in his forties with bright, slightly protruding eyes, and a round cheerful face that Horton instinctively judged to be honest.

'Ebury was a nasty piece of work. He was cocky and clever too.' Colin Anston confirmed his governor's opinion after Horton explained why he was there. He waved Horton into a seat across his desk, which, despite its size, in the small grey office still didn't seem large enough to cope with all the paperwork piled on it. The amount matched that on Horton's desk this morning, which was probably now even deeper. Cantelli would have to write a report on their interview with the TV divers, unless Bliss expected him to waste time on it, given their status. He didn't know what he was going to write up about this investigation, but then maybe there wasn't one here, and Dr Clayton would find both mother and son had died from natural causes.

'What do you mean by clever?' Horton asked, trying not to hear the slamming doors and rattling keys. He couldn't prevent the tightening in his chest and the slightly nauseous feeling rising in his throat, which hinted at the beginnings of an attack of claustrophobia. He'd been fine in Welton's office, because it was situated far enough away from the everyday sounds of the prison, though the journey there had been rough. Not without difficulty he curbed his desire to spring up and walk about. Instead, he crossed his legs and for a moment let his mind dwell on the boat and the big wide open spaces of the Solent. He couldn't wait until Saturday and his holiday. He wrenched his mind back to what Anston was saying.

'Ebury had a knack of getting straight to a person's weakness.

I've seen him wheedle, cajole and manipulate his way into someone's confidence, only for him to turn it against that person and exploit it.'

'That include prison officers?'

''Fraid so, especially the rookies. I've had many a talk with prison officers who have rued the day they thought they were converting Ebury to the good and righteous path only to find they'd been tricked and he'd exploited their trust or betrayed a confidence. Ebury had a nasty streak right down his middle. You had to be firm with him. He'd test you to the limit.'

Interesting. So had Ebury recently got his claws into someone who had finally turned the table on him and killed him? But that wasn't possible with a locked cell door and a diagnosis of natural death, although Dr Clayton hadn't confirmed the latter yet. And it certainly didn't fit with Irene Ebury's death.

Nevertheless, Horton said, 'Was there anyone in particular?'

Anston eyed him suspiciously. 'Why do you ask?'

'Just curious,' Horton rejoined evenly.

Anston looked sceptical. 'Ebury just stopped breathing and died,' he said, correctly interpreting the reason behind Horton's question.

Horton nodded slowly. 'Mr Welton told me about the fight. Do you know what it was about?'

'No.'

'And you unlocked the cell when?' Horton already knew the time but it didn't do any harm to see if Welton and Anston were singing from the same hymn sheet.

'At ten a.m. Ebury was dead. I looked in on him at nine forty-five. He was lying on the bed. I thought he was asleep.'

'Why didn't Mr Staunton look in on Ebury? I understand he locked him in and he was on duty in that wing.'

'He had other duties to attend to. Like the police, Inspector, we are always short staffed and prisons are overcrowded. I was helping out.'

Horton could see that was the truth, but he thought he'd push it a bit further. 'Is there anyone else who might have had a key to that cell?'

Anston glared at him. Pulling himself up, he said sternly, 'Ebury died of natural causes. The post-mortem will confirm that.'

'I'm sure it will.' Horton smiled. 'Could I see his cell?'

'There's nothing in it. His belongings are here.' Anston pointed to a cardboard box. 'We're trying to trace his other relatives.'

Horton wasn't sure he had any. According to Mrs Northwood there were none. 'I'd still like to see his cell,' he insisted, holding Anston's stare, though not really relishing the task. Finally the prison officer capitulated. Clearly not pleased with the request, he showed Horton out, locking his office door behind him as he went.

As they made their way through several locked gates and along echoing corridors, Horton fought off the sickening and dizzying wave of claustrophobia by thinking through what he had learnt about Ebury. Clever, cocky and manipulative. He tried to equate this description with what he had been told about the Ebury who had shot and killed the security officer. Admittedly Ebury had been younger then and maybe more headstrong, but if he had been so clever and manipulative then why hadn't he committed a more sophisticated crime, rather than chasing the security van in a stolen car, holding it up and shooting the officer?

He said, 'Did Ebury ever talk about his crime?'

'We don't encourage that sort of thing in here. Besides sixty per cent of them will tell you they're innocent.'

Horton tried a smile despite his rapidly beating heart and sweating palms. He hoped he didn't look like Boris Karloff on a good day. 'No doubt fitted up by the police.'

They walked through into another wing. The smell of prison mingling with disinfectant turned Horton's stomach. Once again the painful memories of those children's homes came back to haunt him. He forced himself to concentrate on the faces of the men cleaning the landing who were eyeing him curiously. Did he sense their relief at Ebury's death? Maybe he just expected it after what Welton and Anston had told him.

About two thirds of the way down, Anston stopped and unlocked a cell. He pulled open the door and reluctantly Horton stepped inside the small room about twelve by eight feet. His stomach immediately went into a spasm and his pulse raced.

My God, to be locked in here! Not to be able to step outside to see the stars, feel the wind from the deck of the boat, breathe the salty air, make a coffee whenever he felt like it, take a walk . . . The sweat threatened to break out on his forehead and he fought valiantly not to betray his feelings. He didn't want to appear vulnerable in front of Anston because he had a feeling that Anston would revel in it.

With all the control he could muster, he forced himself to stay motionless and survey the blank, cheerless cell, taking in every detail of it: the magnolia-painted brick, the single bed with the rolled-up mattress; the wooden cabinet, table and chair. In the corner beyond the bed was a half-screen door with a gap underneath it revealing the base of a toilet. Opposite was a small basin. There was no window. It was simply a brick box. All trace of Ebury's personality had been scrubbed from the cell and packed away in that cardboard box that Anston had shown him. The prison had acted swiftly. It was less than four hours since he'd died.

With his fear now firmly in check, he said evenly, 'Who told Peter about his mother's death?'

'Ken Staunton. Your colleague, Sergeant Cantelli, is talking to him now in the staffroom.'

Anston didn't miss much.

'Where was Ebury when you entered?'

'On the bed. I could see at once by his colour and the still-ness that something was wrong. I felt his pulse, there was nothing. I raised the alarm and called the doctor, but I knew it was too late.'

'Was there anything unusual about the body? The way it was lying, the smell, the way it looked?'

'He was dead,' Anson replied stiffly, glaring at Horton.

He'd made an enemy there. Not that Horton was unduly worried and neither did he blame Anston for feeling that way. After all, he'd invaded Anston's territory and made accusations against him and his fellow officers' efficiency. Horton would feel justifiably outraged if anyone did that to him. He also saw that the real power in this prison stood before him. Anston was holding this place together, not Geoff Welton.

'Did Ebury leave a diary, any letters or notes?'

Anston shook his head. 'He could barely write and though he was offered literacy classes, he always turned them down.'

'How did he spend his recreation time?'

'He was a good footballer. If he wasn't playing or practising he just laid on his bed, staring at the ceiling, probably thinking up some cruel torment for one of his fellow inmates.'

There was nothing more to be seen here. Anston led him back

to his office. Horton would have liked to have taken Ebury's belongings with him, but Anston wouldn't permit it. He let Horton view them though. There wasn't much, just a couple of photographs, a cigarette lighter, which Anston assured him didn't work, and a silver chain necklace.

'Is this it?' Horton asked incredulous.

'Apart from some girlie magazines, his clothes and toiletries, yes.'

Horton wasn't sure if he believed him, though Anston looked to be telling the truth.

'May I?' He asked, indicating the photographs. Anston nodded his approval.

Horton turned one over. There was nothing written on the reverse. Flicking it back, he found himself staring at a woman who looked to be in her early sixties. Her short silver hair framed a classically featured face with high cheekbones and fine eyes. She was very slim, perhaps a bit too thin, and she appeared tall against the young man beside her, whom he assumed was Peter Ebury. Anston confirmed it. Horton surmised therefore that the woman was Peter's mother, Irene.

She was smiling into the camera, though Horton sensed there was a sadness about her, or was that weary resignation that her son had already descended into a life of crime? This must have been taken not long before Peter Ebury had committed the armed robbery because he looked in his mid-twenties. He was good-looking and fit with a cocky smile. Horton knew from his earlier phone call to the station that by then Peter Ebury had served three terms in prison for theft, assault, and grievous bodily harm.

Horton tried to place where the photograph had been taken. Mother and son were standing outside a block of flats that Horton didn't recognize. Why hadn't anyone visited this woman when she was in the Rest Haven? Surely she must have some friends or relatives in Portsmouth. He wondered what his mother had thought of her when they'd worked together.

The other photograph was of Peter Ebury in a nightclub surrounded by a group of young, heavily made-up but attractive girls of between eighteen to twenty-five, one of whom was sitting on his lap. They all looked drunk, presumably from the champagne that was on the table in front of them. Horton judged it to have been taken about the same time as the picture with his mother.

'Any idea who they are?' He indicated the girls, wondering why Peter had kept this particular photograph.

Anston shook his head, then, as if reading Horton's mind, said, 'Perhaps Ebury wanted it to remind him of what he was missing and would be missing for a very long time. He got life.'

Which meant he would have been mid- to late-forties before he came out. 'Can I get photocopies of these?'

'I don't see why you should want them.'

'We *are* investigating his mother's death,' Horton said swiftly and with an edge to his voice.

'What's suspicious about it?'

Horton sensed there was more than idle curiosity in that question, but Anston's expression was a blank canvas.

OK, so let's give him something to chew over, Horton thought.

'An intruder was seen in her room and her belongings are missing.' He'd already told Anston more than he'd told Welton, but then Welton hadn't asked the question, which confirmed Horton's earlier thoughts that Welton had lost his grip.

'Could be something or nothing.' Anston shrugged.

'Precisely. And until I am satisfied that it's nothing, I'll keep investigating.' He held Anston's steely gaze.

After a moment, Anston raised his eyebrows in a gesture that said, please yourself.

'I'd also like a copy of his birth certificate.'

'It won't tell you much.' Anston opened a buff-coloured folder on his desk and handed the certificate to Horton.

The space where the father's details should have been entered was blank, or rather it said 'unknown'. Much the same as Horton's own birth certificate. Had Peter been the result of a five-minute screw in the back of a car in a lay-by or a shag under the pier after a boozy night out? Or was he the product of a regular relationship? Ebury had been born on 31 August 1974 and the birth had been registered in Portsmouth.

After he'd received the photocopies of the photographs and the birth certificate, Horton thanked Anston and stepped outside the prison, sucking down lungfuls of the petrol-fumed air like a submariner unexpectedly saved from a suffocating death. He didn't mind the sheeting rain that now accompanied the blustery wind. It was a two-minute walk to the car, but Horton would gladly have walked all the way back to the station some four miles distant just to get the stench of prison from him.

In the car, Cantelli said, 'Ebury never took advantage of the listeners service, and he never applied for education either within the prison or a distance-learning course. He shunned the prison visitors, said they were a bunch of self-satisfied, egocentric pricks who could only get their jollies by seeing someone lower in the slime than themselves.'

'Ebury said that?' Horton asked, surprised.

'According to Staunton. I asked if those were Ebury's exact words and Staunton said more or less.'

Horton remained doubtful, but Anston had claimed that Ebury was clever. Though, not clever enough to evade the life of a criminal.

'I managed to have a brief chat with a couple of other officers in the staffroom,' Cantelli added. 'They all thought that Peter Ebury was a pain in the arse and no one's sorry he's gone.'

'Which bears out what Welton and Anston told me.' Horton quickly briefed Cantelli.

Cantelli pointed the car towards the station. 'I asked if someone could have pinched a set of keys to Ebury's cell, copied them and then put them back, but Staunton looked at me as if I should be carted off to the funny farm. He took great pains to run through the security procedure and the prisoners' routine, and, from what he said, I don't think anyone could have killed Ebury.'

Horton, reluctantly, had to agree that it was looking that way. But he still didn't like it. Unless Walters, Seaton and Somerfield came up with something from the nursing home, he would have to accept there was no case to answer.

This was exactly what DCI Bliss told him twenty minutes later. He found her in his office.

'This is where you should be, Inspector,' she said, eyeing him like he was a dung beetle. 'Not deploying uniformed resources without approval from the duty inspector and requesting staff from the scientific services department to take fingerprints and photographs without authorization from me. This amounts to nothing more than a whim.'

'It was hardly that,' Horton retorted, thinking why the hell doesn't she shift her narrow backside out of my chair, sitting there like she's the chief bloody constable. Less than two months ago she was a DI like him.

'A whim,' she insisted. 'An old lady died. It happens.'

'Her belongings are missing and a resident reported seeing someone suspicious in Mrs Ebury's room—'

'They're dementia patients, for heaven's sake. Everyone is suspicious.'

'Oh, I see. So we can forget it,' he said with heavy irony, stung by her supercilious tone. 'Irene Ebury had dementia and has no one left to care about her or her belongings, which don't amount to much anyway. Her dead son is a criminal so he won't be missed. It's obviously not as high profile as two ponced-up television presenters receiving threatening calls, which you will find are a publicity stunt.'

Bliss stood up, her face flushed with anger. 'You know very well what I mean. It's a question of resources and you don't have them to explore every petty crime—'

'I hardly call someone dying petty,' he replied tautly.

Her colour deepened. 'If you can't prioritize your caseload, then you'd better think again about staying in the job.'

That was well below the belt. It didn't even justify an answer as far as he was concerned. He held her stare which was as cold as an emperor penguin but not nearly so cute and thought how he'd love to see the back of her.

Her voice was like barbed wire when she added, 'I've ordered DC Walters to return to the station immediately, and Seaton and Somerfield to resume their usual duties. You might not like the fact that I got promotion, especially when you didn't, or that I am now your superior officer, but you either work with me or you put in for a transfer.'

Like bloody hell I will, he thought. And give you the satisfaction of getting rid of me? He could see that he was a great big nasty thorn in Bliss's neatly tended garden of CID. Well, tough, if she didn't like it, then she'd have to pull him out. She'd get her hands scratched trying, though, and he couldn't see Bliss wearing gloves. She wasn't the type.

'Results, Inspector, that's what we're paid to get. C.A.S.E. = Results. See if you can earn your salary.' With a tight frown, she swept out of room. Well, at least now he knew what the initial R stood for.

Cantelli poked his head round the door. 'You're still walking then?'

'My balls are intact and so is my determination. She told me to forget about Irene Ebury and her stolen belongings, and you know what that makes me want to do?'

Cantelli groaned and rolled his eyes. 'I've sent the photographs off to the photographic unit and I've requested the case notes on the Peter Ebury armed robbery. I'll start looking into Irene Ebury's background this afternoon.'

Horton hesitated. He knew that Bliss's threats wouldn't hold water with Cantelli, but should he tell him about the connection with his mother? He'd never lied to Cantelli and had rarely kept anything from him. In fact, Cantelli was the only person in the station who knew about him being raised in children's homes and with foster parents. But maybe there would be nothing to find. And perhaps he'd explain everything after Thursday when Cantelli had got through the ordeal of his father's funeral. Horton heard the excuses in his mind and shoved them aside.

'Is Walters back?' He glanced at the clock on his desk, seeing with surprise it was almost two o'clock.

'In the canteen. He saw Bliss on the warpath and just kept going straight on.'

Horton didn't blame him for that. Fortunately Bliss's office was in the opposite direction to the canteen. 'Then let's see what he's unearthed.'

FOUR

With his mouth full of chicken and ham pie, Walters said, 'We managed to speak to all the staff on duty before Seaton and Somerfield had to report back and *she* called me in.'

'It's all right, Walters, Sergeant Cantelli is keeping an eye on the door.'

Walters stabbed another chip with his fork and conveyed it to his mouth with a look of relief. 'No one claims to have gone to Irene Ebury's drawer in the basement or to have noticed if the drawer was locked or unlocked. They all think Mrs Kingsway saw Dr Eastwood leaning over Mrs Ebury on the morning she died and the old lady's got confused over the dates.'

But it was the night staff that had been on duty so Horton

knew they'd have to question them. And without Bliss knowing. He took a bite of his sandwich as Walters continued.

'The fingerprint bureau found some prints on the cabinet in the basement and on the door. They took the staff's prints. Mrs Northwood nearly blew a gasket. But they haven't done the night staff.'

'How many are there?'

'Six, not counting the manager who's off sick.'

Marion Keynes would be at home and hopefully not too sick to answer his questions, which he intended to put to her later.

'Go back tonight, Walters, and talk to the night staff. Ask them to call into the station so we can take their prints.'

'Do I have to?'

'You got a date?'

'No, but . . .'

A glare from Horton stilled his protest. Polishing off his sandwich, Horton said, 'How did you get on at Oldham's Wharf this morning?' It seemed ages ago now.

'Nothing was stolen. And there was no sign of a break-in.'

'Then why report it?' Horton asked, puzzled.

Walters shrugged his expansive shoulders and the flesh around his jowl wobbled. 'Ryan Oldham said one of his vehicles had been moved.'

'And that's it?' Horton cried incredulously. 'The driver could have done that!'

'That's what I said. He didn't go a bundle on it. Told me how to do my job. He wants fingerprints, forensics, the lot. I said I'd see what we could do.'

'Which is precisely nothing unless you've got more than that.' He hoped he didn't sound like Bliss. But at least he did have a theft at the nursing home to investigate, not to mention a questionable death, two if you counted Peter Ebury. Scraping back his chair, he said, 'Make an appointment for me to see Dr Eastwood.'

In his office Horton studied the notes he'd made on Irene. She'd been thirty-five when she'd given birth to Peter, which was quite old to have a first child in 1974 when women tended to have them younger. If indeed Peter was her first and only child. Her medical records would reveal this information, but Cantelli would also run a check with the Registrar and HM Revenue and Customs at the same time and get her employment record. He'd also see if could find any record of a marriage.

He looked up as Cantelli and Walters walked into the CID office and settled at their desks. Bliss's reprimand rang in his ears. *They're dementia patients, for heaven's sake.*

Irene Ebury had no one to fight her corner. She deserved more than just becoming another statistic. He'd like to find at least one relative or friend who would stand by her coffin and mourn her passing.

And what about his own mother? There was no record to say she was dead, but perhaps her body had never been identified. Gaye Clayton's words about corpses stacked up in the mortuary made him shiver despite the heat from the radiator. Could his mother be lying in a mortuary somewhere, awaiting the day when someone would claim her? Or had she been buried in an unknown grave without anyone to mourn her death? The thought disturbed him, so hastily he pushed it away and began to shift some of the paper on his desk.

There were three telephone messages waiting for him. He dealt swiftly with one by ringing the person, another by throwing it in the bin, and then paused over the third. It was Mrs Collins again, insisting they investigate her son's death. Daniel Collins had died in a road accident on Christmas Eve. He'd been drunk. No other vehicle had been involved. This was the third time she had rung. On the second occasion he had asked to see the incident report. It might have arrived by now and be buried on his desk somewhere.

He found it and flicked it open. Daniel Collins had skidded off the dual carriage and over Salterns Wharf into the sea. It had been his bad luck the tide had been up. He'd drowned. The autopsy had revealed he had been over the legal drinking limit. End of story. Strange coincidence, though, that it was only about half a mile from Oldham's Wharf.

Horton closed the file. There was nothing they could do, but he wasn't without sympathy for Mrs Collins in her grief. He'd get Walters to ring her back and arrange to visit her.

Cantelli knocked and entered carrying the local newspaper. 'Walters has made an appointment with Dr Eastwood for tomorrow at eleven fifteen. And I thought you might like to see this. Page three.'

Horton found himself staring at a photograph of the two TV divers: Nicholas Farnsworth and Perry Jackson. It had been taken on a location dive from one of the television episodes, though where he didn't know. There were some hills in the background that could have been Dorset, but equally it could have been Cornwall. Farnsworth was smiling into camera, his brow glistening with sea water, while beside him Perry Jackson looked as though he'd just swallowed it. Horton read the headline: TV Diver Shrugs off Death Threats.

'What did I tell you?' Horton said with disgust. 'Those anonymous calls were a pack of lies staged by one of these prats for publicity. And they've got it. Bet one of them went running to the press as soon as we were out of sight. You'll have to buy your own lunches, Barney.' Horton threw the newspaper in his bin and rose, picking up the Daniel Collins file.

'It still could be genuine,' Cantelli insisted, following Horton out of his office. 'I could get that list of contacts from Corinna Denton, just in case.'

'Waste of time.' And there was no need to send an officer around to collect those staff and guest lists. Good, because they had better things to do.

Horton dropped the Collins file on Walters' desk. 'Call Mrs Collins and arrange to see her. But read the file first. We're going to see if we can raise Marion Keynes from her sickbed. I only hope she hasn't got anything infectious. If DCI Bliss asks where we are you don't know.'

'What was all that about?' Cantelli asked, as they headed out of the station.

Horton told him.

'Such a waste.' Cantelli shook his head and folded a fresh piece of chewing gum into his mouth. 'That stretch of road's a notorious black spot. Even sober it can be nasty.'

Cantelli lived not far from Salterns Wharf.

'Did you hear anything about the accident?'

'No. Too busy making sure Santa got his mince pie and glass of sherry. It was tough facing all that stuff this Christmas with Dad going like that, but you can't let the kids down, can you? Poor woman.'

Horton knew he was thinking of Daniel Collins's mother and what her Christmas must have been like. She deserved their sympathy.

Marion Keynes on the other hand didn't. That much was clear from their first encounter, as she glared with open hostility at their warrant cards. When Cantelli asked if they could come in, she shrugged and padded off on fat, splayed feet, leaving them to follow her into a small open-plan room in the narrow terraced house. It stank of stale food, over-stewed tea and cigarettes and looked as though it had been turned over by junkies desperate for a fix. In the midst of the chaos sat two fat boys gazing open-mouthed at a large plasma television screen, where a hyperactive youth in torn clothes was doing an impersonation of someone in excruciating pain. Horton guessed the youth was attempting to sing because there was a microphone glued to his mouth, but he'd heard better sounds coming from a pneumatic drill.

She reached for a packet of cigarettes on the mantelpiece. 'Why are you interested in Irene? She's dead.'

'Could you turn the television down,' Horton said firmly but politely, not much caring for her hard mouth and sharp eyes.

She snatched up the remote control and stabbed at it with a frown. Instantly the two boys howled in protest.

'Upstairs.' She pointed at the ceiling as if her offspring had no idea where their bedrooms were.

Neither child moved. The younger one folded his plump arms across his chest and scowled for the Olympics, whereas the eldest glared at Horton as though he'd willingly stick a knife in him. Maybe a few years from now, Horton thought, he would try. He felt like hauling them up and telling them to do as they were told. Judging by Cantelli's unusually fierce expression and his rapid chewing of gum, Horton guessed he was thinking along the same lines.

Marion Keynes said, 'Take a packet of crisps with you.'

They shot up with a whoop and yell and like two mini tornados whizzed past Horton and into the kitchen.

'Kids!' she said, as the boys returned munching their crisps. 'You give them all these toys for Christmas and they're still bored. You've got to blackmail them into doing everything these days.'

Horton dashed a glance at Cantelli and read in his deep dark eyes, not mine you haven't. A run round the football pitch would do them more good than staring at a television screen, Horton thought, before the gyrating youth started howling above them, as if he'd just taken poison.

'Turn it down,' Marion Keynes yelled, making Cantelli jump. Nothing happened.

As she shook out a cigarette and lit it, Horton quickly glanced at the photographs on the mantelpiece. Marion Keynes was the complete opposite to her husband, who was dark-haired with a keen face, and had the body of a cyclist or runner. There was a photograph of the couple on holiday abroad. He was wearing a scuba diving outfit whilst she was decked out in a swimming costume. The expression 'a beached whale' flitted into his head.

They weren't invited to sit, probably because every chair was covered with clothes, toys or magazines. And the room was stifling hot. The gas fire was belting out full blast, and Horton guessed the central heating was also turned up.

'What did Irene Ebury talk about?' he asked.

'How she was once Miss Southsea, but you had to take everything she said with a pinch of salt.'

Horton thought her voice held a trace of spite. And she didn't look to be suffering from any illness that he could see.

'She used to go on and on about the famous men she'd met and dated when she'd been working in the clubs and casinos. Roger Moore, Ronald Reagan, Dean Martin, you name them, she'd had them all. She even claimed her son was the illegitimate child of Frank Sinatra.' Marion Keynes laughed.

Neither he nor Cantelli joined in.

'You stop listening after a while,' Marion Keynes said sharply. 'I've had enough of it. That's why I'm off sick – stress. I'm handing in my notice. I'll probably go back to agency work. It pays more.' She glanced at the clock on the mantelpiece, but Horton wasn't going to take the hint. If Marion Keynes had stress, then he was Dr Freud. Here was a woman who had fancied a few days off and judging by the state of the room, it wasn't to do her housework.

'Why do you want to know about her anyway? She was just an old woman.'

With an unusual edge of steel to his voice, Cantelli said, 'What time did you discover her body?'

'So, that's it, is it? They're saying it's my fault,' she flashed. 'The bastards! They're covering their backsides. She was dead when I went into her room, and if anyone says any different then they're lying.'

'Who are *they*, Mrs Keynes?' Horton asked wearily. He'd had enough of Marion Keynes already.

'Mr Chrystal and his bloody brothers, that's who. They own the Rest Haven and half a dozen old people's homes on the coast.

They're probably looking for someone to blame in case the family sue, not that Irene's son is in a position to. Did you know he's in prison?' she said with relish.

Horton disliked her considerably, and he didn't much care if it showed.

'What time did you discover Irene?' Cantelli persisted.

'Five thirty a.m.,' she snapped, glaring at him.

'Why did you go into her room at that time?' Horton asked.

'It's when I do the rounds.'

Horton didn't believe her.

'Did you hear or see anything unusual that night?' Cantelli spoke again.

She smiled with a smugness that looked as though it was going to drive Cantelli to violence. Usually the sergeant managed to keep a tight rein on his emotions, despite his half-Italian blood, but this time she'd really got to him.

She took another pull at her cigarette and said with heavy cynicism, 'It *was* New Year's Eve. The ships' hooters and fireworks were going like the clappers, and there was a party in the street.'

Which, Horton thought, would have served to cover up the noise of someone entering the building and killing Irene Ebury. *If s*he had been killed. There was that half landing where the stairs turned. The window looked out on to the flat-roofed extension of the kitchen and the gardens beyond. It was, as far as he had seen, the only window which wasn't double glazed. It made a good entry point.

He said, 'When did you last see Mrs Ebury alive?'

'I gave her her medication at eight thirty and made sure she was in bed. Then I checked that she and Mrs Kingsway and our other residents were all asleep before . . .'

'Yes?' prompted Horton.

'Before we had a drink to see the New Year in,' she said defiantly.

'We?'

'The staff. We cracked open a couple of bottles of wine. Well, why not? It was New Year's Eve.'

'What time did you start drinking?'

For a moment she looked as though she might tell Horton it was none of his business. Then she said, 'Just before midnight.'

Horton doubted that. More like nine o'clock, he thought. Maybe Walters would get the truth from the other staff.

'Why all this interest in her?' she asked.

'What kind of things did she talk about, apart from being Miss Southsea and her movie star conquests?' Horton knew that the easiest way to avoid answering a question was to ask another one.

'Not much. I didn't really listen.'

'When you're on duty, do you use the same office as Mrs Northwood?'

'Yes, why?' She looked both surprised and suspicious.

'And do you always lock it when you leave it?'

'Of course.'

Horton didn't know whether to believe her. She held his stare defiantly, but there was that wariness in the back of her eyes.

'When was the last time you entered the basement?'

She looked startled. 'I'm in and out of there all the time.'

Cantelli looked up from his notebook. 'And when did you last check on Mrs Ebury's belongings?'

She looked at each of them in turn. Her face flushed. 'So that's it! They've been stolen and you think I did it. Who pointed the finger at me? I bet it was that cow Angela Northwood. She's never liked me. Well, they can poke their job.' She stubbed out her cigarette with such violence that Horton thought she'd go through the brick mantelpiece.

'The drawer was forced open. You didn't notice it when you went down there?'

'No, I bloody didn't.'

'Did you show Dr Eastwood up to Mrs Ebury's room?'

She glared at him and folded her arms against her flabby bosoms. 'Yes,' she snapped. 'He arrived about half an hour after I called him.'

'And was Mrs Kingsway awake?'

'I woke her not long after I found Irene dead. I got one of the care assistants, Cheryl, to take her downstairs and make her a cup of tea. That's it. I'm not answering any more questions.' She picked her way through the debris and flung open the door. The wind and rain rushed inside, but she held her ground.

So, it couldn't have been the doctor that Mrs Kingsway had seen bending over Irene Ebury. Perhaps she had dreamt it. Either that or there really had been an intruder.

Turning on the threshold, Horton took a lingering look around the dishevelled room not bothering to hide his disgust. His eyes swivelled to Marion Keynes and she shifted uneasily under his hostile gaze.

'Where does your husband work, Mrs Keynes?'

'None of your fucking business,' she blazed, slamming the door on him.

Cantelli zapped open the car. 'Nice woman.'

'Yeah, pity we don't meet more like her.'

Cantelli smiled. 'What bloody awful kids. She's got no control over them. If they were mine.'

'They certainly wouldn't be spoilt brats like that.'

'Makes you tremble to think what they'll turn out like.'

'We'll probably be picking up the results of it in years to come.'

'Some of those toys were pretty expensive,' Cantelli added, pulling away. 'I know because Joe wanted one of those computer games that were lying around the floor. I couldn't afford one on a sergeant's pay, let alone three that I saw there. Makes you wonder where the Keynes got the money from.'

'Could be bought on credit.'

'Or perhaps she stole Irene's jewellery and flogged it.'

That was a possibility which Horton had already considered. 'I wouldn't put it past her. She's sloppy, uncaring, and unfeeling. The Rest Haven is well shot of her.'

'Why become a nurse?'

'To make herself feel superior, I expect.' Horton caught Cantelli's worried glance. 'It happens, Barney, you know that as well as I do. It's how some people get their kicks by bullying the elderly, frail and vulnerable.'

'But nurses are meant to care,' Cantelli protested.

'Most of them do, but you know as well I do that now and again you come across the odd callous bastard or bitch, who either believes they're put on this earth to rid it of those they consider inferior and weak, or they're evil and greedy.'

'Then I think we should investigate Marion Keynes more thoroughly,' declared Cantelli vehemently.

'Walters will tell us what time the staff really started drinking and if it was just before midnight like she says then I'll resign.' Then Horton had another thought and one he didn't much care for. He recalled the uniform that Mrs Northwood had been wearing: dark trousers and a white tunic type top. If Marion Keynes had pinned up her lank blonde hair, and had had her

back to Mrs Kingsway could the old lady have mistaken her for
a man?

Cantelli seemed to have been following the same train of
thought.

'Do you think Marion Keynes could have killed Irene Ebury?'
he said, easing the car into a queue of rush-hour traffic.

Horton considered it for a moment and found the answer
disturbing. 'I think she could be capable of it. Perhaps she stole
Irene's belongings before Christmas, and sold the jewellery to
buy those presents. Then Irene asks to see her belongings, so
while everyone was getting merry on New Year's Eve, Marion
slips up to Irene's room and finishes her off. Mrs Kingsway
wakes and sees the back of Marion Keynes leaning over Irene's
bed and mistakes her for a man because of the uniform.'

He was glad he hadn't mentioned anything about an alleged
intruder to Marion Keynes. If she decided to return to work, and
she thought that Mrs Kingsway could identify her, then he could
have put the elderly lady's life at risk. That was always supposing
Marion Keynes was a killer.

'We'll see what Dr Clayton gets from the autopsy. In the
meantime it won't do any harm to dig a bit deeper into Marion
Keynes' financial background. Find out what her husband does,
Barney, and how many other care homes she's worked in. Also
get out a full description of the jewellery to all the usual fences
and shops.'

'You going to tell Bliss?'

'What do you think?'

Cantelli dropped him off at the station and headed for home.
Horton pushed back the door to the custody cell block and the
heat hit him like a bomb blast. Along with it came the smell of
sweat, dirt, shit and something indefinable to anyone but a police
officer.

'Has someone died in here and no one's bothered to check?'

'Sorry, sir. Two junkies brought in this morning. Haven't had
a chance to put them through the sheep dip yet.'

If only, Horton thought.

'Oh, and DCI Bliss was asking for you, sir. Wants to see you
as soon as you come in.'

Now what? Who complained? Jackson or Farnsworth? Marion
Keynes perhaps? No, he didn't think so. Probably more like
Colin Anston or Geoffrey Welton from the prison.

Knocking first, then entering her office, he drew up startled. She was clearing her desk. Her usually pale skin was flushed, but it wasn't with anger because Horton could see that under her crisp exterior she was secretly very pleased with herself.

'I've been seconded to the Performance and Review Team,' she said without preamble. 'I shall be working out of head-quarters for the next three months helping to review best investigative practices.'

God help us all, thought Horton, but took care not to let his feelings show. They say that every cloud has a silver lining and at least she'd be out of his hair.

'As from tomorrow you will resume command in my absence. Superintendent Reine's instructions.'

Ah, so not hers and clearly against her wishes. Well, good on Reine. Perhaps he wasn't such a stuffed prick after all. 'I'm being made up to acting DCI?'

She eyed him incredulously.

'So it's the job without the pay or the rank,' he added bitterly. He might have guessed.

Cramming the last of her files into her overcrowded briefcase, and straightening up, she said, 'Detective Constable Harriet Lee has been assigned to help you. She starts tomorrow and will be here on secondment for a while.'

He hadn't heard the name before. She wasn't from this station. 'How long is a while?'

'Until the permanent appointments are announced.'

Which would be at the end of January.

'Where's she from?'

'Headquarters. I'm told she's a highly respected officer.'

Yeah, but not operational, Horton thought, and did she have any experience in criminal investigations? He had been hoping for Seaton or Somerfield on secondment. It was just his luck to get a paper pusher.

He followed Bliss into the corridor where she paused. He couldn't mistake the triumphant gleam in her eyes. He guessed this was her dream come true. But why had she been plucked from here to be set down in HQ? She'd only been a DCI one month, and here for about the same length of time, so hardly long enough to make a name for herself. Perhaps it was that e-mail that had impressed the powers that be: C.A.S.E. = R. Well, Bliss had got a result all right.

He sat in his office and listened to the rain hurling itself with manic fury against the window. There was a great deal puzzling him and it didn't include those threatening phone calls received by the TV divers because that was one case that had got a result, for the divers anyway. They had had their publicity in the local press and no doubt the nationals would pick up on the story tomorrow. No, what he was puzzled by was far more serious. There was the death of Irene Ebury and her link with his mother, Jennifer. What could Irene have told him about Jennifer's disappearance? Probably little was the answer, but it still irked him that he might have missed out on learning some valuable information about her.

Then there was the death of Irene's son, Peter; the mysterious intruder at the Rest Haven Nursing Home as seen by Mrs Kingsway; Irene's missing belongings and Marion Keynes' attitude and extravagant Christmas. But, after reviewing all these in a long and tiresome day, he was left with three key questions. Why had Bliss been unexpectedly sent away? Why was someone from outside the division being seconded to his team? And what did either of those things have to do with the deaths of Irene and Peter Ebury?

FIVE

Tuesday, 8.30 a.m.

The questions followed him into work the next morning. He still didn't have any answers, even after considering them at length on his run last night, and while he'd tossed and turned in his bunk listening to an avenging wind screech and howl through the masts. He'd reread the missing person's file on his mother, thanking God it hadn't been lost in the fire that had consumed *Nutmeg*, his previous boat. But there was nothing in Irene Ebury's statement that hinted why his mother had disappeared and no mention of her son, Peter. Horton hadn't really expected it, but it had been worth checking.

Carefully he had stowed it away under one of the bunks, thinking that he really ought to remove it to his office where it might be safer. And he should also think about getting another boat of his own, instead of living on this borrowed one. Maybe during his holiday he'd start looking for one. But that thought brought him back to his questions because he didn't much fancy sailing away without some answers to them.

He had just finished telling Cantelli about Bliss's sudden departure when there was a knock on his office door and he found himself looking into the deep brown eyes and oval face of an attractive, slender Chinese woman in her early thirties.

'DC Harriet Lee, sir,' she said crisply, dashing a smile at Cantelli.

Horton approved of her black tailored trousers and flat shoes. This was no job for stilettos and a skirt. But had she chosen to wear a red sailing jacket because she knew his passion for the pursuit or was that just him being a cynical, suspicious cop with an overactive imagination?

He waved her into the seat next to Cantelli, making the introduction, unable to shake off this uncomfortable feeling that she was here for a reason, which wasn't to help them out. She returned Cantelli's smile with, Horton thought, genuine warmth.

'Mind if I take my jacket off, guv?' she said.

Her accent wasn't local. There was a slight sing-song element to it and he guessed that she was originally from the north of England.

'You sail?' he asked, as she shrugged out of the jacket, gathering up her sleek raven hair in one hand and pushing it behind her.

'When I can.'

Cantelli shuddered.

'What's the matter, Sarge? Don't you like the sea?' she asked brightly.

Despite his readiness to distrust and maybe even dislike her, Horton couldn't help approving of her directness and her cheerful manner.

'Give me dry land any day.'

'You've got no soul, Sarge,' she teased.

'Oh, yes, I have, but mine's strictly earthbound.'

She laughed and Cantelli beamed at her.

She'd quickly got the measure of Cantelli, Horton concluded. Was that because she'd been briefed? If so, what had her boss told her about him? And who was her boss? He certainly didn't think it was him.

'Where's DC Walters?' he asked, wondering what Lee would make of the lumbering detective. Walters hadn't returned from the Rest Haven by the time Horton had left the station late last night.

'He's probably in the canteen,' Cantelli answered.

'Find him, and ask what he found out from the night staff.' Once his office door was shut, Horton addressed Lee. 'Have you worked in Portsmouth before?'

'Not worked, no, but I know the area. I often come down to race off Hayling Island.'

'You're a member of the sailing club?'

'Look, I'm sorry if I've been foisted on you, guv, but I needed to get back into investigations. I got sick of pushing paper around a desk at headquarters. I've had a bit of a personal problem too – relationship fall-out with a guy I worked with. Nothing I can't handle, but I wanted a change. I'm applying to come back operational as soon as there's a position. My governor knows Superintendent Reine and he said you were short-staffed, so here I am.'

Horton nodded. 'And your governor is?'

'Superintendent Warren.'

She said it without hesitation and without any hint that it wasn't true. Horton hadn't heard of him, but he could check her story.

'Glad to have your help,' he said, wondering if he was and noting that she had skipped answering a question. She'd told him nothing of what she had done at HQ. He could press her, but he didn't think it was worth it at this stage.

His phone rang. She made to leave, but he forestalled her with a wave of his hand.

Horton was surprised to hear Corinna Denton's voice and even more surprised when she told him that Perry Jackson had received another threatening telephone call, this time warning him that if he didn't resign from the programme by the end of the week he'd be dead meat. Why were they persisting in this charade? he thought angrily. Surely they had achieved their aim of getting publicity. The small voice in the back of his mind nagged at him that he could just possibly be wrong. But he'd been around too long and heard too many lies not to smell this one. For appearances' sake, though, he supposed that they had better go through the motions.

He told Corinna Denton that an officer would be with her in fifteen minutes and rang off. Quickly explaining the situation to Lee, he ended with, 'Get over to the hotel and talk to Jackson. Pick up a guest and staff list while you're there. And ask Corinna Denton for that list of family and friends she was compiling for us. People who know they're staying at the Queen's Hotel.' As Lee reached his door, Horton added, 'Take Walters with you.' He would get the update on the nursing home from Cantelli.

He watched her go. She walked purposefully, confidently. Then he picked up his telephone and dialled a number. It was answered on the fourth ring with an impatient, 'What?'

Horton smiled. Ray Ferris had never been known for his courteous manner, but he'd been a whizz at research, much like Sergeant Trueman, who was now with the Major Crime Team and whom Horton would dearly have loved to get working with him alongside Cantelli. 'That's no way to greet a member of the public.'

'Public? You? Andy, what the hell do you want? I'm up to my armpits in paperwork.'

'Told you that you should have refused promotion.'

'And have ended up shovelling shit in CID and having drunks spew up over my best suit? Not bloody likely.'

'Then stop moaning and give me some information. DC Harriet Lee – what do you know about her?'

'Never heard of her.'

'She works in your building.

'So do another hundred people. What does she do?'

'At the moment she's seconded to my team, but before that she was pushing paper around like you.'

'Which department?'

'No idea. That's what I'd like you to find out.'

'Why don't you just ask her?'

'And spoil all the fun?'

After a moment, Ray said, 'Leave it with me.' And he hung up.

Horton wondered if Ray would discover the truth or find what he was expected to find. Now for stage two. Uckfield might have heard of, or even know, who this Superintendent Warren was. And he was back from his holiday. So were Catherine and Emma, Horton thought, pushing back his chair, and no phone call from his solicitor yet.

He made his way to the major crime suite where he found the inscrutable and reassuringly dependable Sergeant Trueman.

'How are things?' Horton greeted him, with half an eye on the office next to Uckfield's where he could see DI Dennings, with the phone pressed to his ear and a deep scowl on his squashed-up face.

'It's pretty quiet for a change. Reckon all the criminals are still recovering from too much Christmas pudding. What about you, Andy? I hear you're looking into the death of an old lady at a nursing home. Anything funny about it?'

Trueman didn't miss much. 'I don't know,' he answered truthfully. 'I just don't like the fact her son has also died – and in prison. Do you remember Peter Ebury, armed robbery, killed a security officer called Buckland?'

Trueman threw himself back in the chair and nodded. 'I do. Buckland was ex-job.'

'A copper?' Horton asked surprised. Cantelli hadn't mentioned that.

'Not for long. He did his probation, but didn't last twelve months after that. He went into private investigations for a while, then turned up as a security officer in 2001, when Peter Ebury shot him.'

'Did this come out at trial?'

'I don't know. Crampton was the arresting officer. He retired not long after, in 2002. Buckland's death hit him pretty hard.'

'Why?' Horton perched on the desk opposite Trueman. They had the room to themselves. DC Marsden must be on leave or on an investigation. Horton hadn't known Crampton, though he'd heard of the name.

'He and Buckland were young coppers together.'

'How the devil do you remember all this?' Horton asked, amazed.

'I remember *that* case because by a strange quirk of fate I used to live next door to Buckland. I was only a boy, of course, when he was in the police force, but in those days you were shit scared of coppers and my dad used to say if I didn't behave he'd fetch Buckland in.' He gave a sigh. 'You'd think that was enough to put me off going into the police, wouldn't you? Guess I must have liked the uniform. Either that or the power.'

'What power?' scoffed Horton.

Trueman smiled. 'Want me to see what I can find out about Peter Ebury?'

'Cantelli's already requested the case notes.' Horton hesitated, then added, 'But you might want to look into Irene Ebury for me?' If Trueman discovered the connection with Jennifer, then Horton knew he could trust him not to blab about it. He recognized that this decision marked a step forward for him. Until now he'd been almost paranoid about anyone at the station discovering even the remotest scrap of information about his mother.

'But I wouldn't want to get you into trouble with your boss,' Horton said sarcastically, nodding towards Dennings' office and stifling his feelings of resentment, not without difficulty.

'He doesn't bother me.'

No, thought Horton. Trueman had the measure of DI Dennings – his bark was far worse than his bite and his intelligence way below that of the average retriever. Though Horton recognized that that was his prejudice speaking, tainted with the experience of having worked with Dennings when he was on Vice.

Quickly he relayed to Trueman what little information he had about Irene and what Marion Keynes had said about her being Miss Southsea. 'See if there's any truth in that, and if you can get hold of any photographs of her.' He was curious to see what she had looked like when younger.

'Leave it with me.'

Horton rose, adding, 'Oh, and Dave, keep it between us. I don't want DC Lee, or anyone else, except Cantelli, knowing what you're doing.'

'Who's DC Lee?'

'Good question.'

Horton rapped on Uckfield's door.

'What?' came a roar.

Horton interpreted that as the command to enter. 'Nice tan, Steve.' He eyed Uckfield's craggy brown face, wondering how he could ever have trusted this man. Of course, he'd known the extent of Uckfield's ambition from when they had first joined the force together. It had included marrying the chief constable's daughter. But when Uckfield had suspected Horton of murder, and had given Dennings the job on the Major Crime Team, which had been promised to Horton, he'd felt bitterly betrayed. It was a taste that stayed with him.

'Good holiday?' Horton had difficulty seeing Uckfield's short bulky figure on a set of skis, and was reminded of that photo-graph of Marion Keynes in a swimming costume. Uckfield in swimming trunks, though, was even harder to picture.

'What do you want?' Uckfield barked. 'I've got a backlog that makes me think every single bloody crime of the century's been dumped on my desk.'

'You will go off and enjoy yourself.' Horton sat without being invited. He wondered what crimes Uckfield was slaving over as Trueman had said it was exceptionally quiet. 'Have you heard about DCI Bliss being moved to HQ?' He could see instantly that Uckfield hadn't, and that he was annoyed he hadn't been told. Although Bliss's temporary transfer didn't directly concern Uckfield, Horton knew the big man would see it as a personal slight that he hadn't been informed. 'You've probably got an e-mail about it,' Horton added.

'Along with five hundred others and most of them junk. It'll take me from now until next Christmas to clear this lot.' He gestured at the paperwork on his desk, which looked even greater than that languishing on Horton's desk. 'What is she doing at HQ?'

Horton told him. Uckfield had now got his emotions under control and listened impassively. He finished by saying, 'I've also got a secondment from HQ. DC Harriet Lee.'

'So?'

'I'd like to know what she did at HQ.'

'Ask her.'

'I have. She worked with Superintendent Warren. I thought you might know him.'

'Never heard of him.'

Horton thought that Uckfield was telling the truth. 'I'd like to know what department he runs.'

'Didn't Lee tell you?'

Evasive. 'Thought you might tell me.' Horton held Uckfield's stare. Before Christmas, Uckfield had been forced to confess that he was having an affair with the constabulary's press officer, Madeleine Dewbury. Horton didn't know if it was still going on and he didn't much care. He wasn't into blackmail, but he was owed a favour, several if he wanted to start counting the times he'd got Uckfield out of the shit.

After a moment Uckfield said tersely, 'I haven't got time for this.' His phone rang. Horton didn't budge. Uckfield reached for it and hissed, 'I'll see what I can find out.'

That was two senior officers Horton had enquiring on his behalf. And two people nosing around might just get him a reaction from Lee or even Superintendent Reine, his boss. When you want to ruffle a few feathers, put a couple of cats amongst the pigeons and wait to see what flies out.

Horton told Cantelli what Trueman had said about Buckland, the shot security officer.

Cantelli frowned, puzzled. 'I don't remember anyone saying he was ex job, but I might have missed or forgotten it.'

That was possible but unlikely as far as Cantelli was concerned. 'You worked with Crampton. What was he like?'

'Fair. A good detective and a good copper. He had a bit of bad luck while he was on the case. His boy got knocked down by a car. He wasn't too badly injured, but I remember Crampton handed the case over to Jempson. By then Peter Ebury was in custody and the case more or less sewn up. Crampton died five years ago. Heart attack. Didn't have much of a retirement, two years.' Cantelli looked troubled. 'And you say he knew Buckland?'

'So Trueman claims.'

'He's probably right then. My memory's not as good as it was.'

Horton scoffed, but he guessed Cantelli had other more personal and pressing things on his mind. 'We'll see what the case notes say.'

'Should be with us later today. There were a lot of resources thrown at that case, I do remember that. But Ebury and Mayfield weren't on the loose for long.'

'There was no doubt they did it?'

'None whatsoever. Caught red-handed.'

So no claims of being framed there. Horton glanced at his watch. It was about time they left for their appointment with Dr Eastwood. As Cantelli headed towards the surgery, Horton said, 'What do you think of our new team member?'

'Seems nice. Bright girl too, and energetic. Walters looked a bit shell-shocked when she marched him off to the Queen's Hotel. She'll keep him on his toes.'

'Pity his poor bloody toes,' Horton muttered, and told him of his suspicions about her appointment.

Cantelli looked surprised, then concerned. 'But why?'

'Maybe someone doesn't want us nosing around Peter Ebury's death.'

'Then why not simply warn us off. DCI Bliss or Superintendent Reine could have ordered us to drop it.' Cantelli dashed him a glance as the penny dropped. 'Bliss did tell you to leave it, and you carried on regardless.'

'Yes. And Bliss must have gone to Reine, probably to complain about my insubordination, or to ask that I be transferred. But someone must already have been in touch with Reine, probably after we'd started asking questions at the prison, and told Reine to let me run with the investigation. It's not a matter of preventing us from nosing around, but wanting us to.'

'If there's something funny about Peter Ebury's death, then why doesn't whoever it is – Special Branch or the Prison Directorate – investigate it themselves?'

Horton stared at the windscreen wipers doing their valiant best to cope with the lashing rain. Cantelli was right. If there was a serious crime being committed in that prison, such as drug smuggling, then declaring Ebury's death as suspicious would mean exposing the prison to the most vigorous investigation, and perhaps someone didn't want that. But that didn't take into account what Dr Clayton might find. *If* she discovered that Ebury's death was suspicious, then whether the prison liked it or not they'd have to submit to a major investigation. And why let him loose on the case if they wanted it hushed up? No, it didn't make any kind of sense and until it did he'd carry on asking questions. Meanwhile he'd keep an eye on Lee.

'What did Walters get from the nursing home?'

'The staff started drinking at ten o'clock on New Year's Eve and not midnight as Marion Keynes claimed, and she was there drinking with them. None of them saw or heard anything unusual, and Walters couldn't find anyone who went to check on Mrs Ebury or Mrs Kingsway all night. Marion Keynes certainly didn't go up there before midnight but she might have done in the early hours of the morning. She returned to her office, after their little party, but no one can be sure what time this was. It was a fairly quiet night patient-wise, or so they claimed.'

'The poor souls were probably drugged up to the eyeballs,' muttered Horton.

'You think so?' Cantelli said sadly. 'I'd hate to see my mum in a place like that.'

Horton had to admit it wasn't the best nursing home he'd come across, but it wasn't the worst either. They still had some questions to ask about it though, and he thought a call to social services wouldn't be out of place.

'No one noticed that Mrs Ebury's drawer had been broken into either,' Cantelli added, expertly manoeuvring the car into a space about the size of a postage stamp, outside a modern building that proclaimed it was the Southsea Health Centre.

So no help there. They were asked to wait in a brightly lit and well-designed reception that looked more like an architect's office than a doctors' surgery. Horton wasn't complaining about that, or the fact that it was devoid of patients. He hated these places even more than he hated hospitals, and that was saying something. He was just getting impatient when a receptionist showed them into Dr Eastwood's consulting room.

'Can we hurry this up? I have a list of patients to visit.' Eastwood said brusquely, without looking up from his correspondence.

Horton remained silent and gestured to Cantelli to do the same. After a moment Eastwood glanced up. He let out an exasperated sigh and threw down his pen. 'What is it?'

Cantelli said, 'You certified Irene Ebury's death as heart failure. Is that normal with dementia patients?'

'Not always.' Eastwood frowned at them. Horton held the emaciated doctor's hawkish stare impassively until Eastwood was forced to divert it back to Cantelli. He answered in a brisk tone. 'Usually with vascular dementia, the patient suffers a series of mini strokes, each one getting slightly worse and coming more frequently until the patient is very ill and bedridden. Pneumonia sets in and that is often is the cause of death. Mrs Ebury also had a weak heart.'

'Did she ever mention her son or any other relatives to you?' Horton asked.

Eastwood's head shot to Horton. 'No.'

Horton wasn't convinced it was the truth. 'We'd like to see her records.'

'They're confidential.' Eastwood's eyes narrowed in his pinched face.

'It would help us with our inquiries.'

'Which are?' Eastwood said archly.

Horton was glad Eastwood wasn't his doctor. 'We are treating her death as suspicious.'

'You can't honestly believe that! Who would want to kill her?'

Horton had had enough. He felt anger boil up inside him at Eastwood's scornful tone. Now, let's see how you like this, you string of caustic humanity, he thought. 'For all I know, you, Dr Eastwood.'

'How dare you—!'

'And how dare you waste my time,' Horton raged, leaning across the desk. 'You either cooperate or I take you in for questioning.'

'On what grounds?'

'We have a witness who claims Mrs Ebury was killed.' Horton stretched Mrs Kingsway's words to suit his purpose.

'That's ridiculous!' Eastwood gave Horton a stare that was like the frozen plains of Siberia. But if he wanted icy then Horton could give him glacial.

Eastwood rose and began stuffing some records into his case. 'Mrs Keynes called me to the Rest Haven at six a.m. and I arrived there at six thirty. I examined Mrs Ebury and gave the cause of death as heart failure. She had heart problems and high blood pressure.'

'We'll see if you're right then, doctor. There is to be an autopsy.'

Eastwood flushed, opened his mouth to say something, then obviously thought better of it.

The doctor's times matched with those Marion Keynes had given them. But there was something puzzling Horton. 'I didn't think GPs did out of hours visits.' He had the satisfaction of seeing Eastwood look put out.

'Mrs Keynes has my home number and thought it best to call me.'

Now, why was that? wondered Horton. Eastwood tried to bluff it out with a cold stare, but Horton could see he was worried. That was another thing that bothered Horton. If Marion Keynes had discovered Irene Ebury at five thirty a.m., then why had she waited until six to call the doctor? He supposed she could have been organizing the removal of Mrs Kingsway from the room. But she claimed she had delegated that to the care assistant, Cheryl, and although the old lady would have taken some time to get out of bed it could have been done by the time Dr Eastwood arrived even if Marion Keynes had called him the moment she discovered Irene.

'Now, I have patients to visit—'

'Just one more thing,' Horton said, noting the relief on Eastwood's face. 'Did Irene Ebury have more than one child?'

'I've already said her medical history is confidential. When, or if, you can prove that a serious crime has been committed, then you can see her notes, but only if you have a warrant and only those parts of her record that are relevant to your inquiry.'

'Her son died yesterday.'

Eastwood was genuinely surprised. After a moment he said, 'She only had the one pregnancy that went to full term.'

And that must have been Peter. Horton heard what Eastwood wasn't saying. Had Irene had a series of miscarriages or abortions even? Not that that helped them or was relevant. He had wondered if she might have other children somewhere, or perhaps given up a child, or children, for adoption.

'And her GP before you?'

Eastwood snapped. 'Dr Mason. Somerton Health Centre.'

Horton felt a familiar jolt. That had been his health centre as a boy and his mother's, which indicated that Irene must have lived in the same area as them. Had Irene helped his mother get that job in the casino?

He hoped that Dr Mason might be more amenable. He asked Cantelli to drop him back at the station and then to visit the Somerton Health Centre.

'See if you can find out who Irene's social worker was. She must have had one to help her move to the Rest Haven. If they're not still around, then there must be a file on her. Make an appointment for us to see it.'

In his office, Horton called Anston at the prison, only to be told they hadn't unearthed a single relative. There was no word from Ray Ferris or Steve Uckfield about DC Lee, but maybe it was too soon. He saw her stride into the CID office and in her wake followed a heavily perspiring and panting Walters.

Joining them, Horton said, 'If I didn't know better, I'd say that DC Lee has made you walk back from the Queen's Hotel.'

Walters took a large handkerchief from the pocket of his trousers and mopped his forehead as he flopped heavily into a chair.

'Only from the car park,' Lee replied.

'Yeah, but it's the pace she walks at,' Walters grumbled. 'Makes Paula Radcliffe look like she's strolling in a marathon.'

'So how did you get on with the divers?'

'The call was made to Mr Jackson's hotel room, but it didn't go through the hotel switchboard, which suggests that, like the others, it came from another hotel room or was made by one of the staff. It was a man and Mr Jackson claims it is the same caller as before. He seemed very unnerved by it. He said he had no idea who is doing it.'

'Do you believe him?'

She thought for a moment. 'Yes.'

Horton wasn't convinced, but he told Lee to start checking out the names on the lists that Corinna Denton had given her and for Walters to take the hotel staff list. His phone was ringing and he hurried back to his office hoping it was Ray Ferris. It wasn't.

'Why did you go to the airport yesterday morning?' Frances Greywell sounded cross.

Well, tough. Why shouldn't he see his daughter?

He said: 'I like aeroplanes.'

There was silence for a moment and he could imagine her rolling her grey eyes. 'Catherine is saying that Emma cried all the way home; that you upset her and it's not fair on the child.'

Shit. Horton gripped the telephone and felt his heart somersault as he imagined Emma's tears. He told himself that Catherine was lying. The last thing he wanted was to hurt his daughter.

'This is not good for us, Andy. Catherine's lawyers will use the fact that Emma seeing you unnecessarily upsets her.'

'Rubbish,' he dismissed, but he knew that what she said was true. There had to be a reason why Catherine was being so obstructive. Cantelli said it was jealousy. Maybe he was right and Catherine was jealous of his love for Emma and hers for him. But that didn't help him. He shouldn't have gone to the airport, it had been a mistake, but it was too late for that now. He didn't want to jeopardize his chances of seeing Emma. He took a breath to calm himself.

'Tell Catherine, through her lawyer, that I'm sorry. I won't try to see Emma again without it being agreed.'

'You mean it?'

Frances Greywell sounded surprised and sceptical. He didn't blame her for that.

'Yes. But see if you can arrange for me to see Emma as quickly as possible.'

'OK. I'll be in touch.'

He sat back, wondering what would happen next, and was thankfully shaken out of his morbid thoughts of a life without his daughter by a brief knock on the door. Lee entered.

'I've just had a Mrs Collins on the line.'

Horton groaned silently. He knew the poor woman was distraught over losing her son in that car accident on Christmas Eve. He wasn't being harsh, but he thought he'd dealt with it. 'I told Walters to see her.'

'He said he hasn't had time.'

'Did he even call her?'

Lee shrugged, which Horton interpreted as no. Bloody Walters. But then he had kept him rather occupied.

'She's adamant her son's death was no accident. And there's something else. It might not mean anything, but it is interesting in light of what Walters has told me about your investigations at the Rest Haven Nursing Home.'

Horton's attention heightened. 'And that is?'

'Did you know that Daniel Collins worked there?'

Did he indeed! Now that was interesting. But what was even more remarkable and puzzling was the fact that none of the staff had mentioned him.

SIX

As Horton headed for the Collins's house with DC Lee, he recalled Angela Northwood saying they were a care assistant down, but she had made no mention that it was Daniel Collins and that he'd been killed in a tragic accident. Of course she had been tired and Mr Kingsway bellowing at her probably hadn't helped. He didn't see how Daniel Collins's death could have any bearing on the deaths of Irene Ebury and her son, but it was another factor that disturbed him about that nursing home.

He said as much to Lee, then swiftly filled in the gaps that Walters had left out during their twenty-minute journey across the city to Southsea. Pulling up outside a semi-detached house facing a cemetery, she said, 'Not the best place to live when someone you love has just died.'

Horton stifled the usual copper's black sense of humour, which would have drawn the retort, 'Handy for the funeral though,' and climbed out. The rain had eased to a fine drizzle, which a blustery wind seemed intent on tormenting. He let his gaze drift up the facade of the solid, well-kept Edwardian semi, a smaller version of the nursing home in Whitaker Road and about a half mile away, and saw the fresh white net curtains, a polished door handle and neatly tended garden. The gate squeaked as he pushed it back and he steeled himself to meet a mother's grief.

Mrs Collins showed them into a high-ceilinged and comfortably furnished living room, where the air was heavy with the smell of bereavement. There were no signs that Christmas had been celebrated here, only photographs of Daniel Collins and condolence cards. His eyes fell on the curly-haired little boy holding a trumpet and the teenager on holiday, then recent photographs of a grown man of thirty with dark hair and square spectacles, who was clean shaven with a slightly awkward look about his oval face. Horton could see the resemblance to his mother: a slim lady in her early fifties, with light brown hair cut in a short bob. Her eyes behind her glasses were full of anger, which Horton knew hid her pain. Despite this she looked tired, but not as tired as the middle-aged, balding man sitting quietly in the opposite chair with a bewildered look on his unshaven, lined face. Daniel Collins had been their only child.

After the introductions and the invitation for them to take a seat, Horton said gently, 'The post-mortem results confirm your son died of drowning, Mrs Collins.' He had quickly reread both the incident report and the post-mortem report before leaving the station.

'But *how* did he drown?' Mrs Collins said irritably. 'That's what I want to know and what I want you to investigate. And don't tell me Daniel was drunk, because I don't believe it. Daniel didn't drink. None of us do.'

But there had been alcohol in Daniel's bloodstream. Not an immense amount according to the autopsy report, which hadn't been conducted by Dr Clayton but enough to take Daniel Collins over the breathalyser limit. He might not have been paralytic, but Horton knew that drink affected different people in different ways.

He caught Lee's expression and guessed what she was thinking.

Lots of children lied to their parents, even when they were in their thirties. It was pointless to contradict her. Maybe Mr Collins had tried and given up, though judging by the state of him, Horton thought it was taking all his effort to continue breathing. His heart went out to them. How would he feel if it were Emma? He knew the answer to that by the sickening lurch in his stomach.

Horton sat forward. Quietly he said, 'What do *you* think happened, Mrs Collins?'

For a moment she seemed taken aback. Then there was a minute relaxation in her shoulders, barely detectable, before she was ramrod stiff again. All her grief was being held in and Horton guessed that if she gave into it for just one moment she would be completely overwhelmed.

'Someone forced him off the road on to the Wharf and into the harbour.'

'There was no evidence of any other car being involved. No tyre marks, no witnesses.'

'Doesn't mean there wasn't anyone,' she said stubbornly, flashing him an angry look.

'And how do you explain the alcohol found in Daniel's bloodstream?' He waited for her to say the pathologist had got it wrong.

'Someone must have given it to Daniel against his will.'

'Heather,' Mr Collins stirred himself to speak. His tone was one of weary resignation as though he'd heard this a thousand times already, which Horton guessed he had.

'Are you saying that someone spiked Daniel's drinks?'

'It happens.'

It did. And because Daniel didn't normally drink he could have become drunk more quickly on what other men might have been able to handle. Horton wasn't going to say that though. He wondered if anyone had checked Daniel's movements before the accident. He doubted it. There would have been no cause to, until now. And the only reason he was interested was because of where Daniel Collins had worked and his suspicions concerning Irene Ebury's death.

'Where did Daniel go on Christmas Eve?'

Taking her cue that he was treating this seriously, Lee took her notebook and pen from her rucksack, which had been slung over her shoulder.

Mrs Collins studied Horton for a moment, then took a breath.

Horton saw the tears in her eyes and the relief on her face. He was glad of his decision to help even if it led to nothing more than confirming this had been a tragic accident.

Clearly with an effort at holding herself together, she said, 'He went out just after eight thirty and said he would be back before midnight. When he didn't return we were upset, weren't we, Dad?'

Ted Collins nodded but didn't speak.

Mrs Collins continued. 'The next thing we know the police are at the door at two o'clock in the morning to tell us our son was dead.' She took a deep breath as her voice quavered.

Horton left a pause before continuing. 'Did he say where he was going?'

'No, and I didn't ask. It was his business.'

'I wish we had,' Ted Collins said quietly.

'Well, we didn't and that's the end to it,' his wife snapped.

'Did he call you during the night?'

'No. He always saw Christmas Day in with us. It was tradition. If he didn't come home, then something must have happened to him. Someone must have prevented him. Even if Daniel had been held up somewhere, he would have rung.'

She was implying that Daniel must have been held against his will, but Horton thought Daniel could have been so drunk that he had lost all track of time and had forgotten to call home.

'How did he seem when he left here?' asked Lee.

Mrs Collins eyes flicked upwards to Lee's. 'Fine.' The word came out in a choke, but she cleared her throat. 'He said, "I won't be long," and that was it.'

There was a short pause before Lee asked gently, 'Did he have a girlfriend, Mrs Collins?'

Horton watched the couple's expressions. Mr Collins looked sad, and Mrs Collins surprised.

'No.'

Horton this time. 'Did he take anything with him when he went out?'

'Only his jacket.' Mrs Collins frowned, puzzled, as though she was remembering something. Finally she said, 'Now you come to mention it, he did seem a little excited.'

Horton wondered if that was the benefit of hindsight speaking. 'Did anyone call him?'

'They might have done on his mobile.'

Horton could check that with the phone company.

Mrs Collins added, 'He could have been meeting someone who spiked his drinks and then forced him off the road. Perhaps he was chasing Daniel in another car.'

'Do you realize what you're saying, Mrs Collins?' Horton asked solemnly.

'Yes. Daniel was killed by someone. I'm not saying it was deliberate; maybe it was high spirits that got out of hand. But my son was killed and not accidentally, and I won't rest until someone takes notice of me and does something about it,' she finished defiantly, glaring at him.

OK, thought Horton, holding her gaze. She could be right.

'We'll need some details and to look at his room,' he replied firmly.

Mrs Collins opened her mouth, maybe to continue protesting, then his words and the tone of his voice penetrated her anger. Her shoulders slumped. The tears began to well up in her eyes. 'You'll investigate?' she stammered, surprised.

'Yes.'

'Oh, thank the Lord. Thank you.' A sob caught in her throat and exploded into a heart-wrenching cry. The sight of her grief tore at Horton's heart. He rose as Mr Collins put his arms around his wife. She buried her head on his shoulder, and he turned his face into her hair. They cried together. Probably, Horton thought, for the first time since hearing the dreadful news.

Lee swiftly departed in the direction of the kitchen. Horton tried to shut out their sorrow and instead concentrate on the photographs of Daniel Collins. There was one taken on holiday – Cornwall judging by the rugged scenery and sweeping bay – and another on a small yacht with Daniel in his twenties. He wasn't smiling in either photograph. He looked a fairly studious, solemn kind of man.

Lee returned with a glass of water.

Ted Collins took the glass and, easing his wife away from him, said, 'Heather, drink this.'

She stopped sobbing and took it in both hands. After a sip, she pulled herself up, took a handkerchief from the sleeve of her cardigan and said briskly, 'Tea, Inspector?'

'Please.' He didn't want one, but he knew that it would give her something practical to do. 'Perhaps Mr Collins would like to show us Daniel's room while you're making it.'

They both rose. She headed down the passageway to the kitchen and Ted Collins led the way upstairs.

'Tell me about your son,' Horton said, knowing this was going to be difficult for the man, but that it might also be therapeutic.

'He was a quiet lad, a bit shy, but very caring. He was a qualified nurse, used to work at the hospital until a year ago,' Ted said over his shoulder, as they came out on the landing. 'His mother worshipped the ground he walked on. It's very hard for her.'

And hard for you too, Horton thought, stepping into a large bedroom at the front of the house with a stone bay window that overlooked the cemetery. It was very neat. The double bed was made and Daniel's clothes were presumably stacked away in the white laminate fitted cupboards either side of a fireplace that clearly wasn't used judging by the small cannonballs that were placed in the hearth. The room was painted cream and there were only a couple of pictures of bland seascapes on the wall, which could have been anywhere in Britain. Nothing remarkable or very personal here. There was a door opposite the cupboards, which Horton guessed led into a bathroom or shower room.

Ted Collins headed for it and opening it said: 'This was Daniel's lair, as we called it. We had this door put in especially to connect the two rooms, some years ago.'

Now this was more interesting. Horton stepped into another good-sized room with a single window, once again giving on to the front. His eyes took in and registered the laptop computer on the desk that faced the window. Opposite the door, one complete wall was covered with shelves containing storage boxes of varying sizes from those resembling a shoebox to others that clearly held magazines. They were all labelled. Amongst them was a row of books. On the back wall was a cabinet with a hi-fi on top of it and beside it an easy chair. Horton noted the room's almost clinical neatness, but it was the photographs on the wall that really took his interest. They were stunning under-water pictures.

'Marine photography was Daniel's hobby,' Mr Collins said sadly but proudly, following Horton's gaze.

And he had been very good at it. Horton crossed to look more closely at them. One was of a wreck with a shoal of fish in front of it, and the other two were of thick fleshy tube-like masses of white and orange clinging to rocks. Some kind of coral, he guessed. His mind flicked to the television divers. Strange that Daniel should also be a diver, but it was not significant as far as Jackson and Farnsworth were concerned. Daniel definitely couldn't have made those threatening calls.

He turned to see Ted Collins struggling with his emotions.

'Can you give us a moment? We'd like to look round with your permission and then we'll be down for that tea.'

'Of course.' Ted Collins halted at the door. 'Even if you don't find anything, I want to thank you. This means a lot to us.'

'Sad,' Lee said with a sigh.

Horton silently agreed. He crossed to the computer desk, noting that only the laptop was allowed to despoil its surface. The drawers contained pens, pencils, paper clips, stationery, all very neatly placed. No diary. 'What's your gut reaction?'

'Daniel Collins could have met his end, just as the report says he did.' Lee opened the cabinet. 'He could have had a secret life away from here. One in which he boozed and whored. He could be a mummy's boy, and the type that grooms underaged girls for sex on the Internet.' Lee crossed to the computer. 'He could have been having an affair with a married woman, or been gay, but whatever we discover – even if it's just the fact he was a secret drinker and couldn't stand another Christmas Eve with his parents – it'll break their hearts again. Despite the connection with Rest Haven, I think we'll find a lover, and one he didn't want his parents to know about.'

He looked up. 'You really believe that?'

'It's a strong possibility. There's some expensive camera equipment in here.'

He crossed to examine the shelves. The boxes were labelled with dates and place names: the Solent, Isle of Wight, Cornwall, Devon, Cyprus, Singapore. They contained CDs, also labelled. Horton guessed they held photographs Daniel had taken whilst diving. Apart from photography and diving magazines, Daniel's reading material consisted of books on underwater photography, photography in general, marine archaeology, and a couple of Clive Cussler novels.

If there was something going on at the Rest Haven, and Daniel had discovered it, would that have been enough for someone to kill him? Horton wondered. He picked up a novel and flicked through it. It would depend on what it was, he considered. What could warrant taking a man's life, or two lives if you counted Irene? he thought, stashing the book back on the shelf. But then he knew people could kill for something as small as a paper clip.

Could Daniel have discovered Marion Keynes stealing Irene Ebury's belongings and threatened to go to the police? Could Marion Keynes, and possibly her husband, have plied Daniel with drinks and forced him off the road in order to silence him? He felt cold at the thought. He knew he had to consider it as a possibility.

Lee was poking around in the desk. 'There's no address book. I guess he kept that on his computer.'

'We'll ask if we can take it with us, and get Daniel's mobile phone number before we leave. I'd like a record of his calls. Let's have that tea.'

Heather Collins now looked weary beyond the point of tiredness. Her grieving had begun, leaving her a shell of the woman she had been when he had first seen her. He took his tea and sat down, resisting the temptation to look at his watch. Instead he subtly looked at the clock on the mantelpiece. It was almost two thirty. He wondered how Cantelli had got on with Dr Mason and whether he had also had time to discover what Marion Keynes' husband did for a living. Was it too early for Trueman to have got information on Irene Ebury? And had Ferris or Uckfield found out more about DC Lee? What had Dr Clayton discovered from the post-mortem on Peter Ebury and how was she getting on with Irene's? It was time to get back to the station, but he had a few more questions to ask first.

'Did your son belong to a diving club?'

Despite her grief, Mrs Collins looked surprised at his question. 'Yes, the Eastney Sub-aqua Club.'

Horton knew it. It was almost opposite Southsea Marina, his old home, and he had a hankering to get back to it, even on his borrowed boat. On Saturday he would sail her back there.

Lee said, 'Has Daniel ever been married or engaged?'

It was Mrs Collins who answered. 'No. And now . . .' She pushed her hand to her mouth to prevent herself from crying.

Horton quickly said, 'I'd like a list of all your son's friends with their addresses. That way we can discover if Daniel saw any of them on Christmas Eve.'

Heather and Ted Collins nodded.

'I'd also like to take his computer,' Horton continued.

Ted rose and left the room.

'Did Daniel ever talk about his work at the Rest Haven?'

'Not much, Inspector. He should have stayed in hospital nursing, but he didn't like the shift work or the long hours as his hobby always came first. And they've put nurses on contracts now so there's no job security.'

'Were there any residents that he was particularly close to or who he talked about more than others?'

She shook her head. So no help there, Horton thought. 'Was he worried about anything at work?'

'I don't think so. He never said.'

Mr Collins returned and handed the computer to DC Lee.

Horton asked gently, 'Have you arranged the funeral yet?'

'It's on Thursday. Ten thirty at Portchester Crematorium, then back here afterwards.'

The same day as Cantelli's father's funeral; that was at twelve thirty. If he was also going to attend Daniel's, then it was going to be a grim day. He put down his mug and rose.

'It would be helpful if you could work on that list of names right away and telephone it through to DC Lee.' Horton handed Heather Collins his card. 'You can reach her on the main CID number. If she's not there, call me.'

At the door, Heather Collins hesitated. Horton could see her struggling with something. After a moment she said, 'Do you know why I was so convinced that this couldn't have been an accident?'

Horton suspected he was going to hear how she'd had a dream or a premonition. He was wrong.

'I was diagnosed with breast cancer just before Christmas. Daniel was devastated, even though I tried to reassure him I'd be fine. So you see, it was even more important to him to be with me this Christmas Eve. Oh, I know what's going through your mind – then why did he go out? He said it was for me. He wanted to make sure I had the best possible treatment and was going to see to it that I did. It doesn't matter now. But thank you for taking us seriously, Inspector. It means a lot to us.'

He smiled reassuringly but his smile vanished as he climbed into the car. Something about Mrs Collins's statement had struck him. He glanced at Lee as she pulled away. Had the same thought occurred to her? She showed no sign of it. But Horton wondered

if Daniel had been going out to blackmail someone to fund his
mother's treatment privately, and that 'someone' had a connection with the nursing home. Again Marion Keynes sprang to
mind. But would she have had enough money to pay Daniel?
Horton doubted it from what he'd seen of her house and he knew
that care assistants, and even nursing home managers, didn't earn
a fortune.

There was an alternative. Had Daniel decided to tell Marion
Keynes that he wouldn't betray her to the police if he could have
a share in the sale proceeds of Irene's jewellery? But even then
he doubted that they would have fetched much, so perhaps other
residents' jewellery had gone missing? And there was something
else troubling him. If Daniel had been murdered – and Horton
discounted the improbable theory that Daniel had been forced
off the road by another driver – then how the devil had his killer
done it?

SEVEN

'The Daniel Collins fatality, Christmas Eve – anything odd
about it?' Horton addressed Bob Wellsley, the uniformed
officer standing on the other side of his desk. It was late
afternoon and Horton had read and reread the report until he
knew it backwards.

Lee was trying to tease something out of Daniel's computer,
and Walters had almost finished going through the lists that
Corinna Denton and the Queen's Hotel had given him. So far
he'd discovered bugger all.

Horton guessed that Walters didn't really know what he was
looking for anyway, and Horton wasn't so sure himself. If
someone had a grudge against Perry Jackson, then it wasn't going
to come to light simply by checking criminal records. It would
mean questioning anyone who had a connection with the TV
diver, and that would take for ever, not to mention more staff.
Horton simply didn't have the resources.

Cantelli had returned from Dr Mason with the disappointing
news that Mason had been as unhelpful as Dr Eastwood.

'You'd have thought there was a code amongst them to obstruct the police as much as possible,' Cantelli had said. 'Either that or our friend Eastwood called Mason and warned him.'

'Why would he do that?'

'Because he didn't like you?' volunteered Cantelli cheerfully.

Probably, but Horton wasn't going to lose any sleep over that. So unless Dr Clayton found anything from the autopsy, or they discovered that the belongings of other residents were missing, the investigation would go nowhere.

'There doesn't appear to be anything suspicious about it,' Bob Wellsley answered. He was a solid dependable man, thorough, middle-aged and very experienced. If Wellsley hadn't sniffed out anything, then maybe it was an accident after all.

'His mother's adamant that someone forced him off the road.'

'There were no skid marks on the road and no witnesses have come forward.'

Horton knew that. He had the photographs of the scene spread out on his desk, but they were of the car and none of Daniel Collins because the fire fighters had got him out in the hope that he might still be alive. The front of the car was crumpled, but not as much as Horton had expected, so the impact couldn't have been severe. All the car windows were open.

'Where's the car now?'

'In the compound, sir.'

'Has it been examined?'

Wellsley looked surprised. 'I thought it was a drunk driver.'

'It might still be, but there's an element of doubt.' Horton would get the forensic team on to it. He studied the schematic that Wellsley had drawn. 'So Collins was heading in the direction of Southsea and presumably home. Any idea how fast he was travelling?'

'The absence of skid marks indicates that he wasn't speeding. I would say he simply veered off the road.'

Horton frowned. 'Why veer to the left and up on to the wharf? He would have had to drive up the slope into the small car park before going over the top. Why not veer to the right and into the crash barrier?'

'A vehicle could have been travelling northwards. Collins was drunk, thought it was closer than it was, or he was blinded by its headlights, he wrenched the wheel over to his left and ended up bounding up the wharf and over the edge, his reactions dulled by the drink.' Wellesley scratched his nose and added,

'It could have been a bird, perhaps a swan from Salterns Lake, or brent geese flying low, and Collins swerved to avoid them.'

Unlikely, thought Horton, but Wellsley continued. 'There is another theory, not that I go along with it . . .' He hesitated.

'What?' prompted Horton. He was prepared to go with anything at this stage.

'The ghost.'

He gave Wellsley a sceptical look.

'Yeah, I know, but that part of the road is supposed to be haunted by the victim of a previous traffic accident. Sometimes in the rain and fog, drivers have claimed to see it and there's certainly been more accidents on that stretch of road than anywhere else along it, and more fatalities there than on any other road in Portsmouth.'

'We'll discount the spook. Was there anything inside the car or the boot?'

'Only the usual documents, which were rather wet: insurance, MOT certificate, breakdown services details, and the spare wheel and tools in the boot.'

'No mobile phone?'

'No. Could be at the bottom of the sea.'

And the tide went out exposing mud where the incident had occurred. Raising his voice, Horton called, 'Walters! Got a job for you.'

Wellsley left with a grin, guessing what fate Horton had in store for the overweight detective. Horton briefed Walters and countered his grumbles with the advice that he get himself a pair of fisherman's waders. Then he called the scientific services department and asked if they could examine Daniel's car, before turning his thoughts to the interview with the Collinses. There was something bugging him, but he couldn't think what it was, and though he sat for a few minutes trying to grasp it, it still eluded him.

He rose and stared out of the window, watching the rain slanting down on to the overflowing drains in the station car park. Were none of these strands going to hang together? Was he completely off his trolley for even bothering to follow up the Eburys' and Daniel Collins's deaths? Bliss would have thought so. Why hadn't anyone at the Rest Haven mentioned Daniel's death? Perhaps he hadn't been very well liked.

And why hadn't Ray Ferris or Steve Uckfield got back to him

with any news on DC Lee? If he could just get it clear in his mind that her secondment was genuine and Bliss's departure a gift from heaven, then he could settle down to trying to solve some of the other hundred and one cases clogging his desk.

His head was thudding. Cantelli was right. He needed to take some time off. Next week he would. He pulled his blinds shut and marched into the CID office, swiftly crossing to Lee. Cantelli was on the phone.

'How are you getting on?'

'Not much so far. Just some rather lovely photographs. We really need to access his e-mails and view his Internet record.'

'Leave that for now. Go to the Rest Haven, find out if Daniel Collins was the only male working there and what the staff thought of him. Did he know or ever speak to the owners? Oh, and while you're at it, get some feedback on what the staff think of the owners, Mr Chrystal and his brothers. Also check the register of the residents' belongings with what is in the drawers, see if anything else has gone missing.'

Lee plucked her jacket from the back of her chair and left without protest or comment.

Cantelli came off the phone. 'Ian Keynes is a lorry driver. He's worked for Ryan Oldham for the last eighteen months.'

Horton considered this. 'Oldham's Wharf is less than half a mile from Salterns Wharf, where Daniel died. Years ago Oldham's used to operate out of Salterns.'

'So?'

Cantelli was right. Where did that lead them? Nowhere.

'Neither Marion nor her husband has a criminal record, but their credit rating is very poor. I've just got Marion's previous employment record. I'll start checking it out to see if she left anywhere under a cloud. The Chrystal brothers own four nursing homes in the area including the Rest Haven. The abbreviated accounts at Companies House show a fairly healthy profit. And I've got the Commission of Social Care Inspector Report for the Rest Haven. It's not bad, but like I said before, I wouldn't put my mum there.'

'What's wrong with it?' Horton asked, interested, sitting in Walters' vacant chair.

'The inspector visited unannounced in July last year following a few adverse comments from relatives.' Cantelli briefly consulted his notes. 'He said there wasn't regular supervision of the staff,

the residents' social and emotional needs weren't being indi-
vidually assessed and new equipment and furnishing was needed
in several of the residents' rooms.'

Horton could back that up by what he'd seen.

'He also said that the delivery, storage and management of
medicines needed improving,' continued Cantelli. 'I think it's
about time they got another visit.'

'OK, but wait until we've finished our investigations.'

'Oh, and the photographic unit called and said there's nothing
they can get from the photocopied photos I gave them of Irene
and Peter Ebury. They need the originals.'

And Horton thought they had little chance of getting them.
'Did you make that appointment with Irene's social worker?'

'Yes, but it's not the same one who was handling her case
when she moved to the nursing home. She left a year ago.
Tomorrow morning, nine thirty.'

Horton rose, glancing at his watch. 'Well, we might not need
to keep it if Dr Clayton confirms death by natural causes. Come
on, let's see what she has to say.'

They were shown into Dr Clayton's office by Tom, the whistling
mortuary assistant.

'I was just beginning to think you weren't coming,' Gaye greeted
them, looking up from her computer screen. She nodded a farewell
to Tom and gestured them into the seats across her desk.

Horton was surprised to see that her office was still full of
Christmas cards; they were spread out on filing cabinets and
blue-tacked to the walls. Christmas seemed like a lifetime ago
to him.

She swivelled her chair across from the computer screen. 'First,
Peter Ebury, cause of death, respiratory failure. He looked pretty
healthy and I wouldn't have thought he would keel over with
that, but it's what he died of. I've sent his organs for further
tests and I've taken blood samples, but it looks as though he
died a natural death and prematurely. Bit of a waste.'

Cantelli said, 'His whole life was a waste.'

So that was the puzzle over Peter Ebury's death solved, thought
Horton despondently. 'And Irene Ebury?'

Gaye gently swung her chair round, tapping a pencil against
her mouth. 'Irene Ebury was in a poor state: thinning arteries,
weak heart, cancer in one of her lungs, and it was a heart attack.'

Although he'd been expecting that news he nevertheless felt a bitter blow of disappointment. He was also annoyed that Dr Eastwood's diagnosis would be borne out.

'Could it have been induced?' he asked, more in hope than anticipation.

'You mean brought on by a shock? Possibly. Alternatively she could have been injected with air. Because of her poor health it wouldn't have needed much to cause an embolism, but it would have required a skilled person to inject the air into her by using a syringe.'

Horton brightened up at that. 'She was in a nursing home. Plenty of people there who could have done it.' He was thinking of Marion Keynes.

Gaye raised her eyebrows. 'If she was injected with air then it's almost impossible to detect. I looked for froth around the heart and in the blood vessels, but I couldn't find any.'

So, dead end. He could sign off both these deaths and forget about Lee being sent to keep an eye on him. What an idiot he'd been. 'Looks as though I was wrong on both counts.'

'What about the missing jewellery and the intruder?' Cantelli said.

'Sounds like one of those murder mystery games,' Gaye commented.

Horton said, 'We'll continue to investigate the missing jewellery with Marion Keynes as our prime suspect. As for the intruder –' Horton shook his head – 'Mrs Kingsway must have imagined it.'

'And Daniel Collins?'

Was his death simply a tragic accident after all? wondered Horton. Probably, but he might as well ask whilst he was here.

'Your colleague did an autopsy on a Daniel Collins who died on Christmas Eve. His car went over Salterns Wharf. He worked at the nursing home where Irene Ebury died. I've read the autopsy report but wondered if you could tell me anything more about it.'

'I doubt that,' she answered, tapping into the computer. 'Daniel Collins, aged thirty-four, drowned. Toby Simmonds did the autopsy. It seems straightforward. His body's been released to the Chapel of Rest. Want me to take another look?'

Horton hesitated, saw the grief-stricken faces of Mr and Mrs Collins and said, 'No.' They'd been through enough already.

'Why the interest? Apart from the nursing home link, that is?'

Horton gave her a brief summary of what Mrs Collins had said. Gaye looked sorrowful. 'I expect she's just finding his death hard to come to terms with.' Her green eyes swivelled to Cantelli. 'And how are you coping, Sergeant?'

Cantelli gave a sad smile. 'I keep telling myself that Dad was old and he'd had a good life, but it doesn't make it easier.'

'No,' she answered quietly, then added, 'Inspector Horton tells me the funeral is on Thursday. I'd like to come if it's OK with you?'

Cantelli brightened up. 'Of course it is. The service is at the cathedral. The Roman Catholic one that is,' he added. 'At twelve thirty. Dad's being buried in Milton cemetery and then it's back to the restaurant in Southsea for the wake.'

Gaye didn't need to ask which restaurant; there was one in Southsea owned by the Cantellis and run by Barney's brother, Tony. Following her promise to be there, they returned to the car.

'Do we keep digging?' asked Cantelli.

Horton thought of that other funeral on Thursday morning. He saw the Collinses' faces when he told them he'd stopped the investigation into Daniel's death. It didn't bear thinking about. They still had Daniel's computer, his car was going to be examined. Walters might return with something from his mud bath and DC Lee could unearth some interesting information from the Rest Haven. He wondered if he'd just seen a pink pig flying overhead. 'For now.'

'Irene Ebury *was* Miss Southsea in 1957,' Trueman said, following Horton into his office. He handed over a newspaper cutting. Horton gave a soft whistle.

Peering over his shoulder, Cantelli said, 'They made real women in those days.'

'Better not let Charlotte hear you say that.'

But Irene had indeed been good-looking, thought Horton, staring at the curvaceous eighteen-year-old. Her long blonde wavy hair curled on to her shoulders, she was wearing a one piece light-coloured swimsuit, which could have been white, but Horton couldn't tell because it was a black and white photograph, and high-heeled court shoes. She was being crowned by a dark-haired man in his late forties wearing a sharp suit. Reading the caption under the newspaper article, Horton saw he was the actor, Dale Bourton.

'Ever heard of him, Barney?' Horton asked.

'He was a heart-throb in the fifties and early sixties, labelled the English Gregory Peck. Starred in a couple of British movies, then seemed to disappear from the scene. I'll look him up on the Internet.'

Horton could see that Trueman had more. He gestured for him to continue.

'She left Portsmouth in 1958 and worked in London at a couple of nightclubs until 1963, then there's no record of employment, or address for her, until she showed up back here in 1973, pregnant with Peter. She never married and she lived in Mile End for a while before being given a council flat in Jensen House.'

Horton started. It was where he had lived with his mother. Here was another connection between the two women, not only had they worked together but they'd lived in the same tower block. And that disturbed him. 'What number?' he asked warily.

'Fifteenth floor. Number one hundred and twenty.'

My God! The same floor even and a couple of flats down from his childhood home! He looked again at the picture. He couldn't recall Irene Ebury, but then he'd only been a child and more interested in other things, like football. He'd returned to Jensen House before Christmas, trying to retrieve some memory of the day his mother had disappeared. He hadn't been successful in that, but he had found his neighbour of 1978 still living there. Would Mrs Cobden recognize Irene? It was worth asking. He also wouldn't mind pushing the newspaper cutting underneath Marion Keynes' nose just to show her that Irene hadn't been making it up. And if she hadn't invented that, then maybe Mrs Kingsway hadn't been imagining this intruder either. After what Dr Clayton had told him though, there didn't seem any case to answer. But his copper's sixth sense was twitching worse than a rabbit's nose.

He briefed Trueman on the results of the post-mortems.

'Do you still want me to poke around?' he asked when Horton had finished.

'Only if you haven't got anything better to do.'

Trueman rose. 'Superintendent Uckfield's been out most of the day. I'll squeeze it in when I have time. And it beats wading around in mud.' He jerked his head at the door, smiling. Horton looked up to see a very wet and filthy Walters waddling in carrying a large plastic bag full of what looked like scrap metal, drink cans and food cartons. Walters wasn't waving a mobile phone and neither did he look very happy, so Horton guessed he hadn't found it and turned to Cantelli.

'For God's sake, Barney, stop him from coming any further. The cleaners will have a fit if he trails all that dirt through here.'

'I think they've already probably gone on strike if he's walked through the station like that.'

'Take that bag over to scientific services. Then shoot off home, Barney, and tell Walters to do the same, and quickly.'

Horton called the scientific services department and told them about the bag, but not that every item inside it would be caked in the mud of Langstone Harbour. He wasn't that brave or foolish. They'd soon find out. He checked his desk but there was still no message from Uckfield or Ray Ferris about DC Lee. And there was no case file on the Peter Ebury robbery. That should have been with him by now. He'd get Cantelli to chase it up tomorrow.

He sat back, and as the rain drummed against the window, he let his mind roam through the events of Lee's first day on the team looking for one small thing – a word, a glance, a gesture – anything that told him who she really was and what she was doing here. He could find none.

He sighed. Maybe there was nothing to find, just like Dr Clayton's results showed. But his mind refused to admit that. If the deaths were suspicious, then all the victims had been killed so expertly that it couldn't be detected.

He posed himself some theories. What if Irene's stolen jewellery was a distraction and the real purpose of the theft had been to take her photograph album? Could there have been an incriminating picture in it? He didn't mean pornographic, just something that would expose a secret. Could the missing photographs and letters have any connection with when Irene had lived in London or where she had been between 1963 and 1973?

The outer door swung open and Lee marched in. He beckoned her into his office.

'Well?'

'Daniel Collins was a quiet man. The staff and residents liked him. He didn't socialize with the staff outside work and didn't talk very much about his personal life, except for his marine photography. He only worked days so I didn't think there was any point hanging around to talk to the night staff.'

'Had anyone ever seen Daniel Collins drink alcohol?'

'No. And as far as any of them know Daniel didn't know the owners. They very rarely see them. Everything is left to the manager, Mrs Northwood, to deal with.'

'How did she react when you asked her why she hadn't mentioned Daniel's death to us?'

'She said that she'd been too tired and worried about Mrs Kingsway to think about it. And then there was the shock of finding Irene's belongings missing and dealing with that obstinate inspector of mine and she asked doesn't he ever give up. I told her I hadn't known you for long, but from what I'd seen, I didn't think you were the giving-up type, not as long as there was a sun in the sky, even if it was obscured by rain, fog and cloud.'

Her words brought Horton up sharply. Lee was right. And though he couldn't *see* exactly what was wrong because it was shrouded by too much happening, he could feel it, sense it and smell it. He couldn't let the matter of Dr Clayton's autopsy reports put him off. And he couldn't let the fact that Lee might not be all she was making out to be stop him. There was something wrong at that nursing home and he was going to find out what it was.

'What about the residents' belongings?' he asked.

'They're all there. Only Irene's are missing.'

It was as Horton had thought. Tomorrow Trueman might get some more information on Irene, and he'd take that press cutting and show it to the old lady in the tower block. There was also the interview with social services.

'You'd better get off home, Lee.'

She rose but hesitated. 'I asked the staff where Daniel could have gone Christmas Eve; almost without fail they said there was only one place, the sub-aqua club at Eastney. I thought I could go there now and have a word with the members. It beats staring at the walls of a hotel bedroom.'

Lee was right. He should have thought of it himself. There was, however, one flaw. If Daniel had been at Eastney, then there would have been no need for him to have been on the dual carriageway and certainly not travelling south into Portsmouth.

Still, if Lee wanted to visit the sub-aqua club whilst off duty, then who was he to stop her? But she wasn't going alone. He rose.

'I'll join you.'

He'd heard the saying that the Chinese were inscrutable, but he wondered if he had just detected a flicker of disappointment in Lee's brown eyes.

EIGHT

Horton stared up at the two-storey brick building in front of him. There were lights shining from the upper floor and a handful of cars parked in the spaces in front of it, but there was one car in particular that drew his attention and made him groan. It belonged to Nicholas Farnsworth, the TV diver. He hoped that the man wasn't going to bend his ear about those bloody anonymous telephone calls. And if Farnsworth was here, then perhaps Jackson and Corinna Denton were too. Maybe this hadn't been such a good idea after all.

After Lee's brief introduction to a bodiless voice on the intercom, they stepped inside a rather gloomy and deserted entrance lobby which reeked of sea, salt and sweat. Horton peered down a long dark corridor directly ahead of him, but could see nothing except the sign on the wall that told him it led to the equipment room. From above he could hear the rumble of conversation and the occasional burst of laughter.

Despatching Lee to the equipment room, he followed the sound of laughter to the top of a staircase and pushed open a door. A blast of warmth, light and conversation hit him like a slap in the face and along with it the smell of alcohol and after-shave. There were about twenty people, mainly men, in the spacious room. Some were talking at the bar but the majority were around Farnsworth. Thankfully, Horton could see no sign of Jackson or Corinna Denton.

'Inspector Horton, to what do we owe this pleasure?' Farnsworth chimed brightly, spotting him and switching on his television smile. His insincerity set Horton's teeth on edge.

The others fell silent and looked curiously at Horton. Amongst them was a petite woman in her thirties with the most remarkable smudgy blue eyes he had ever seen. 'I didn't expect to find you here,' Horton said, contriving to make it sound as though Farnsworth was slumming it.

'It's a diving club, and I *am* a diver,' Farnsworth rejoined unruffled, though Horton detected a hint of annoyance.

'Which is why I am here to ask questions about the death of Daniel Collins.'

Farnsworth showed no reaction, but the woman with the smudgy eyes looked startled. On the others, Horton witnessed a mixture of sadness, bewilderment and wariness. One of the men stepped forward.

'Can I help you, Inspector? I'm Gary Manners, the club secretary.'

Horton took in the broad shoulders, powerful head and sharp grey eyes. Manners seemed to be in his mid-forties and had an air of authority about him that Horton guessed came from more than just his position here.

'When was the last time you saw Daniel, sir?' he asked.

'The evening before Christmas Eve,' Manners replied crisply.

Horton could see that he had everyone's attention now, and Farnsworth didn't much like it. Well, tough. 'He was in here drinking?'

'Daniel didn't drink,' the small woman chimed, her voice like a whip cracking.

'Never?'

'Never.'

The others murmured agreement. So that seemed pretty much confirmed. Then why drink Christmas Eve? Could it have been a reaction to his mother telling him she had breast cancer? After all, that was enough to turn anyone turn to drink.

'How did Daniel seem?' he asked.

It was Farnsworth who voiced what Horton knew they were all thinking. 'Why the questions, Inspector? Is there something suspicious about this man's death?'

Horton swivelled his gaze to Farnsworth. 'Did you know him?'

'No.'

Horton thought that rather strange given that it was a small club. But maybe Farnsworth didn't come here that often. Or perhaps Farnsworth thought himself above acknowledging someone like Daniel Collins. At that moment Lee chose to enter.

Her bright smile swept the room and Horton saw a few of the men follow her with appreciative eyes as she made straight for Farnsworth.

'Nice to see you again, Detective Constable,' Farnsworth said smoothly. 'Can I buy you a drink, *if* Inspector Horton will allow it?'

'Orange juice would be great,' she answered, without looking at Horton. The crowd dispersed and Horton was left facing Gary Manners.

'How often did Daniel come here?'

'Nearly every weekend when he wasn't working, and a couple of evenings a week. He was a care assistant in a nursing home, but then you probably know that.'

'Did you ever go out diving with him?'

'Once or twice. He dived with Nathan Lester quite regularly.' Manners scanned the crowd. 'He's not here, otherwise you could have had a word with him.'

'Do you know where I can find him?'

'He has an antiques shop in Highland Road. If he's not there, you might be able to get him in the marine archaeological offices in Fort Cumberland. I don't know where he lives.'

Horton could easily find that out. Lester might be able to tell them more about Daniel. 'How did Daniel seem when you last saw him?'

'Fine. His usual self.'

'And that was?'

'Quiet, watchful, thoughtful.'

'More so than usual?'

'Not really. Daniel wasn't the type to get drunk and kill himself. It must have been an accident.'

'So how do you account for the alcohol found in his body?'

'Maybe he drank something which contained alcohol without realizing it.'

Maybe, thought Horton. 'Have you any idea where he might have gone on Christmas Eve?'

'Sorry, no.' Manners' eyes flicked beyond Horton. 'Now, if you'll excuse me, I need to talk to Nick.'

'He's their most popular member. The bastard!' came a voice from behind Horton.

He spun round to find the petite woman with the smudgy-blue eyes glowering across the room. At first he thought she was referring to Manners. Then following her hostile stare, he saw it was directed at Farnsworth.

'I'm Daisy Pemberton,' she said, stretching out a hand. Horton found her grip almost knuckle crushing. 'I was Nick's girlfriend until about ten minutes ago. He dumped me in the car park, but I refused to scuttle away with a broken heart. He didn't like me coming in, but it's my club as well as his.'

He wouldn't have put her down as Farnsworth's type, but then how did he know what the man's preferences were, though he imagined them to be tall with long blonde hair.

She said, 'You'd better tell your buddy that she's flirting with a serial two-timing bastard.'

Horton glanced in Lee's direction and saw her laugh at something Farnsworth said. Then Farnsworth drew Lee away from Manners with a light touch on her back. For a moment Manners' guard came down and Horton caught a glimpse of anger in his expression. Then he quickly recovered his composure and turned towards another member with a smile.

'DC Lee can handle it,' Horton said. 'So who *is* the other woman in Farnsworth's life?'

'You're a copper, work it out for yourself.'

His mind flashed back to the Queen's Hotel and that interview with Jackson and Farnsworth. Of course, he should have seen the signs then. 'Corinna Denton.'

'No wonder you're a detective! Well, no point in my hanging around now.'

She turned to leave, but Horton forestalled her. 'Can I buy you a drink?' She could tell him more about Daniel Collins and hopefully Lee would get some information from the other club members, if she could bear to tear herself away from Farnsworth.

Daisy eyed him keenly. After a moment she shrugged. 'OK. Dry white wine.'

He ordered a Coke for himself and steered Daisy to a vacant table by the large window. Out on the black sea beyond he could see the pinpricks of the red and green of the buoys in the channel and in the distance the faint lights of a container ship.

'How often does Farnsworth come here?' he asked, putting his full attention on Daisy. It wasn't a chore.

'A few times a year, when he's not diving around Britain on that bloody stupid programme, or giving after-dinner speeches and acting the big TV personality.'

So, perhaps Farnsworth hadn't been lying when he said he didn't know Daniel Collins. Their paths might never have crossed.

She added, 'And to think I fell for Nick. I must have been mad. I mean just look at him.'

Horton did. Farnsworth was smiling at Lee as he spoke, but every now and then his eyes would flicker up and beyond her as though seeking a wider audience. Lee seemed not to notice, but Horton knew she had. He was beginning to think she was a very good cop. Why only a DC? As her temporary boss he ought to see her file. Maybe he'd request it tomorrow. He wondered if he'd be allowed to see it though.

'He's not even a good diver,' Daisy said scathingly. 'Not like Daniel, who was also a very talented photographer.'

'I've seen some of his pictures. What was Daniel like?'

Now, down to the real business of his visit here.

'You don't think his death was an accident, do you?' she declared bluntly, holding his gaze. He knew that lying to her, or fobbing her off, wasn't going to get him what he wanted.

'There are certain facts that don't quite add up.'

'Such as?'

'Like him being drunk, though there is an explanation for that. His mother had just told him she'd been diagnosed with breast cancer. Maybe he hit the bottle in his anger and sorrow. Not being used to drinking, it wouldn't have taken much for him to get intoxicated.'

But Daisy was shaking her head. 'No. Daniel wouldn't have reacted like that.'

'Then how would he have behaved?' He was really interested.

'He would have been upset, of course. But Daniel was always very calm and practical. He would have researched every known treatment for breast cancer, organized his mother's care, even drawn up a timetable for her. He would have spoken to the doctors, and made sure she lacked for nothing. He was very thorough, always erring on the side of caution, which was why he was a good buddy on a diving trip. You just knew you'd be OK. Oh, it used to get up my nose sometimes; he'd double and triple check all the equipment. He was almost obsessive about it, like he was about his photography. He was very painstaking.'

Horton recalled Daniel's bedroom and office. Daisy's words bore out what he'd seen there, everything in its place, everything labelled.

'He wasn't an emotional man then?'

'He might have been inside, but he never showed his emotion, to me anyway. He might have done to others. I didn't know him outside this diving club. But I just can't see him getting drunk and then driving a car. If he did have a drink, which I find rather difficult to believe, though even saints are tempted, then he wouldn't have driven, his personality wouldn't have allowed it. It would have been too risky.'

'He might have been too drunk to think rationally.'

'You're wrong. That wouldn't have been Daniel's nature.'

'You seem very certain.'

'I should be. I'm a psychologist.'

He tried to hide his surprise but he wasn't quite quick or clever enough for Daisy Pemberton.

'It's OK,' she said, pushing a hand through her short dark hair and grinning. 'I'm off-duty. And I specialize in sports psychology.'

That didn't make any difference to him. A psychologist was a psychologist whatever branch she majored in. And he'd had a bellyful of them as a boy. Enough to put him off for life, which was a pity because he found himself rather attracted to Daisy Pemberton.

After a moment she added, 'Daniel's drink could have been spiked by someone he thought was his friend but who wasn't.'

With deepening interest, Horton saw her eyes flick to Farnsworth. Farnsworth said he hadn't met Daniel. Was he lying or was this Daisy's spite talking?

'Why would someone do that?'

'No idea.' She tossed back the remainder of her wine. Rising, she said, 'Want another?'

'No, thanks.'

'I was thinking of drowning my sorrows, but now I shall celebrate my release from hero-worshipping. And I've just seen someone rather interesting walk in.'

Horton watched her cross the room, where she hailed a tall fair man in his late thirties. Horton didn't think Daisy was going to be without a boyfriend for long.

He gave Lee the nod. Outside he breathed in the crisp night air. The temperature had plunged considerably since the morning, but at least it had stopped bloody raining. Zipping up his sailing jacket against a stiff breeze that had veered to

the north-east, he walked slowly out of the car park considering
what Daisy had said. The more he thought about it, the more
convinced he was that she had deliberately planted the idea of
Farnsworth being involved with Daniel's death in his mind.
Either as a form of revenge or an experiment to see whether
he'd take the bait.

He stared across the road at the masts in Southsea Marina,
wishing that all he had to do was slip across there to his boat.
Instead he had a twelve-mile drive to Gosport Marina. 'Sorry,
guv, couldn't get away,' Lee said, hurrying across the car park
and zapping open the car. Climbing in, she continued. 'I checked
out the lockers. Daniel didn't have one. I asked Gary Manners,
and he said that Daniel had his own dry suits, regulator, masks,
fins and snorkel, which he must have kept at home, but he
hired the rest of his equipment from the club, which also has
its own RIB.'

'And Farnsworth? What did you get from him other than a
hand on your back and an invitation to dinner?'

'Which I declined.'

'Pity.'

'There are some sacrifices that one has to make in the name
of the job, but spending an evening fending off that self-important
creep is one too many.'

'Where's your sense of duty?'

She smiled. 'Apart from spouting on about the diving series,
and how much fan mail he receives, all I could get is that he's
divorced and lives in Haslemere.'

Which was about an hour's drive from Portsmouth and easily
commutable. Horton guessed that Farnsworth had chosen to
stay in the Queen's Hotel rather than drive daily for two reasons:
one, so that he could spend his nights with Corinna Denton
and two to take advantage of the television production
company's expense account and indulge in a spot of free luxuri-
ous living.

The door of the club opened and Farnsworth stepped out with
a mobile phone pressed to his ear. He climbed into his car without
noticing them and started it up. Then, still on his phone, he drove
out of the car park.

'Do you want me to go after him?' Lee asked.

'No. Call traffic and see if they can get to him whilst he's
still using his mobile. Oh, and ask them to breathalyse him.'

That would give Farnsworth publicity all right, but Horton doubted it was the type the golden boy wanted.

'Where was Farnsworth on Christmas Eve?' he asked, when she came off the radio.

'With Daisy Pemberton.'

And it didn't need any stretch of his imagination to guess what they'd been doing. He doubted if attending midnight mass was on their itinerary.

'Did you get anything else on Daniel Collins?'

'No.'

He relayed what Daisy had told him, by which time they'd reached the station where Lee dropped him, before heading off, presumably to her hotel.

Horton stared at the paperwork on his desk, wondering when on earth he was going to have time to tackle it. Tomorrow was the answer, he thought, picking up some files and plonking them in his in-tray. A note fell out and reaching for it Horton saw with excitement that it was a telephone message from Ray Ferris. He had called at seven thirty-two, two hours ago, and asked to be called back on his mobile. Checking his office door was tightly shut against the empty CID office, Horton called him from his mobile.

'DC Lee worked in the Operational Planning and Policy Unit,' Ferris said without preamble.

So she was telling the truth, Horton thought, with an edge of disappointment. 'How long for?'

'Six weeks.'

Not long. 'Her boss?'

'Superintendent Warren.'

'OK. Thanks, Ray.' He'd been wrong. It wouldn't be the first time and he was certain it wouldn't be the last either. He was about to ring off when Ferris stalled him.

'That's the official version.'

Horton was suddenly alert.

'Can you talk?' Ferris quickly added. 'And I don't mean in your office.'

Horton rose, his pulse quickening. 'Hang on.' Swiftly he crossed the CID room until he was standing in the empty corridor by the coffee machine. 'And the unofficial one?'

'I haven't told you this, and don't ask where I got it from. She's from the Intelligence Directorate.'

Horton felt cold. Intelligence Directorate dealt with major and complex crimes such as drugs or people trafficking, money laundering, tracking international criminals and extortion on a national and international scale. Why here, why now? What the devil was going on?

'If I end up back on the beat, it's you I'll come hassling.' And Ferris rang off.

Horton exhaled. Collecting his plastic cup of coffee, he returned to his office, mulling over what he had just learnt. So he'd been right about Lee. That didn't make him feel any better.

Ignoring the ringing phone in the CID office and then his own, Horton trawled his mind, going back over the events of yesterday before Lee had been sent in and Bliss shoved out. What had happened before then to warrant such drastic and prompt action from the Intelligence Directorate? He'd said to Cantelli that he suspected Lee's arrival was due to the fact that although Bliss didn't want him to investigate Irene Ebury's death, someone wanted him to run with it. Now he knew who. But how could a nursing home involve such a heavyweight organization as the Intelligence Directorate?

He ran through the sequence of events at the Rest Haven: Mr Kingsway's bellowing; climbing the stairs to Mrs Kingsway's room; his viewing of the room where she and Irene Ebury had slept; the trip to the basement . . . No, hang on. Slowly he put down his coffee. Of course! He'd looked out of the window of Irene Ebury's room and seen that curtain twitch in the house opposite.

He sat up, his mind racing, trying to grasp the significance of that, and then he recalled the burly man in a waxed jacket walking on the opposite side of the road. What an idiot he'd been! He should have seen the signs – hadn't he been on enough undercover operations to spot them? That nursing home had been under surveillance and still was for all he knew. But why? Whatever the reason, it had to be something big. And did that involve Daniel Collins? Yes. Otherwise why would DC Lee want to follow up his death and visit the sub-aqua club?

Horton delved into the papers on his desk and retrieved the road traffic report on Collins's death. Once again his phone rang, but he ignored it and the caller left no message. He read through the report carefully already knowing what he would find, or rather what he wouldn't. Nowhere did it mention that Daniel Collins worked at the Rest Haven and yet Lee had said he did. She had claimed that Mrs Collins had mentioned it on the telephone but had she? He could easily ask her. His eyes flicked to the clock and with surprise he saw it was almost ten thirty. It was too late to call her now. He didn't want to disturb her, though he guessed her nights were now already very disturbed.

Daniel had died on Christmas Eve, so had that been when the Intelligence Directorate had stepped in? Or had it been after Irene Ebury had died? Then another more chilling thought struck him. If there was any truth in this mysterious intruder that Mrs Kingsway had seen bending over Irene Ebury, had it been one of Lee's colleagues checking out Irene's belongings? For what though?

Horton rose and paced the floor, the blood pounding in his ears. Could their involvement have any connection with his mother? No, it wasn't possible. But the thought made him hot under the collar.

. He wrenched opened the blinds and thrust back the window, letting the frozen air cut through him like a knife. Somewhere, amongst all that he'd learnt so far about the Eburys and Daniel Collins, was buried some vital piece of information that had connections to a major crime and he was missing it. So, too, was the Intelligence Directorate, otherwise why send Lee to work with him?

His phone rang and this time he snatched it up to find the custody clerk on the other end.

'I've been trying to get hold of you, Inspector. I heard you wanted to be informed about Nicholas Farnsworth.'

He'd forgotten all about him. 'Has he been booked in?'

'And out again.'

'Why? His breathalyser test must have been positive.'

'It was when he was pulled over, but it was negative when he was tested again here. We had to let him go.'

Horton cursed and rang off, then thought that it didn't really matter. He had other more important things to think about, and top of his list was fathoming out just exactly what the Intelligence Directorate was after at the Rest Haven Nursing Home and why the hell he was being kept in the dark.

NINE

Horton's anger and curiosity kept him tossing and turning for most of the night, so that by the time DC Lee arrived the next morning he had unearthed three cases left over from Christmas, which would keep her occupied for days and away from the Rest Haven and Daniel Collins. Maybe then she, or her boss, would be forced to let him into their confidence.

He wondered if Uckfield knew about the Intelligence Directorate's investigation. He hadn't when Horton had spoken to him earlier about Lee, but he might now have been put in the picture, as Horton suspected Superintendent Reine had been. Maybe he should see the boss and ask him outright. But if Reine had been sworn to silence, then he wouldn't break that; Horton had learnt that with ambitious men like Reine and Uckfield loyalty to their superiors far outweighed any loyalty to their subordinates. He was just about to summon Lee to his office when his phone rang.

'This is Ryan Oldham. Get over here now. There's something you need to see, and don't send that moronic fat bastard.'

The line went dead and Horton, fuming, stared at his phone. The moronic fat bastard he took to be Walters who had gone to Oldham's Wharf on Monday to investigate an alleged break-in. Well, if Oldham thought he could simply command and he would come running then he had another thought coming.

He called reception and demanded to know why the call had been put directly through to him only to be told that Oldham had insisted on speaking to a senior detective immediately or he'd call 'the bloody chief constable'.

'That's no reason not to warn me first,' Horton said crossly.

'Sorry, sir, but the switchboard's going ballistic this morning. Everyone's finally woken up after Christmas. And there have been so many accidents on the roads in this God-awful weather that we're stretched to breaking point.'

Not completely appeased, Horton slammed down his phone

and marched out to the CID office. He didn't have time to investigate Oldham's claims of moving trucks. Then he reconsidered. Oldham's Wharf was very close to where Daniel Collins had died. Maybe visiting the scene of the incident would give him inspiration; it often worked that way. And he recalled that Cantelli had said Marion Keynes's husband, Ian, worked as a lorry driver for Oldham. Cantelli could have a word with Keynes. Perhaps he'd let something slip about Irene Ebury's stolen belongings. OK, so he'd have to put up with Oldham ranting about trucks that had mysteriously moved in the night and suspected burglars, but he could handle that. It meant forgoing the appointment with social services though. Damn. All his intentions of keeping Lee at arm's length looked set to go out of the window. He couldn't send Walters because he wouldn't have a clue what questions to ask. There was no contest.

On their rather torturous route to Oldham's Wharf, Horton brought Cantelli up to speed with his and Lee's visit to the sub-aqua club, but said nothing about Lee working for the Intelligence Directorate. It wasn't that he didn't trust Cantelli, but he wanted to find out first if Uckfield was now party to the secret, and see if he could wheedle some further information out of him.

Cantelli said, 'It's a wonder Farnsworth hasn't been on to Superintendent Reine this morning, bleating about his arrest for drink driving.' He swung into a muddy road that led to Oldham's Wharf and drew to a halt on the rough ground that served as a car park.

Horton peered through the torrential rain at the lorries trundling into the yard. Beyond them he could see a high bank of shingle and a couple of crane-like machines towering over it. The rain was almost horizontal and there would be scant protection from it in Oldham's yard except in the three Portakabins to the right of the large iron gates. He must have been mad to come here. He should have sent Lee with Cantelli; how would Ryan Oldham have reacted to her? he wondered with a slight smile. But he had never been one for ducking out of an unpleasant task and leaving it to his subordinates. He wished, though, that he was wearing his motorbike boots and leather trousers – a wish that was reinforced as he stepped out and straight into a puddle. He pulled up the collar of his sailing jacket, but before he'd even gone five paces he was drenched. Cantelli, with hat, raincoat and wellington boots, looked more suitably attired.

He noted that there were no CCTV cameras over the car park, but as they headed towards the yard he saw one over the electronic gate. He'd never been here before, but he'd run some dinghy sailing courses for kids in the sailing centre just to the right of Oldham's.

A shape loomed at them from one of the Portakabins and Horton found himself facing a solidly built square man in his late forties, with granite features, wearing a voluminous heavy-duty waterproof coat, green Hunters – which were almost completely covered in muck – and a yellow hard hat.

'About bloody time,' he boomed. 'Follow me.'

Oldham, Horton assumed, falling into step behind him, as he stomped across the busy yard oblivious to the rain. With a longing glance at the shelter he was leaving behind, Horton thought with envy of DC Lee in a nice, warm, dry office drinking coffee with a social worker. His feet were soaked and he had long since lost all feeling in his toes. His trousers looked as though they'd been dipped in a bath full of sludge and the water was cascading off his head and over his nose like it was Niagara Falls.

Oldham was heading for the shore, where Horton could see a dredger waiting to unload its cargo of gravel. It had obviously come up the harbour on the high tide. About twenty feet from the quayside Oldham abruptly drew up.

'There.' He flung out a podgy finger. Horton followed its direction and found himself staring into a pit about five feet deep and twelve feet square. Focusing his eyes in the streaming rain, he blinked and ran a hand over his sodden face. To his horror, he was staring at what looked remarkably like a human hand protruding from the gravel. This he hadn't expected. He glanced at Cantelli, who paused mid chew.

'You could have said on the telephone,' Horton grumbled.

'And be called a liar like before. Not bloody likely and before you say anything, I told the lads not to touch it. Not that they'd want to, if it's for real, but I haven't got all day to stand around here gawping at it. That dredger needs unloading, so hurry up and do what you have to do.'

Horton didn't like to tell him it wasn't that simple, but before he called in the heavy squad he ought to check that it was a human hand and not a plastic one, otherwise he'd have to emigrate to avoid the ribbing.

'How do I get down there?'

'That steel ladder over there. You'd better wear a hard hat. Scott,' he bellowed, and a muscular man in his thirties appeared almost from nowhere. 'Give us your hard hat and get yourself another one.'

Oldham handed it over to Horton, who adjusted it before beginning a careful descent of the slippery ladder. In the pit he felt the rain even keener, cutting into his flesh, but that was probably his imagination and apprehension.

His feet sunk into the soft gravel almost up to his knees. He didn't think he could get any wetter or dirtier not unless someone decided to throw a bucket of slurry over him. This was his penance for sending Walters out into the mud of the harbour.

As he waded his way closer – thinking Phil Taylor of SOCO would have a fit if he could see him – he noticed a piece of blue material around the wrist. The material didn't look like cloth but some form of latex or rubber. His heart contracted. Could it be a diving suit? If so, then one particular diver sprang to mind. Shit! Perry Jackson. He touched the hand and the icy flesh made him recoil. *It couldn't be him. Those telephone calls had been a publicity stunt, hadn't they?*

'Who is it, Andy?' Cantelli called out.

Horton heard the anxiety and excitement in Cantelli's voice. He glanced up and caught the sergeant's concerned expression.

'Can't see yet, but it's a man judging by the size of the hand and wrist.' *Too big a hand to be Jackson's?*

With difficulty, his cold, wet fingers fumbled inside his jacket for a pair of latex gloves. Putting them on proved almost impossible, but eventually he managed.

Oldham shouted, 'Can't you get a move on?'

Ignoring him and with his heart thudding against his ribs, Horton carefully began to clear away the gravel around the hand. His heart quickened as more of the rubber became exposed. Yes, it was definitely a diver. His mind was racing. If this was Perry Jackson, then what the blazes was he doing here – dead? And if it wasn't him, then who could it be? Daniel Collins had been a diver and he'd died not far from here, and last night he'd been in the sub-aqua club asking questions about Daniel's death. Had he somehow instigated this?

The yard seemed to have fallen quiet and even the weather seemed to have abated, yet he knew neither had. The hand and wrist extended to an arm, but that was as far as he dared go before spoiling the scene of the crime even further, *if* this man had been killed and he had no real evidence of that. He could have met with an accident and fallen into the pit, but Horton doubted it, unless Oldham had started kitting his employees out in diving gear.

Horton's spine pricked with unease as he climbed back to the surface. He mentally replayed the last call that Jackson had received: 'Resign from the programme by the end of the week or you're dead meat.' *But it was only Wednesday.*

At a nod from Horton, Cantelli pulled the mobile phone from his coat pocket and stepped away.

'Who the hell is he?' demanded Oldham.

'No idea. We'll have to wait for the doctor and the scene of crime team.'

Oldham glared at him. 'Are you saying you can't move him?'

'Sorry. This could be a crime scene.'

Oldham snorted.

Raising his voice against the howling wind, bleeping trucks, engines running and concrete churning, Horton shouted, 'Were there any signs of a break-in this morning?'

'That loading shovel's been moved.' Oldham pointed to a truck to their right, which had a big scoop-like shovel attached to it. It was the same type of truck that Walters said Oldham had reported as having been tampered with on Monday. Perhaps Taylor and his scene of crime team would get something from it. But Horton knew that the rain would have washed away most, if not all, of the external evidence.

Oldham didn't strike him as a man given to fancies and para-noia and if he said a truck had been moved, and none of his men had admitted to moving it, then Horton guessed it had. Maybe for the grizzly purpose of dumping the body in that pit. For a moment he wondered if he should call the Queen's Hotel and check if Perry Jackson was there, then thought better of it. He didn't want to alarm anyone. He was still hoping it wasn't Jackson's body in the pit. But if it wasn't, then who was it?

'Did anything show up on your CCTV?'

'No. Not last night or Sunday night, when we had the first break-in and that idiot showed up.'

'Is there any other way into the yard?' Cantelli asked, coming off the phone and giving Horton a slight nod that told him that SOCO were on their way, along with Dr Price.

'No. It's fenced on all sides except seaward, of course, where the dredger is. Wish I'd let the bloody thing unload now and bury the poor sod.'

'I'm sure you don't mean that.'

Oldham sniffed. Perhaps he did, thought Horton. Their killer – if this man had been killed – had been unlucky because if Oldham's dredger had disgorged its cargo, then the body might not have been discovered for days, weeks even.

'What do you dredge for?' Cantelli shouted above the wind.

'Marine aggregates, sand and gravel, the sort you use for your patios, and driveways, and for building houses.'

'Business is good?' Horton asked.

Oldham turned and waved a hand around the yard. 'What do you think?'

To Horton's mind it looked as though it was thriving. He was puzzled that none of Oldham's staff had stopped working to gaze at the somewhat unusual, not to mention shocking, discovery of a body on the premises, but maybe they were scared of Oldham. He had a reputation for being a tough businessman and he was probably a very demanding employer.

'Can someone walk around the perimeter with Sergeant Cantelli to see if an intruder could have entered that way?' Well, Cantelli had the wellingtons and the hat.

Oldham nodded at Scott, who set off at a brisk pace with Cantelli following, trying to keep up. 'Look, can't you move him? I've got to unload that dredger.'

'Sorry.'

'Then I'll send my angry customers to you.' And Oldham stormed off.

Horton was glad to see the scene of crime van sweep into the yard, and behind it a patrol car. Taylor and his crew sensibly stayed put whilst PCs Seaton and Allen began the almost impossible task of erecting a canvas tent in the pit in the atrocious weather. It would have been laughable if the reason for them being here hadn't been so serious, Horton thought, watching them. There was no sign of Uckfield or Dennings. Cantelli wouldn't have notified the major crime team until they were absolutely certain this was murder. Horton hoped it wasn't, and he sincerely hoped it wasn't Perry Jackson down there, but he wasn't about to take bets on either.

Finally the tent was up. Seaton and Allen were drenched to

the skin and looked appealingly at Horton. 'Join the club,' Horton muttered, before detailing Seaton to log everyone who entered the tent and Allen to talk to the men in the yard to find out if any of them knew about the mystery of the moving truck. It sounded like a Miss Marple mystery, he thought, once again climbing into the pit, only Miss Marple would probably have solved the case by now and remained dry in the process.

He stepped just inside and Taylor handed him a scene suit. Against the sound of feet crunching on gravel and the canvas snapping in the wind like rifle-shots, he watched silently as the photographer and videographer did their stuff. Then Taylor and his assistant, Beth Tremain, slowly and carefully began to uncover the gravel that hid the body. Horton found himself holding his breath. He tried to prepare for what he was about to see. He thought of those anonymous threatening telephone calls, his visit to the sub-aqua club last night, Daniel Collins's body being fished out of his car not half a mile from here, and a chill ran through him that had nothing to do with the weather and how wet he was.

Taylor had outlined the body without uncovering it. It didn't look like Jackson's build. Too tall. But he could be mistaken, or perhaps he was just hoping that. Then Taylor began to clear the gravel that covered the head. Horton's body was so rigid with tension that he felt it might snap. Then a voice and a blast of wind and rain swept through the tent along with the smell of alcohol.

'You could have picked a better day to find a body,' Price said, coming up behind them.

'There's an obstruction on his face,' Taylor said, in his usual mournful manner.

'What kind?' Horton could feel his heart thudding against his ribcage.

'Don't know. Hang on.'

Horton watched, feeling as if he were in the grip of a nightmare and couldn't escape. Gradually Taylor's skilled fingers uncovered the face. Across the nose and eyes was a diving mask. A regulator was pushed into the poor man's mouth. The head, forehead and neck were covered with a diving hood that resembled a balaclava. He couldn't tell who it was.

'Want me to remove the paraphernalia?' Price volunteered, stepping forward after the photographer indicated that he'd got his shots.

Horton nodded and held his breath. His heart was going like the clappers as Price bent over the body. He pulled the regulator from the mouth and then carefully removed the diving goggles, easing them over the back of the head. With a sinking heart Horton gazed on a face he knew all too well, and one that a great many people in the United Kingdom would also know. But it wasn't Perry Jackson he was staring at. Instead Horton was peering into the dead face of his co-presenter: Nicholas Farnsworth.

TEN

'Looks like you've cocked up,' Uckfield said half an hour later.

Horton winced inwardly at the accusation and felt guilt rush in to replace reason.

'You should have treated those threatening telephone calls seriously,' Uckfield added.

It was what Superintendent Reine would say, not to mention the media. Horton groaned silently. He hadn't liked Farnsworth, but he hadn't wished for him to turn up here, dead. Had he really got it so wrong? Obviously, he thought, following Uckfield's scowl as it studied the recumbent figure of Farnsworth.

But why Farnsworth? If those threatening calls had been genuine, then the body lying before him should have been Perry Jackson. Was Farnsworth's death nothing to do with those calls, but everything to do with Horton's visit to the sub-aqua club last night? Had Farnsworth known something about Daniel Collins's death and was that why he had left the club hot on their heels with a mobile phone pressed to his ear – to warn Daniel's killer and sign his own death warrant? Or was he simply looking for an excuse to offload his guilt?

Perhaps Farnsworth had also received threatening calls but had chosen to ignore them. Was this a vendetta against the TV divers? Bloody hell, he didn't know. In fact, he was fast coming to the conclusion that he knew bugger all about anything. Maybe he should simply hand everything over to Uckfield and DC Lee. But he didn't like to admit defeat, and he didn't much fancy

leaving a case with such a stain on his judgement. Maybe if he
hadn't been in such a foul mood when he'd first met Jackson
and Farnsworth, brought on by his emotional reunion with his
daughter at Heathrow Airport, he might have treated the incident more seriously. No. It was pointless speculating and beating
himself over the head with guilt. There was still time to get some
answers before Saturday. And he was determined he would.

Dr Price had given the time of death as somewhere between
twelve to four hours ago. That was a wide margin. But Horton
could narrow that down. Farnsworth was still alive at nine thirty-
five when he had left the station. Had he come straight here to
meet his killer? That would put the time at approximately
ten p.m. Or had his killer transported the body here and dumped
it in the pit? He couldn't help thinking that if that second breathalyser had proved positive, or if he had questioned Farnsworth,
then he might have been alive now. But he'd been caught up
with the news about DC Lee, and he hadn't thought that
Farnsworth mattered. That was a mistake he was going to have
to live with.

'You'd better brief me, *fully,* but for heaven's sake find somewhere out of this sodding weather,' Uckfield growled, as they
stepped outside the tent.

Horton scanned the yard and saw Ryan Oldham giving PC
Johns a hard time at the entrance. Johns was capable of handling
that. As Uckfield crossed to Dennings, Horton made for Oldham.

He broke the news bluntly. There was no need to tiptoe around
men like Oldham.

'What the hell is Farnsworth doing in my yard, dead?' Oldham
bellowed.

Long years of listening to liars and cheats had fine-tuned
Horton's senses, and he detected something that told him Oldham
was familiar with the TV diver.

'You know him?'

'Of course I do. I've seen him on the television.'

There was more, but Horton judged now wasn't the time to
push it.

'We'd like the use of an office until the mobile incident suite
arrives.'

'Do what you bloody well like – you will anyway. How long
will you be?'

'Could be all day.'

Oldham snorted and, shouting to Scott to follow him, stormed off towards a Portakabin.

Horton saw a very wet Cantelli talking to the driver of a lorry, which had just pulled up. If only this bloody rain would stop, he thought, turning and heading for the same Portakabin as Oldham. Not that it made any difference now; he was soaked to the skin.

Uckfield joined him. 'What the hell was Farnsworth doing *here*?' he demanded, stepping inside.

And that was the million-dollar question that was bugging Horton. The upper reaches of Langstone Harbour, where the tide receded to expose mud and sand, was hardly the place to go diving. If you wanted to discover wrecks and other historical artefacts in the harbour, then you simply waited for the tide to go out.

Horton addressed a woman behind a desk. 'Is there some-where we can talk in private?' Through the thin partition in the office beyond, Horton could hear Oldham talking to Scott and he wasn't being very complimentary about the police.

'There's the kitchen. It's just through there.'

They'd have to talk quietly, he thought, because it was only in the next room. 'Can we make ourselves a drink?'

'Help yourself.'

Horton flicked on the kettle and spooned coffee into two mugs as he told Uckfield about Daniel Collins's death nearby. He said nothing of Ray Ferris's discovery about DC Lee.

'But Collins's death was an accident,' Uckfield said, obvi-ously irritated.

Now, how do you know that? Horton hadn't mentioned it being an accident, and the road traffic incident report would hardly have landed on the head of the major crime team's desk. Maybe Uckfield had just assumed it. Like hell he had! Someone had told him, and probably at HQ yesterday. He guessed that Uckfield had been summoned there after he'd made some enquiries about DC Lee. A guess that became a conviction when Horton saw a slight shiftiness in Uckfield's eyes.

'Was it an accident?' Horton said evenly. 'It's beginning to look very doubtful. And before you say anything, I've got no hard evidence to support that, just a feeling.' The kettle boiled and Horton turned away. As he poured water into the two mugs, he said casually, 'Did you find out anything about DC Lee?'

'She comes highly recommended by Superintendent Warren.'

'You've spoken to him?' Horton said, once again facing Uckfield.

'Yes. She got involved with an officer there; it all went pear-shaped so he thought a spell away from there and being operational would do her good.'

So Uckfield was sticking with the cover story. Horton handed him his coffee, seeing only Uckfield's usual scowling countenance. But he'd swear on oath that Uckfield was lying.

'You'll have to make a report on why you ignored the threats to Farnsworth's life.'

'*He* wasn't threatened. It was his co-presenter who got the calls.'

Uckfield dismissed that with a wave of his hand. 'It's the same difference.'

'No, it's not, Steve, and you know it,' Horton was stung to retort. 'And my money's still on it being a publicity stunt.'

'Well, I hope you're right, because if you aren't then this other presenter – what's his name . . .?'

'Perry Jackson.'

'Could be at risk.'

Horton doubted it, but he remained silent.

After a moment Uckfield said, 'This doesn't look good for you. It's bound to be a high-profile case, with Farnsworth being a television personality. We'll get hammered by the press. I'll do my best to cover your backside, but . . .'

With immaculate timing, saving Uckfield from making a comment that Horton knew would drive him to a cold fury, Cantelli put his head round the door.

'Any chance of a cuppa? My feet are so cold they hurt.'

Uckfield looked about to explode and deny Cantelli's request when his mobile phone rang. Brushing past Cantelli, he exited with a glare at Horton and a 'Yes, sir,' into his mobile phone.

Cantelli let out a breath as Uckfield banged the door on them. He picked up a tea bag and tossed it into a mug. 'I see he's his usual cheerful self. Holiday must have done him good.'

Horton wrapped his frozen fingers around his own mug and took a sip of the hot coffee. 'What did you get?'

'The perimeter wire is intact. The site foreman says the CCTV cameras hardly ever work and even if they do they don't always bother to put a tape in. Last night was no exception. No recording.

The business is doing well and Oldham isn't a bad boss; tough but fair is the consensus. You know where you stand with him is the general opinion.'

Which is more than you do with Uckfield, Horton thought with bitterness. Uckfield would sell his soul, not to mention sacrifice his old friends on the high and mighty altar of promotion.

Cantelli removed the tea bag with a spoon, squeezed it out and left it on the drainer, after looking for and not finding a bin. He spooned in three sugars and stirred. 'I also had a word with Ian Keynes, Marion's husband.'

That must have been the lorry driver that Horton had seen Cantelli talking to.

'When he knew who I was, he accused me of upsetting his wife with our allegations of theft. It was bluster. He's a surly beggar and he was definitely uneasy about something.'

'The nursing home will have to take a back seat for the moment.' Horton didn't like leaving it, but he didn't have a choice. Once Uckfield mobilized his full team, though, Horton might be able to get back to it. By then it would be too late, he'd be on holiday. But how could he sail away, metaphorically and literally, with all this hanging over him? He should be able to and maybe he might have done if it hadn't been for the Intelligence Directorate's involvement.

Cantelli nodded solemnly. Horton could see that he understood, but liked it about as much as he did.

'Could Farnsworth's death be due to natural causes?'

'Is the sun hot?'

Cantelli shivered elaborately. 'Not at the moment.'

Dr Price had removed Farnsworth's hood to reveal a livid mark on the throat. Price wouldn't speculate as to what had made it and neither would he confirm it was the cause of death. He was just there to certify death, he had said tetchily. The rest was down to Dr Clayton. Horton thought it looked as though Farnsworth had been strangled and that, and how the body had been found, had been enough to call in the major crime team.

'Where is the rest of Farnsworth's diving gear: aqua lung, spare regulators, lines, fins? Where's his car?'

'Could be parked at the sailing club next door. Want me to check?'

'I'll do that, and for goodness' sake stop stirring. You'll go through the bottom of that mug.'

Cantelli tapped the spoon on the side and took a sip. 'Maybe he came here by boat.'

The thought had already occurred to Horton. 'Then where is it? Why come here? And who moved that truck, if Oldham is to be believed?'

'You think he's lying?' said Cantelli, blowing on his tea to cool it down.

'Perhaps the reports of the break-ins are phoney to make us think there was an intruder when really Oldham was planning to kill Farnsworth. He knows Farnsworth and I don't think it's just from the television programmes as he claims.'

'But why would he want to kill Farnsworth? And why is Farnsworth dead when it was Perry Jackson who received those threatening telephone calls? They're not even alike; different build, hair and eye colour, so it can't be a question of mistaken identity.'

Horton thought of that hood and mask that had covered Farnsworth's face. The build was wrong, yes, but in the dark, in panic, with the victim wearing a diving suit, maybe the killer struck out and realized afterwards he'd cocked it up. Or there was an alternative. Had Perry Jackson staged those calls and killed his co-presenter? His motive? Perhaps he didn't like Farnsworth getting too much of the limelight.

He said as much to Cantelli, then added, 'You'd better break the news to Corinna Denton and Perry Jackson. Get details of their movements yesterday and last night. And there's that cameraman, Jason Kirkwood. Make sure you talk to him. They're all suspects until we say they're not. And watch closely for Jackson's reaction. I'll send Lee over to the hotel to help you.'

'Is it all right if I go home and change first? I don't think the Queen's Hotel will want me dripping all over their nice posh carpets.'

'Need you ask?'

'What about Uckfield?'

'What about him?'

Cantelli smiled and put down his mug of tea. 'I'm on my way.'

Horton stayed inside the Portakabin long enough to call Lee.

Before he mentioned anything about Farnsworth, he asked her how she had got on at the social services offices.

'Irene Ebury set fire to the council flat where she lived three times. She was a smoker and she'd fall asleep forgetting where she'd left the fag, or she'd leave something on the stove. On the third occasion the neighbours complained and she was referred to social services. A medical report confirmed dementia. She insisted she was fine. She hadn't left anything on the cooker and she would never fall asleep smoking, but she did admit to liking the odd gin or two. Eventually, when she was found at Fratton Station one night in her nightie and dressing gown, she was sent to St James' Hospital for a mental assessment and it was considered that she was a danger to herself and the other residents. The social worker and doctor recommended her to be moved to a specialist nursing home catering for dementia.'

'Who helped her to move?'

'Her social worker, Naomi Bennett, but she doesn't work for social services any more. Shall I locate her?'

'Later.' Horton then told her about Farnsworth's death. There was silence and he wondered for a moment if he'd been talking into thin air. Not going according to your plan, he thought gleefully, before reminding himself that Farnsworth was dead. 'Sergeant Cantelli will meet you at the Queen's Hotel. Wait for him outside.'

Would they pull her off his team now that there was a murder case which would take priority certainly over any investigation he might pursue into the nursing home? But if it was Daniel Collins's death the Intelligence Directorate was really interested in, and not Irene Ebury's, then maybe her boss would leave her where she was, especially if there was a connection with Farnsworth's death. And that connection was the sub-aqua club and the proximity of where the two bodies had been found.

He stepped outside to see that the media had arrived. PC Johns was doing his best to keep them at bay. A member of Oldham's staff must have alerted them. Soon they would be here in their droves.

Horton found Uckfield at the edge of the pit. He told him that he'd dispatched Cantelli and Lee to the Queen's Hotel. 'I'll check the sailing centre car park for Farnsworth's car and if it's not there I'll put out a call for it.'

'I'll brief the press.' Uckfield made to turn away when Taylor hailed them.

'We've found something that will interest you.'

Wondering what it could be, Horton stepped inside the tent with Uckfield and stared at Farnsworth's body, feeling once again that stab of guilt. Taylor had uncovered the legs and arms and as Horton's eyes followed the direction of Taylor's gesture he started with surprise. Three fingers of Farnsworth's left hand were missing. He was damn sure that Farnsworth had had the full complement of digits last night.

'Why the devil do that?' Uckfield voiced Horton's thoughts exactly.

But maybe he could take a guess. 'It could be a jilted lover.' He thought of Daisy Pemberton. Surely she wouldn't be strong enough to have attacked and killed Farnsworth, and he couldn't see her hacking off fingers. 'Or an outraged husband or boyfriend,' he added.

'Then why not just hack off the third finger of the left hand?'

'Maybe it was easier to slice them all off. Especially if the killer was in a hurry.'

Taylor said, 'I can't see them lying around, but they could be in here somewhere.'

'I want a thorough search made of this whole yard, even if it means removing every single grain of gravel.'

Oldham wasn't going to be very pleased about that thought Horton, hoping he wasn't the one to tell him. He stared down at Farnsworth. What had he been doing here and at night? It could hardly have been to steal gravel, even if he was building a patio. And he couldn't have had a secret assignation with another lover, not wearing diving gear. If he could find the answer to that question then he might also have the answer to the second one, which was who had killed him. If they were very lucky then maybe the person whom Farnsworth had called on his mobile phone after leaving the sub-aqua club last night was the killer. Horton hoped so, but he wasn't holding his breath. Nothing was ever that straightforward.

ELEVEN

'Farnsworth called Corinna Denton,' Cantelli said an hour later.

So no joy there thought Horton. He didn't have Corinna marked out as her lover's killer, but then he could be wrong.

Cantelli continued. 'I've taken a quick look around Farnsworth's room. There's a laptop computer, no mobile phone though and no letters or diary. His rucksack's there with his publicity photos, but there's nothing to throw any light on his death. I've locked the room and the interconnecting door to Corinna Denton's and told the manager that no one is to go in. I've also phoned the Surrey police and asked them to send someone out to Farnsworth's house in Haslemere, and to make sure it's sealed off. I thought DI Dennings might already have done that, but apparently he hasn't.'

That didn't surprise Horton. With the phone crooked under his chin, he swung round in his seat and turned over his wet T-shirt on his office radiator. Along with his socks, shirt and trousers they were generating enough steam to rival a Turkish bath, filling his office with a smell like wet PE kits, reminiscent of school and a time in his life he'd rather forget. Or the changing rooms at Portsmouth football club, where he'd once been an apprentice, which was a much more favourable recollection. He'd managed to find some dry clothes: a pair of uniform trousers and police issue sweatshirt, and he kept a pair of trainers in his office in case he had the chance to go for a run during the day.

'Who's the next of kin?'

'Corinna says Nick's ex-wife, Annette Hill. She reverted to her maiden name after the divorce. There were no children. And she says that Nick's parents are both dead. There are no brothers or sisters. I've got Annette Hill's address. She lives in Bournemouth.'

Horton was surprised, not that Farnsworth had once been married, but that he'd still kept his former wife as his next of kin. He would hardly name Catherine as his, if she chose to marry Edward bloody Shawford – or any man come to that – after their divorce.

Once again, with the phone crooked under his neck, Horton quickly transcribed the address that Cantelli relayed to him. 'I'll ask Dorset police to inform her. We'll need a formal ID.'

'Don't we need two people?'

Horton raised his eyebrows. 'You're not thinking of bringing Annette Hill and Corinna Denton together?'

'Could be interesting. Annette is a lecturer in marine archaeology at the School for Conservation Sciences at Bournemouth University. Farnsworth met her on a dive when she was a student. Maybe she didn't like her ex-husband messing around, hence the fingers being chopped off.'

Cantelli had a point. Horton said, 'How long have they been divorced?'

'Seven years.'

'Then it's taken her a long time to work up a head of steam. How's Corinna taking the news?'

'She's very cut up. Blames herself for Farnsworth's death. Says she should have called us earlier, but she didn't realize that he was missing. Farnsworth called her last night at about nine thirty-five to say that he was going to be late and not to wait up for him.'

So what had made Farnsworth change his plans that night? Was it something that someone had said in the sub-aqua club? Or was it his questions about Daniel Collins? On the other hand Farnsworth could already have made an appointment to see someone and hadn't wanted to tell Corinna until the last moment.

'They rowed,' Cantelli continued. 'Corinna accused him of having another woman and slammed the phone down on him.'

Maybe she was right. Horton wouldn't put it past Farnsworth. Perhaps there was another of Farnsworth's women who was disappointed he hadn't shown up last night. To Horton's reckoning Farnsworth must have met his killer soon after his release from the station, otherwise he would have missed the high tide; always given Farnsworth had gone there by sea. There had been no sign of his car in the sailing centre car park when he'd checked.

Cantelli was saying, 'She waited all night for him to call her to apologize or creep into her bed but he didn't do either. This morning she thought sod him. She didn't go into his room and she didn't call him. Now she thinks that if she had done she might have saved his life.'

'Unlikely.'

'That's what I told her.'

'And the cameraman, Jason Kirkwood?'

'Hates the sight and sound of Farnsworth and doesn't blame someone for killing him. Said Farnsworth had it coming and that it was probably some irate husband or lover. In his opinion the killer deserves a medal.'

'So where was he last night?'

'In the hotel, drinking at the bar until ten thirty. Lee checked. The barman remembers him. Then he claims he was in his room, alone, all night. I told them both not to leave the hotel without informing us. Kirkwood seemed to like the idea of the production company picking up his bills whilst he continues to live in the lap of luxury. The press look as though they're setting up camp in reception, Andy. I take it Superintendent Uckfield will call a conference.'

You bet he will, thought Horton. Any chance to get his face on the television. And he was welcome to it. It was a chore that Horton didn't relish. And he knew they needed all the help they could get to gain information about Farnsworth's whereabouts the previous night. He'd called Ray Tomsett, the harbour master, on his way back to the station in the patrol car. Ray hadn't seen any boats in the channel the previous night or early this morning and he'd had no reports of anything untoward. He said he would ask the fishermen and bait diggers.

'Did Farnsworth make a will?'

'Corinna doesn't know. It never came up in their conversations.'

'No, I can see how it wouldn't,' Horton said wryly. Farnsworth was the type to think he was immortal.

'Perhaps they'll find one at his house in Haslemere. He must be worth a few bob.'

He probably was, but Horton didn't see that as a motive for killing him. 'Where's Perry Jackson?'

'With a man called Nathan Lester at Fort Cumberland. Corinna was going to call him, but I said we'd break the news to him ourselves.'

'Good.' Horton recalled that Nathan Lester had been the name that Gary Manners, the secretary of the sub-aqua club, had given him as one of Daniel Collins's diving partners.

'Pick me up, Barney. Tell Lee to bag up any personal papers and bring them back to the station, and to get Farnsworth's computer over to the computer-crime unit. Oh, and give me Farnsworth's mobile phone number.'

Cantelli relayed it. Horton rang off, but he didn't replace the receiver. Instead he dialled another number. It took a while to be answered but eventually a tired voice greeted him.

'I'm sorry to disturb you, Mrs Collins,' he said, after quickly announcing himself. 'But there's something I need to check with you. When you phoned in and spoke to Detective Constable Lee before we came to visit you, did you mention to her where Daniel worked?'

'I can't remember. I'm sorry. I was so angry and upset. I might have done. I'm not sure. Is it important?'

'No,' he reassured her. He hadn't really expected any other answer.

'Is there any news?'

'Not yet, I'm afraid.' He could hear her disappointment in the short silence that followed. 'Did Daniel ever mention a man called Nicholas Farnsworth?'

'That's the television diver. Daniel used to record and watch the programme.'

'Nothing more than that?'

'No. Why?'

He hesitated for a moment, then thought that she'd find out soon enough. 'We're investigating his death. His body was found this morning at Oldham's Wharf.'

Silence. When she eventually spoke, her voice shook. 'Do you think this man's death has something to do with Daniel's?'

'It's too early to say. I'll keep you informed. Meanwhile if anything occurs to you that you think might help us, please let me know.'

'I will.'

He knew she wanted to ask more questions, but he didn't have the answers to give her, and maybe she sensed that. Plucking his sailing jacket from the radiator, he wondered if Lee had seen Daniel Collins going in and out of the Rest Haven whilst it was under surveillance. Was it still under surveillance? Only one way to check, but that would have to wait.

To Walters he said, 'Any joy with Collins's list of friends?'

'There's only a handful and no one saw him on Christmas Eve, or have any idea where he went. And they all say Daniel Collins never touched alcohol.'

He gave Farnsworth's mobile phone number to Walters and told him to check Farnsworth's calls and see if he'd ever rung Daniel Collins. Then he dived into the canteen and bought a couple of packets of sandwiches. He doubted that Cantelli would have eaten and even if he had, the sergeant would always eat again. He'd never seen a man put away so much food and stay resolutely wiry.

In the custody block Horton addressed a slender woman in her early fifties. 'Who was on duty last night when Nicholas Farnsworth was booked in?'

She consulted her computer. 'John Gatcombe.'

'Did Farnsworth kick up a fuss, seem upset, worried or angry?'

'John didn't say when I took over this morning. Farnsworth was hardly here five minutes before he was released according to this.' She nodded at the computer screen.

No help there then. He would need to talk to the arresting officer, though he also made a mental note to talk to John Gatcombe when he came on duty that night.

Horton checked the time. Cantelli would be here any moment, but he'd wait for him. Quickly he doubled back and headed up the stairs of the new extension to the major incident suite where, across the crowded room, he could see Trueman inscribing on the crime board.

'Where's Dennings?' Horton asked, after weaving his way through the additional personnel drafted in for the investigation.

Trueman had written up the time of the autopsy; two fifteen p.m. Besides that was a photograph of Perry Jackson and Nicholas Farnsworth taken from yesterday's newspaper and a picture of Farnsworth's body both with and without the diving mask. There was also a close-up of the mutilated hand and again Horton considered the significance of those missing fingers, though he couldn't come up with any new ideas.

'Still at the scene,' Trueman answered.

Horton's mind conjured up Dennings facing Oldham; an exchange he wouldn't have minded witnessing. Two bull mastiffs squaring up to each other flitted into his head and made him secretly smile before knocking on Uckfield's door.

Horton quickly relayed his telephone conversation with Cantelli. 'We're off to interview Jackson. As far as I'm aware he doesn't yet know the news about his buddy.'

'If you get anything before three o'clock call me. I'm giving a press conference.'

Horton couldn't resist asking Uckfield if his latest sexual conquest would be present: their PR lady, Madeleine Dewbury.

'She will, and you can wipe that smirk off your face. It's over between us,' Uckfield hissed, his eyes flicking beyond Horton to the door. 'Only she doesn't know it yet. I haven't had a chance to tell her, so keep it shut.'

'Anything you say.'

Uckfield picked up his phone, clearly indicating their conference was over and Horton headed to the rear exit to find Cantelli waiting for him.

'Like the gear,' Cantelli said, eyeing Horton's clothes.

'We can't all be snazzy dressers like you.'

Cantelli grinned. As the sergeant drove to Fort Cumberland, Horton ate his sandwiches and considered the meagre facts surrounding Farnsworth's death. It didn't get him very far. It was still too early to speculate, even if he had more to specu-late with. He wondered how Daisy Pemberton would take the news.

He asked Cantelli if Corinna Denton had mentioned her, but was told she hadn't talked about any other woman in Farnsworth's life except his ex-wife. Cantelli brought the car to a halt at a set of tall iron gates. Beyond them Horton could see the grassy expanse and scattered brick buildings of the eighteenth-century bastioned Fort Cumberland.

Cantelli spoke into the intercom and as they threaded their way through the grounds Horton was transported back to the hot August day two years ago when he'd brought Emma here on one of the Fort's open days. He could smell the dry grass and taste the salt in a gentle sea breeze. He felt her small hand in his as they followed the guide around the buildings and into those dank tunnels where he had tried so desperately hard to hide his fear of being closed in. Then they'd gone for an ice cream along the seafront and a swim. Catherine had been working. He wondered, sadly, if he would ever be allowed to spend such blissful days with his daughter again.

Cantelli drew up in front of a red-brick building that was a much later addition to the original Fort built in 1740. It had guarded the entrance to Langstone Harbour and had been used by the Royal Marines until about twenty-five years ago.

Inside Horton asked to see Nathan Lester and was directed to an office not far from the entrance. He wondered how they could have missed it until he saw that it was actually built into the grassy banks of the fortifications.

There was a bicycle propped up against the bank and a saloon car tucked away almost out of sight of the main road. Horton peered inside the car, grateful that the rain had finally stopped, though the wind wrapped damp fingers around his face. There was nothing inside it to tell him it was Jackson's, but he couldn't see Jackson riding a bicycle.

Cantelli noted the registration number, as was his habit, and Horton pushed open the door and stepped inside a small, narrow office crammed with books and paper, but devoid of human beings. The room smelt unused and damp. He could hear the murmur of voices and made for their direction, pausing to listen at the door before thrusting it open.

The two men inside started in surprise. Perry Jackson swivelled round in his seat, frowning, while the other man, whose wiry frame was dwarfed by the desk at which he was sitting, widened timid eyes in a face that reminded Horton of a squirrel. Horton guessed he was in his mid-forties. His limp brown hair was flecked with grey and his complexion oily and tinged with an almost bluish hue, as though he hadn't properly shaved himself.

Jackson snapped, 'What is it now, Inspector? Can't you see I'm in a meeting?'

The wiry man's nervous expression deepened. Horton waited for Jackson to introduce his companion, but he made no move to do so. 'Mr Nathan Lester?' he enquired.

'Yes. Why? What's wrong?' Lester started like a frightened rabbit.

Irritably, Jackson exclaimed, 'It's not those wretched phone calls again?'

Horton eyed him coldly. Jackson didn't flinch. OK, he'd asked for it. Brusquely Horton said, 'Mr Farnsworth's body was found this morning at Oldham's Wharf. We're treating his death as suspicious.'

There was a stunned silence. Nathan Lester opened his mouth to say something but no sound emerged. He had gone deathly pale, his eyes were wide with astonishment, his face rigid with alarm, whereas Jackson was still frowning. He recovered first.

'Is this a joke? Because if it is—'

'I don't joke about such serious matters, Mr Jackson,' Horton said sternly.

The penny finally dropped. 'Nick's dead?' Jackson repeated, as though trying to take it in.

Lester looked as though he wanted to slide under the desk.

After a short pause, Horton said, 'When was the last time you saw Mr Farnsworth?'

Jackson hesitated before answering, but Horton thought it was more a case of recovering from the shock of the news rather than thinking up a lie. 'About eight o'clock last night. He said he was going to the sub-aqua club.'

'And after that?'

'Back to the hotel, or so I assumed.'

'He said nothing about going to Oldham's Wharf?'

'No. I've no idea what he was doing there.'

'And you, sir?' Horton swivelled his gaze on Lester, who flushed and shook his head. 'When did *you* last seen Mr Farnsworth?' Horton watched Lester's Adam's apple rise and fall as he gulped.

'Not since before Christmas.'

Horton knew it was a lie. Lester wouldn't look at him. His pale eyes dropped to the file open on his desk and when they lifted they flitted between him and Cantelli and back to Jackson. There was a thin line of perspiration on his upper lip.

'When exactly?' Horton pressed.

'The twenty-second of December. We had a drink in the sub-aqua club.'

Horton could check that. He guessed though that that much was true. But what was Lester not saying? Studying the frightened man, Horton could see there was a lot more. It had been rather fortunate to find Jackson here, he thought, but he reckoned he'd get more out of Lester away from Jackson.

He asked him to wait outside and Lester seemed only too glad to escape. A few moments later Horton could hear Lester moving about in the next office. He'd liked to have sent Cantelli out there to see what he was doing, but he wanted him here observing Jackson and taking notes.

Horton eased his way through the narrow gap between the desk and wall and managed to squeeze his body into the space that Lester had vacated. Cantelli positioned himself to the right of Horton in the corner and took out his notebook.

'Why do you think Mr Farnsworth was killed when those threatening calls were directed at you?' asked Horton.

Jackson's eyes narrowed. 'You can't think Nick's death has anything to do with them?'

'What else are we supposed to think?' Horton replied steadily, thinking come on, time for the truth.

Jackson shifted and sucked in his breath. Horton could see that he'd finally got the point.

'We didn't think you'd take them so seriously. We thought they'd just send a bobby on the beat and we could milk it in the papers.'

'Are you saying that *you* made those calls?' He'd been right all along, but that didn't minimize the fury he felt.

Jackson had the decency to blush, though his eyes were shining with defiance. 'Nick made the first two, but he swore to me that he didn't make the third or fourth. I didn't believe him.'

And that must have been why they were arguing when he and Cantelli had shown up on Monday.

'The whole thing was Nick's idea,' Jackson said hastily and with distaste. 'He was always coming up with stunts. He said it would make the programme more exciting, and raise our public profile.'

'Oh, I think he's done that all right.'

'I call that remark bad taste and totally out of keeping,' shouted Jackson, springing up. But there was no room for him to do much more.

Horton leaned forward across the desk and gave him an icy stare. 'And I call wasting police time by using schoolboy pranks irresponsible, childish and extremely dangerous. How do we know that his killer didn't read about them in the newspaper and think he'd have a go at fulfilling the prophecy, but he got the wrong diver?'

Jackson went white. Fear hovered in the silence. Horton could hear the wind whistling round the building. After a moment Jackson eased himself back in the chair. When he spoke the belligerent superior tone had vanished and in its place was anxiety. 'You think someone might want to kill me?'

'If the third and fourth calls weren't made by Farnsworth then it's possible. It's also possible that you were the intended victim and not Farnsworth.' Or was Jackson the murderer and using the threatening phone calls to throw the scent off himself? His reactions seemed genuine enough, but that could be play-acting. 'Is there anyone you can think of who would want to kill you?' asked Horton bluntly.

'Of course not, and neither can I think of anyone who would want to kill Nick. Surely there's been some mistake. Couldn't it have been an accident?' he asked with the air of a desperate man.

Horton's answer was in his expression.

'I must speak to Corinna.' Jackson reached for his mobile.

'In a moment. We understand that she and Nick were lovers.'

'Yes. Have you spoken to Jason? Not that he'd care about Nick. He's probably glad he's dead. He never did like Farnsworth especially since Corinna . . .' Jackson halted, then shrugged, 'No doubt you'll find out soon enough. Corinna was Jason's girl before Farnsworth grabbed her from under his nose.'

That was news. Jason Kirkwood had an alibi until just after ten when he had retired to his room. Was there enough time for him to have met Farnsworth and killed him after then? He would have just managed to catch the tide, so yes, Horton guessed it could be possible. Even more so if he had arranged to meet Farnsworth by car at or near Oldham's Wharf. But that still didn't answer the questions why had Farnsworth been wearing diving gear and why kill him at Oldham's Wharf?

And what about Jackson's alibi? thought Horton. He seemed very keen to push Kirkwood at them.

'Can you tell us your movements last night, sir?' he asked briskly.

'For God's sake! This is ridiculous. You can't suspect me!'

'Just tell us where you were between eight p.m. and ten this morning.'

'In the hotel,' Jackson replied stiffly.

'Can anyone vouch for you?'

'Do they have to?' he said in a withering tone. When neither Horton nor Cantelli replied, he was forced to continue. 'I was alone in my room. The staff will tell you they saw me at breakfast this morning with Corinna.'

No alibi then. Farnsworth had trusted his killer enough to meet him and Jackson fitted that bill. Then Horton had another thought. Perhaps it had been another of Farnsworth's stunts, which had backfired. He'd ended up falling into that pit and Jackson had hastily made it look like murder by hacking off his colleague's fingers. It would be interesting to see what the post-mortem revealed.

'Do you own a boat, Mr Jackson?'

'Yes, but what has—?'

'Where do you keep it?'

'I have my own berth adjoining the house.'

'Which is where?

'Hythe Marina, Southampton, *if* you must know. Look, just what are you driving at?'

Jackson could have brought his boat to one of the nearby marinas or moored it on a buoy. He could have used it to take Farnsworth either dead or alive to Oldham's Wharf. Horton would ask Sergeant Elkins of the Marine Support Unit to check if it was still in the marina. And if it was, could Jackson have had enough time to dump the body, then pilot the boat home to Southampton this morning before returning to Portsmouth by car? It was perfectly feasible. Another thing that Elkins could check up on.

Horton said nothing of this to Jackson, instead he said, 'Southampton's less than thirty miles away. Why are you staying in the Queen's Hotel when you could have driven here daily?'

'I hardly think that's your business,' Jackson sniped. 'If you really must know,' he added tersely, 'there is a considerable amount to do in preparation for the series. It made perfect sense to get as much done as we could in a week. And have you seen the traffic on that motorway every morning? Well, then you know that commuting is a nightmare. I chose to use my time productively not stuck in a car on the M27.'

Jackson was now clearly annoyed and exasperated at the line of questioning. Fear had touched him when he thought he might be the next victim or the intended one, but what Horton hadn't seen was any kind of sorrow over his partner's death. And there was a great deal that Jackson should be asking him, which he wasn't, such as how had Nick Farnsworth died? Who could have killed him? But then perhaps he already knew the answers.

'Did Mr Farnsworth own a boat?'

'He preferred to use other people's. Cars were more his taste. Now, if you don't mind, Inspector, I have a great deal to do. There are calls I need to make.'

Horton held Jackson's hostile stare, looking again for a small glimmer of grief. He didn't find it. There was a lot more that Horton wanted to know about Jackson and his relationship with Farnsworth, but he judged that now was not the right time to discover it.

He rose. 'We'll need to talk to you again. Please let us know if you intend checking out of the hotel.'

Jackson was already reaching for his mobile phone before Horton had extricated himself from the desk, but at the door Horton paused, and in true police fashion said, 'Oh, just one more thing. Who inherits Mr Farnsworth's estate?'

'I haven't the faintest idea.'

Horton contrived to look surprised. 'Wouldn't he have made a will, diving being a dangerous pastime?' He saw, with satis-faction, Jackson flush at the word 'pastime'.

Clearly restraining himself with difficulty from rising to the insult, Jackson said, 'He might have done, but that doesn't mean to say he told me about it.'

No, thought Horton, perhaps he hadn't. He heard Jackson address Corinna, as he closed the door and turned to find Nathan Lester hovering nervously in the outer office. Leaving Cantelli taking an obsessive interest in a wall chart next to the door of the office, Horton asked, 'Where is everyone?'

'Oh, no one works here. This is just a resource centre for the divers registered on the Marine Archaeological Project.'

'And you're one of those divers?'

'Yes, so are Perry and Nick. How did Nick die, Inspector?'

Looking anxious and pale, Lester had asked the question that Jackson should have done. Horton wasn't yet prepared to divulge any information surrounding Farnsworth's death.

'How well did you know him?' he asked.

Lester sat down heavily. 'We've been diving together a few times. I can't believe he's dead.' He withdrew a handkerchief from the pocket of his casual trousers and blew his nose noisily.

'What is the Marine Archaeological Project?' Horton asked. He could still hear Jackson's voice rumbling in the background.

'There's a group of us that dive in and around the Solent area. We register what we find on a central database.' He pointed to the computer. 'We're making a map of the underwater heritage in order to help preserve it. Nick was our patron. He'd managed to get some funding for it and get all this equipment donated. He was due to speak at an international conference in June about the project.'

He ran a hand through his hair. Horton thought his face seemed to have grown thinner in the last twenty minutes.

'Perhaps Mr Jackson will step in?'

Lester looked anxiously towards the door and dropped his voice. 'Perhaps he will, but it won't be the same.'

Horton thought there was something strangely akin to hero worship in Lester's voice. And, seeing how distressed he was over Farnsworth's death, Horton was beginning to wonder if it was more than that. On Lester's part at least. Horton had no doubts as to where Farnsworth's sexual proclivities lay.

He also wondered how Jackson felt about Nick being chosen to speak at such a prestigious conference. Horton had a couple more questions, but not about Farnsworth. He said, 'Did you know Daniel Collins?'

'Yes.' Lester looked surprised. 'He died in a car accident on Christmas Eve.'

'When was the last time you saw Daniel?'

'Just before Christmas. The twenty-first.'

'Did Mr Farnsworth know him?'

'I don't think so. Nick never said.'

'He didn't go diving with him?'

'No. If you want to know who Daniel went diving with, then you can check the sub-aqua club's record book.'

Manners hadn't mentioned that. Horton looked blank and Lester elaborated. 'Every diver has to check his equipment, sign to say he or she has checked it and then log the time they leave, state their intended dive location and sign in again on their return. It's good diving practice.'

Cantelli was indicating that Jackson was coming off the phone. Horton thanked Mr Lester and took his leave.

Outside Cantelli said, 'Jackson didn't sound like he was comforting Corinna Denton from what I overheard. He was more worried about where this left him and the programme.'

And was Jackson glad to rid himself of Farnsworth? Horton's phone rang. It was Trueman.

'We've found Farnsworth's car. It's in the car park at Southsea Marina. The recovery unit's on its way.'

Horton stared north across the grass of Fort Cumberland. He could just see the masts of the boats in the marina. Had Farnsworth's killer dumped the car there or had Farnsworth driven it to the marina after being released? He could have met his killer and together they could have travelled by boat to Oldham's Wharf, even in the appalling weather of last night.

To Trueman he said, 'We'll be there in thirty seconds.'

TWELVE

'Anything?' Horton asked, as Cantelli peered inside the Range Rover.

'No sign of any missing fingers. If that's what you mean.'

'Pity.'

Cantelli smiled. 'And there's nothing lying about on the seats. It's locked,' he added, trying all the door handles.

'Call Elkins and ask him to check if Jackson's boat is at Hythe Marina and if it's been taken out over the last twenty-four hours. Then pop across to the sub-aqua club and check those diving records.' He hoped someone was there. 'Get copies of every dive Farnsworth made. And while you're there also get a copy of Daniel Collins's dives. I'm going to have a word with the marina staff.'

Horton found Eddie, a lithe 53-year-old with a weather-beaten wrinkled face in the marina office. Horton asked him if any boats had left the marina last night.

'No. Why? Something up?'

'You could say that.' Horton gave him the news about Farnsworth's death, leaving out the bit about the fingers and how the body had been found, although not *where* it was found. It would be in all the newspapers and on the radio and TV anyway. It was still troubling him that Jackson hadn't been curious about that.

Eddie said, 'It was silent as the grave here last night. Oh, except for a nice little yacht, which came in yesterday afternoon, and an even prettier party on board. A dark-haired girl with smouldering eyes and bit of a sharp tongue.'

Horton's interest picked up on that. Hundreds of girls could meet that description, but he could name one who matched it perfectly. 'Daisy Pemberton.'

'You know her?' Eddie asked, surprised.

'I've met her.' She hadn't said she'd arrived by boat, but then why should she? Had Farnsworth returned after being released to apologize or make it up with her? Or perhaps all that stuff about being dumped had been an act for his and Lee's benefit? Could Daisy Pemberton have motored to Oldham's Wharf and killed Farnsworth? But Eddie had said nothing had left the marina. And somehow Horton just couldn't see Daisy Pemberton as a murderer. He also didn't have Farnsworth down as the apologizing type.

'Where is she?'

'Pontoon J. It's called *Sunrise*.'

Horton quickly made his way there, wondering why Daisy had chosen to arrive yesterday. Was there anything sinister in that or had she just been hoping that Farnsworth would go sailing with her? How could a woman like Daisy have fallen for such a slimeball? he thought, punching in the security code to the pontoon. But then he didn't know how his estranged wife could go for an overweight, balding, puffed-up, pompous prat like Edward Shawford.

Thank God Shawford hadn't gone on holiday with her and Emma over Christmas to Cyprus. It was bad enough thinking of Emma being with him on ordinary days without imagining him spending Christmas with her. But why hadn't he? Horton wondered. Was the romance over? If so, how did he feel about that? Pleased, yes, but it was too late for him and Catherine to resurrect their marriage.

His thoughts had taken him to *Sunrise*. Eddie was right, she was a lovely yacht. Not brand new, but obviously well cared for. She was far bigger than *Nutmeg* and about five times more expensive. Psychologists must be well paid, he thought, if Daisy actually owned this yacht.

'Hello!' he called out.

'Hello yourself, Inspector,' a voice inside echoed back. 'Come on board.'

'How did you know it was me?' he asked, after sliding open the hatch and climbing down into the cabin. She was dressed in jeans and a large red sweatshirt, which seemed to accentuate her dark looks and make those smudgy blue eyes even more appealing. Or was that just the way she was studying him? He just couldn't see her killing Farnsworth, and as for chopping off his fingers . . . OK, so that was possible. There was something gritty behind the urchin face and determined chin and though the eyes were beguiling they were also intelligent, cool and assessing. In front of her, across the table, were spread papers and a laptop computer, alongside which there was a mobile phone.

'I saw you by Nick's car. What's he done now? Forgotten to renew his licence?'

'Did you see him last night after he left the club?' he asked as casually as he could, yet to his ears he still sounded like PC Plod asking dumb questions.

'No. Close the hatch; it's freezing. I must have been mad to come here in January.'

'Why did you?' he asked, after doing as she requested.

'Why do you think?' She gave a wry smile.

'You could have stayed with him at the Queen's Hotel.'

'I could have done, but those kinds of places are not my style.'

Was that true? he wondered, eyeing her curiously. Perhaps Farnsworth had put her off because of his affair with Corinna Denton. He could see Daisy following his train of thought.

'It was my idea to come by boat. I happen to like sailing. Please sit down, Inspector. You make the cabin seem even more cramped than it usually is.'

'It's bigger than my boat *Nutmeg*,' he said, before he could stop himself.

'You have a yacht?'

Damn. He hadn't meant to reveal anything about himself. But what did a little thing like that matter. 'I had,' he added, sliding on to the bench seat and facing her across the narrow table in the centre of the cabin. He realized too late that he was already saying too much to a woman who was trained to hear nuances and interpret body language, just as he was.

'You sold her?'

His knees brushed against hers and he shifted his body so as to angle his legs to avoid contact. She appeared not to notice, but he had a feeling she had registered the gesture and thought it interesting as well as significant.

'Someone set fire to her.'

Suddenly he was back there, listening to the footsteps on the pontoon, knowing he had only seconds to escape his assailant, fear constricting his throat and sending his heart into overdrive. He recalled the heat of the fire on his back before he'd dived into the icy black water and couldn't prevent himself from shivering at the memory.

'How awful,' she said gently.

He pulled himself up, knowing he had given some hint of his fear and cursed silently for exposing himself so quickly and easily to someone who would instantly see his weakness. For a moment he had lost control. And control was everything. It was the way forward, the only option. Perhaps one day, because of it, he'd lose everything he valued – love, friendship, his daughter – until he was completely alone. The thought swam up in him, terrifying and isolating, reminding him of the pain of the loneliness of his childhood. The fire had consumed all he'd had left to remind him of his mother except his memories, and they weren't much except anger.

His mind flitted to Irene Ebury. He hadn't forgotten her and her son. Now, with Farnsworth dead, he considered whether Daniel Collins was the linking factor between them all. Common sense told him that he was looking at three different cases. First, the Ebury deaths were, as Gaye Clayton had pronounced, due to natural causes; secondly, Daniel's death was most probably an accident; and the thirdly, Farnsworth's had been murder and that case took priority.

'When did you notice Mr Farnsworth's car in the car park?' he asked, bringing himself sharply back to the case in hand. He had to keep his wits about him with Daisy Pemberton. The last thing he wanted was her peering into his soul.

She eyed him shrewdly. 'This sounds like an investigation.'

He remained silent, hearing the wind howling and drumming through the masts and seeking out vulnerable places in the cabin, where it sneaked through and sent blasts of chill air.

She raised her eyebrows. 'This morning. I thought Nick must have gone out in the Solent with someone. Why?'

'What time did you return to your boat last night?'

'Not long after you left. The man I thought might be interesting turned out to be a complete wally. I left the club at nine. I didn't leave the boat until this morning when I went to buy some groceries. That's when I saw Nick's car.'

He eyed her carefully. Was she telling the truth? He hoped so. 'Is there anyone here he would have gone out to sea with?'

'He didn't mention anyone to me. Why the questions, Inspector? Has something happened to Nick?' She held his gaze, but before he got the chance to reply, she added, 'I can see it has.'

'He was found dead this morning.' He knew that sounded blunt, but he wanted to see her reaction.

She widened her eyes so that they appeared like two huge magnetic saucers drawing him in. Then her brow furrowed. She took a breath and said in a curious, rather than shocked, tone, 'How?'

It's what Perry Jackson should have asked but didn't. 'I can't say, but we're treating his death as suspicious, Ms Pemberton.'

'Daisy. You mean that Nick was murdered.' It was expressed as a statement devoid of surprise. And she didn't look as if she was about to burst into tears; instead she seemed to be considering the facts calmly. Too calmly? he wondered. Had she not felt anything for him? He was puzzled by her reaction and very curious.

'We won't know for certain until the autopsy.'

'Poor Nick. He'll hate being cut up. He was so vain.' She paused for a moment and sadness touched her eyes. 'But you need to know who could have killed him.' He could see her mind racing to put together the facts. Or was she thinking about an alibi? No, she didn't look wary or nervous, and she certainly didn't look upset.

'Could it have been a random attack?' she asked enquiringly.

He considered her question, one that had already occurred to him. Farnsworth could have disturbed the intruder who Oldham claimed had entered the yard and been killed to prevent his identity from being exposed. And he supposed that Farnsworth's fingers could have been hacked off by accident, or to make it look like premeditated murder, but that still didn't explain what Farnsworth was doing there in the first place and what the intruder was after.

'It's possible—'

'But doubtful. And I'm a suspect. Well, I didn't kill Nick, and I didn't see him last night. What about lover girl, Corinna? Didn't she see him?'

There was no bitterness in her voice. She'd got over her romance very quickly.

Horton said, 'She claims she didn't and I'm inclined to believe her. Mr Farnsworth was brought in last night for drink driving, but his second breathalyser test proved negative and he was released.'

Daisy frowned, puzzled. 'So where did he go?'

'His car's here.'

She waved the suggestion away with a dismissive sweep of her hand. 'His killer could have driven it here.'

He'd thought of that himself. 'Why?'

She eyed him cunningly. 'Well, I don't think it would be to implicate me, but then who can tell?'

Horton couldn't help thinking that a psychologist would be a very good liar. 'Who knew you were here?'

'Apart from the marina staff, only Gary Manners and Nick, but they could have told anyone.'

It was a perfectly reasonable answer and yet he felt uncomfortable with it. 'Could Mr Farnsworth have been seeing another woman as well as Corinna?' he enquired.

'I wouldn't be at all surprised. In fact, he probably had a couple on the side even when he was whispering sweet nothings in my ear. Thank God I didn't love him. Sorry, that sounded heartless, especially now he's dead. I was furious at being dumped, yes, but I wasn't upset. It was my pride that was hurt rather than my emotions. You see, I thought that maybe I could help him.'

Horton's ears pricked up at that.

'Nick was suffering from NPD,' she added. 'Narcissistic Personality Disorder. He had a grandiose sense of self-importance and an unhealthy preoccupation with success, fame, and power. I see that surprises you.'

Horton was convinced he hadn't shown any reaction to her pronouncement and yet she had seen something in his expression that had betrayed him. This girl was sharp. Too bloody sharp! He shuddered at the thought of how easily she might be able to read him.

'NPD was only recognized in the UK in the 1990s,' she continued. 'And then only because the government became concerned about the high number of attacks on people from those suffering from severe personality disorders. NPD seemed to be blamed for a great deal of them. It's been accepted in the States as a personality disorder since the 1980s. I expect you know all about it.'

He called to mind a conference he'd attended not long after the Brian Blackwell case in 2004. Blackwell, aged nineteen, had stabbed and bludgeoned his parents to death at their home in Merseyside and had then gone on a spending spree. He had been obsessed with fantasies of success, power and brilliance, claiming that he was a world-class tennis player when he wasn't. Horton put this with what he'd seen and heard of Nicholas Farnsworth.

'You're saying that Farnsworth didn't have any feelings for anyone, but could simulate them if required and that he needed to be admired.' He thought of Nathan Lester and his theory that Lester had hero-worshipped Farnsworth. Maybe he hadn't been far out on that.

'Yes. And with his obsession for success and fame, he probably drove Perry Jackson mad.'

And that gave Jackson a stronger motive. Had Jackson finally got sick of being manipulated by Farnsworth? He said, 'Did you deliberately seek Farnsworth out in order to study him?'

Daisy shook her head. 'No. I met him by chance at the diving club in July and recognized him from the television programme. I could see instantly that he fancied me and I must admit I was attracted to him. I didn't know then that he was narcissistic. I found him overwhelmingly charming and loving, which is, of course, typical of NPDs. Then gradually alarm bells began to ring and I diagnosed the illness, mentally of course. I thought at first that I might be able to help him get treatment. Not that I would have told him so in that blunt way, because Nick couldn't see that he was ill or wrong at all. On the contrary he was always right, and everyone else was inferior and inadequate. I began to make notes and I've been writing up his case.' She indicated the laptop. 'And now I suspect that one of his victims has killed him.'

'Wouldn't they be too insecure to do that?' Horton asked, thinking back to what he'd learnt at the conference. The psychologist who had lectured them there hadn't been anything like Daisy Pemberton. If she had been then Horton doubted if any of his male colleagues would have heard a word she said. They'd have been too busy in their own fantasy land.

'It depends on how long ago Nick ditched whoever it is, or when they walked out on the relationship. Of course, that would have taken some doing, but it wouldn't have been impossible, not if they'd had help from a friend or relative. Planning Nick's death could have given this person back the confidence that Nick had drained from them.'

'How would Nick have behaved?'

'At the start he would have been whatever the other person wanted him to be: charming, funny, sexy, vulnerable, you name it. Once he'd hooked his prey he'd change. Whatever traits you had that he found attractive he would gradually undermine.

With me it was my intellect, which was why I rushed back here after ditching the wally last night and began writing. Nick would lie, cheat, drink and could become violent, though he was never that with me. He might have been with someone else, particularly if the relationship went on for longer. Corinna Denton should consider herself lucky. She's had a narrow escape. Not that she'll see it like that.'

No, but had Jason Kirkwood seen the change in Corinna and so had set out to kill Farnsworth? He had no alibi after ten o'clock, knew how to handle a boat, and he was a diver. But how many others had Nick destroyed that Horton didn't know about?

'Would Nick have behaved the same way towards a man?'

'Yes, if it meant getting what he wanted.'

And was that a greater control over the television programme? A good reason for Jackson to have killed his co-presenter. He would like to have asked Daisy for her professional opinion about the missing fingers, but he couldn't yet. Not until he had completely ruled her out of his investigations. But if she had diagnosed Farnsworth's personality disorder correctly then he could consult the university forensic psychologist who occasionally assisted them.

He said, 'Nick was found at Oldham's Wharf. Do you know what he might have been doing there?'

She thought for a moment. 'No. But Ryan Oldham and Nick had a bit of a set-to a few months ago.'

Horton was surprised at this new piece of information, though it confirmed what he had thought earlier. Oldham had known Farnsworth a lot better than he had admitted.

'I overheard Nick talking to Oldham on the telephone,' Daisy continued. 'When Nick came off the phone he said that he would show Oldham a thing or two. Nick's NPD meant "showing him" would involve destroying the one thing that Oldham valued above all else, and that turned out to be his business. Or it would have done only now that Nick's dead the plan's scuppered.'

It occurred to Horton that Daisy could be making this up.

'I see I have your interest, but not your conviction that I'm telling the truth,' she said drily.

Again he didn't think he'd shown any reaction. She was clever and quick. Or perhaps he was losing his touch.

She gestured at the laptop. 'I can let you have my notes on Nick if it would help. And if it will make you believe me.'

'Go on.'

'Five months ago Nick accused Ryan Oldham of raping the seabed by extracting aggregates and disturbing the heritage and environment. It got in all the national newspapers and on the television. I'm surprised you didn't know about it.'

That would have been August when Horton had been on suspension, living on *Nutmeg* and sailing to escape his loneliness and despair over his failed marriage and wrecked career. What with that, and weaning himself off the booze, following the news had not been top of his priorities. He guessed this had occurred when Cantelli had been on holiday, otherwise he would have remembered it.

Daisy said, 'I believe Nick was going to make life even more difficult for Ryan Oldham by claiming at the conference he was due to speak at this June that Oldham's business was destroying important wrecks and the marine life in the Solent. Nick was devious and very clever.'

'But not clever enough to stop himself being killed.'

'No,' she said solemnly. After a short pause she added, 'I'm sure if you told me how he died I might be able to help more. That could be the key to his killer.'

Horton wasn't going to fall for that, though he had to admit he was tempted. 'All I can say at this stage is he was discovered wearing his diving suit.'

'Mmm, not much there.'

'What about his background, upbringing?'

'He was in the Royal Navy. I've seen photographs of him in uniform, so that much is true. According to him he was doing something top secret, but then he would say that. And not having your powers of investigation, I haven't found out what rank he was and what he did. Perhaps we can exchange notes?' she asked coyly, eyeing him in a way that made his loins stir, but the small voice of caution, ever present when it came to women and relationships, told him he was treading on thin ice, especially with this one.

She gave a small shrug and continued. 'He was married, once, to Annette in 1995. Nick was in the navy then. She's now a lecturer at Bournemouth University. I called her before Christmas, but she wouldn't speak to me. Nick told me that he got divorced because she was stifling him, but I reckon the woman came to her senses when Nick left the navy and she saw what he was really like. The marriage lasted three years and they were divorced in 2001, no children. Nick left the navy in 1996 and according to the press cuttings and official biographies on him he took a sales job with a double glazing company and then became an estate agent in Haslemere in 1999 where he worked until he joined the TV programme in 2006.'

So now they had several thousand motives as to why he was killed, Horton thought, wryly. And it would take for ever to trawl through every property transaction and dodgy double-glazing deal Farnsworth did between those years.

Daisy said, 'He worked for Deansworths and was one of their most successful agents. He earned a great deal of money, which was how he was able to buy an expensive house on the outskirts of Haslemere. Not that I've ever been there. Nick and I tended to meet on board my boat.'

It was said without any trace of embarrassment or defiance, but Horton didn't like to think of Farnsworth and Daisy 'meeting' anywhere, let alone here. He made sure he did not to betray his thoughts and kept his body still and his expression impassive. Maybe this time he had fooled her because she gave no hint that she'd read a reaction. The contents of Farnsworth's house would be examined very carefully, along with Farnsworth's past and finances, which was a job for DI Dennings and his team.

'Do you know if he left a will?'

'I doubt it. Nick would have thought himself immortal.'

Which confirmed Horton's own view. 'How long are you staying here, Miss Pemberton?'

She smiled at, he guessed, his refusal to call her Daisy. 'Until Saturday. I'm off to the States on business on Sunday.'

Horton would have thought there were enough sports person-alities in Britain to keep her occupied, but maybe in the States they paid more for psychological counselling or whatever she did with them.

He thanked her and promised to let her know the outcome of his investigations if they were completed by Saturday. Heading up the pontoon he felt a mixture of relief and regret that she was leaving before he resumed his berth in the marina.

The police vehicle recovery unit was covering Farnsworth's car with a grey tarpaulin sheet prior to getting it on to the breakdown truck. He found Cantelli chafing his hands and stamping his feet in the biting north-easterly wind.

'What did you get from the sub-aqua club?' he asked.

'Farnsworth went diving with Nathan Lester and Gary Manners several times in the summer. Daniel Collins also went with Nathan Lester over the summer months until September, but he never went diving with Farnsworth.'

There didn't seem much there of note. Horton told Cantelli what Daisy Pemberton had said finishing with, 'I'd like to talk to Farnsworth's ex-wife.'

'You can't unless you fancy going to the Caribbean. Trueman's just confirmed she left for a dive when the university broke up for Christmas and isn't expected back until Saturday.'

Shame. So she was crossed off his list of suspects. But they'd get the Caribbean police to check that she really was there.

He glanced at his watch. By now Uckfield would be in the middle of his press conference and it was too early for Dr Clayton to have completed the autopsy on Farnsworth. He'd like a word with Jason Kirkwood, but first he wanted to check out if Daniel Collins had ever mentioned Nicholas Farnsworth to his work colleagues.

That would also give him an excuse to investigate that other matter that was niggling away at the back of his mind: whether the Rest Haven Nursing Home was still under surveillance by Lee's mates from the Intelligence Directorate.

THIRTEEN

I t wasn't. He could see that instantly. There were no vans with darkened windows parked in the street, no twitching curtains and no strange men walking up or down.

Cantelli went off to the Rest Haven whilst Horton slipped across the road to the bed-and-breakfast hotel opposite. Twenty minutes later he was climbing into the car, where Cantelli was already waiting for him, having learned that an oriental-looking young woman and a burly man had taken the room opposite the Rest Haven on 29 December and had left on the afternoon of 5 January – Monday – when he and Cantelli had shown up there in answer to Mr Kingsway's complaints. During that time, according to the hotel owner, the young woman hadn't been very well and had hardly left the room. That wasn't surprising, thought Horton.

He hadn't given the real reason for his inquiries; instead he'd told her that he was looking for somewhere to stay whilst his aunt was in the Rest Haven. It was the same reason that DC Lee and her partner had given.

'Daniel Collins never mentioned Farnsworth to any of the day staff,' Cantelli said, turning on to the seafront. 'They only know Farnsworth through the diving programme that Mrs Kingsway's such an avid fan of.'

'It was a long shot.' Horton stared out to sea. The Isle of Wight stood out starkly, always a sign of bad weather approaching. He could see the town of Ryde climbing the hill and the shapes of the houses along Seagrove Bay. Cantelli hadn't questioned his trip to the bed-and-breakfast hotel and now Horton wrestled to put the information he'd just learnt with the other scraps he'd gleaned about Lee, which wasn't much at all. Maybe Cantelli would come up with something. He told him what he'd just discovered.

Cantelli looked incredulous. 'But what could be going on there that warrants the Intelligence Directorate's involvement?' he asked, puzzled.

It was a question Horton had already asked himself several times. He said, 'It has to be something to do with the Eburys; the Intelligence Directorate pulled out on the morning of Peter Ebury's death thinking they were no longer needed there.'

'Then why put DC Lee with us?'

'Scared we might stumble on something and ruin their investigation I reckon.'

'And does it involve Daniel Collins?'

Horton wondered about that. 'Possibly.' But why and how he didn't know.

'And Farnsworth?'

'No. I think it's just a coincidence that he and Daniel were both divers.' Though the close proximity of their deaths still rankled with Horton.

'You mean the Eburys and Daniel Collins could have been professionally silenced?'

Horton stared ahead. 'It's possible.' Especially, he thought, if a major criminal was behind whatever the Intelligence Directorate were investigating. 'Let's just tread carefully, eh, Barney, and keep this to ourselves for now?'

'I'll make out like I'm tiptoeing through a minefield. I just hope there are no unexploded bombs lying in wait for us,' Cantelli said, swinging into the car park of the Queen's Hotel. 'Do you think Marion and Ian Keynes could be involved in what's going on at the Rest Haven? Angela Northwood doesn't much care for Keynes. She claims she's lazy and a poor manager of staff. She confirms Keynes *was* on duty Christmas Eve.'

Horton thought of the slovenly, overweight Marion Keynes with her spiteful tongue, and of what Mrs Collins had said the night Daniel Collins had died: *he wanted to make sure I had the best possible treatment and was going to see to it that I did.*

'It's possible,' he said. 'We'll talk to her again.'

Horton quickly scanned the reception area of the Queen's Hotel for journalists and was relieved to find there weren't any. They were probably all at Uckfield's press conference. They made their way to Kirkwood's room. Outside Horton said, 'Talk to Corinna again, Barney. Find out what she knows about Farnsworth's relationship with Nathan Lester and the marine archaeological project, and see if she knows of or has heard of Daniel Collins.'

Horton knocked once, got no answer, and was about to knock again when the door opened.

'Found out who killed him yet?' Kirkwood said, leaving Horton to close the door behind him.

Kirkwood flopped down on the bed where Horton could see he was working on a laptop computer. His faded jeans hardly stayed up on his slender hips and he was wearing an overlarge grey T-shirt. With his pale green eyes, slightly sallow complexion and short auburn hair, he looked little more than twenty-five, though Horton guessed he was older.

Horton eyed the dishevelled room with distaste. There were clothes scattered on the floor and papers on the dressing table and chest of drawers. The room smelt of sweat, sleep and stale beer as well as the remains of a hamburger, which he could see in a carton on the bed.

'Why did you make those last two threatening calls to Mr Jackson?' It was a guess, but a good one, and Horton saw instantly he was spot on. Kirkwood's head came up. He looked as if he was about to deny it, but after a moment he shrugged his skinny shoulders.

'It seemed like a good idea at the time. Thought I might get them worried.' His attention returned to his computer.

'You *might* have managed to get one of them killed.'

Kirkwood scoffed. 'How do you make that out?'

'The press coverage could have given our killer the idea.'

'Then Nick shouldn't have started it. It was a stupid idea. Nick was full of them.' Kirkwood didn't bother looking up from his computer screen.

Horton had had enough. Sternly he said, 'Mr Kirkwood, do you think I could have your full attention, or would you rather answer these questions at the station, where you will be free from distractions?'

It did the trick. Kirkwood sighed, pushed down the lid of the laptop and shifted his narrow backside up the bed so that he was leaning against the headboard. 'Fire away.' He folded his arms and eyed Horton curiously.

'When did your engagement to Ms Denton break up?'

Kirkwood's expression darkened. 'August, but the bastard had been screwing her since June. He took great pleasure in telling me that. And it was while we were filming the *Diving off Dorset* series. I should have left him trapped in a wreck, the two-timing scheming git.'

'Instead you lured him to Oldham's Wharf and killed him?'

'You're kidding.' Kirkwood's lips formed the edge of a smile, then obviously seeing that Horton was serious, he quickly added, 'Of course I didn't.'

'You quarrelled though.'

'Wouldn't you? I told Corinna not to be such a bloody idiot. She said she and Farnsworth were in love.'

Those pale green eyes weren't so relaxed now, thought Horton. Here was a man who'd had his pride severely dented and his ego crushed. Horton knew what it was like to be tossed aside and compared with the next lover and his body stiffened involuntarily. He had wanted to tear Edward Shawford, his wife's lover, to pieces and had only just managed to stop himself. Had Jason Kirkwood felt the same way and killed Farnsworth? Quite frankly, though, looking at him, Horton didn't think Kirkwood strong enough either mentally or physically to get the better of Farnsworth.

Kirkwood said, 'You have to understand Nick. He took pleasure in taking what he wanted from people, using them for his own purposes and then spitting them out again when he'd finished with them or got bored. He would have done the same with Corinna if someone hadn't done us all the favour of killing him.'

It was pretty much what Daisy had told him. Horton sat on one of the two chairs that faced the bed. 'What would Farnsworth have wanted from Corinna, apart from sex, that is?'

Kirkwood winced, but said sharply, 'Me off the programme and more of a say in who should be his co-star.'

'He didn't get on with Perry Jackson?'

'They hated each other's guts, but they were contracted to do the series. This is the third and there's another three planned. Nick probably thought he could get rid of Perry before the next series was filmed. It's my guess that Nick made those first two calls to scare Perry and force him to quit.'

'And you played along,' Horton said scathingly.

'Yeah, but only to surprise Nick. I didn't want to scare Perry. I thought that Nick would have to admit he'd made the first two calls and look rather childish.'

Horton studied the scrawny young man and thought he was telling the truth. 'Why didn't you leave the programme when Corinna told you about the affair with Nick?'

'Why should I?' he declared hotly. 'I wasn't going to give *him* the satisfaction of seeing me out of a job. OK, so I admit it hurt like hell to be around those two, in fact it made me feel physically sick, but I wanted to be a thorn in that bastard's flesh for as long as I could, and until I secured another position.'

'You have no alibi for last night.'

'So?'

Kirkwood didn't seem bothered about it. Maybe he had hung around hoping to pick up the pieces after Farnsworth had chewed up and spat out Corinna. Horton had the feeling that Kirkwood was still genuinely in love with her. Time to take a different tack.

'Did you know Daniel Collins?'

'Never heard of him.'

It looked and sounded like the truth. Nevertheless Horton asked, 'Where were you on Christmas Eve?'

'London.'

'All day?'

'Yes. I had an interview for a job, and I got it. Filming off the Caribbean beats the shit out of filming in the Solent. I went out to celebrate that evening with my mates. Why do you want to know?'

Kirkwood couldn't have killed Daniel, but he'd reserve judgement on Farnsworth's death. Returning to his original line of questioning, Horton said, 'Why didn't Farnsworth and Jackson get on?'

'It wasn't always like that. They started off as great buddies; in fact Jackson got Farnsworth the job.'

Horton was somewhat surprised at that; hiding it he said, 'How? Explain the process.'

'The production company, Phantom, circulated an e-mail to all the diving clubs in the UK asking for expressions of interest. There were several auditions, which didn't include demonstrating diving expertise because Phantom was initially looking for someone who looked good in front of a camera, and Farnsworth did. Bloody good, in fact, even though it pains me to say it, the smooth git. Then he went on a dive with me and Perry—'

'Jackson had already been recruited?' asked Horton, trying to get the facts clear in his mind.

'Yes. The programme was his idea initially and he sold it to Phantom. He was on the panel to interview Farnsworth.'

That was news to Horton.

'Then about six months ago Nick found out who Perry's new girlfriend was and he wasn't very pleased. He didn't like having a taste of his own medicine.'

Surely that wasn't Daisy.

Kirkwood said, 'Annette Hill, Farnsworth's ex.'

'How do you know this?' Horton asked sharply.

'I overheard Nick and Perry rowing. We'd returned from a dive. Corinna had gone off to make a few calls and the three of us were sorting out the diving gear. Nick criticized something that Perry had done on the shoot. Corinna was beginning to let Nick have his own way. She was meant to be directing, but she caved in to most of Nick's suggestions, which meant Nick was in more shots. Perry was being elbowed out. Corinna would relay instructions to me on who and what to shoot, and I did as I was told even though I could see it wasn't right. On this occasion Perry flipped. He called Nick all the names under the sun, told him that he was going to get him thrown off the programme and when Nick laughed and said Perry had no chance, Perry told him he was dating his wife and she had said something like, it's nice to be in a relationship where both parties get to have an orgasm.'

Nasty. 'How did Nick take that?'

'He went silent, stared at Perry and stormed off.'

'And after that?'

'They only spoke when they had to. But if I know, or rather I should say knew, Nick, he'd have been plotting and planning a way to get back at Perry.'

And Horton wondered if he had found one. Daisy had said that Farnsworth would find something that his victim valued above everything else and then destroy it. Annette Hill was out of the country so Farnsworth hadn't killed or maimed her. Was her relationship with Perry Jackson still on? He needed to find out. But what else was dear to Perry Jackson? It had to be the programme. If Farnsworth had told Perry he was able to get him slung off it that could have precipitated his death. Horton only had Kirkwood's word for this, but it fitted with what Daisy had told him.

'We'll need someone to formally identify Mr Farnsworth. Maybe you could accompany Corinna.'

Kirkwood looked about to say with pleasure, and then realized it might not be a good move, so he simply nodded.

'We'll send a car for you when we're ready.'

He left Kirkwood to his laptop computer and found Cantelli in the corridor.

'Corinna knows of Nathan Lester but she claims never to have met him. And she's never heard of Daniel Collins. All she knows about the marine archaeological project is that Farnsworth is its patron and helps raise money for it.'

Which confirmed what Lester had told them. He briefed Cantelli on his interview with Kirkwood. 'He's got motive for Farnsworth's death and no alibi.'

'My money's on Perry Jackson,' Cantelli said.

Horton agreed that he was a strong contender. 'We'll need to speak to Annette Hill in the Caribbean to confirm Kirkwood's story.' Horton consulted his watch. 'Let's see what Dr Clayton can tell us about Farnsworth's death.'

FOURTEEN

'He was killed by a forceful blow to the throat, which compressed the vagal nerve causing the heart to stop. Death would have been instantaneous,' Gaye Clayton told them twenty minutes later.

Horton peered at the photographs spread across her desk, which had been taken before her knife had cut into the dead man's flesh.

'It was a karate chop delivered with the side of the hand.' Gaye made a slicing gesture with her right hand. Cantelli winced.

Well, that ruled out Daisy Pemberton, Horton thought, rather relieved. He shuffled the photographs around to get a better look. She was far too small to deliver such a blow to Farnsworth's throat, even if she were a karate expert. But maybe Farnsworth had been crouching down when he was struck. Was it possible to inflict a blow severe enough at that angle to kill? And what about Jason Kirkwood? Weedy he might look, but perhaps he was lethal with the edge of his hand. Then there was Perry Jackson.

'It was one of the silent kill methods used by commandos in the Second World War,' Gaye continued. 'And it's taught to troops undergoing training in unarmed combat. You're not necessarily looking for a serviceman or woman, or even someone ex-service though, anyone trained in martial arts could have done it.'

'And the fingers?' asked Cantelli, staring down at the photographs showing the stumps on Farnsworth's hand.

'Sliced off by a sharp knife with a serrated edge. Divers usually carry knives so it could either have been the victim's own knife or his killer's.'

And given what Horton had just learnt from Daisy about Farnsworth's Narcissistic Personality Disorder, his theory that the killer had severed the fingers as a message – that's what you get for messing around with my fiancée or wife – it was possible. Kirkwood again?

'Any idea of time of death?' he asked hopefully.

'Between nine last night and two this morning is the nearest

I can get for you. It's difficult to say whether he was killed in situ or moved. But if he was moved, then judging by the pattern of lividity, which is rather limited because of the tightness of the diving suit, it must have been very soon after death.'

Which meant that he must have been killed either at or quite close to Oldham's Wharf.

'There's not a lot more I can tell you, Inspector. He certainly didn't put up any kind of struggle. He wouldn't have had time to react.'

And his killer had taken that into account. Horton was disappointed at the lack of information. He hoped the forensic examination would get something from Farnsworth's car or Taylor from the scene of crime, but he wasn't holding his breath.

'Did you get a chance to look at the PM report on Daniel Collins?' he asked.

'I did. My colleague was right, death by dry drowning. As Collins entered the cold water it caused his throat to constrict and shut off supply to the airways.'

'Anything unusual strike you?'

She eyed him curiously. 'You think the two deaths are linked?'

'Only by the fact that they were both divers and died fairly close to each other.'

'I think you had better rule that out, Inspector,' she replied firmly.

Horton recalled the photographs taken at the scene of the incident. 'The car windows were open.'

'He probably thought the fresh air would help to sober him up when we all know it only makes things worse. You step outside after a skinful and wham; you don't know what year it is, let alone what day of the month. There was enough alcohol in Daniel Collins's bloodstream to dull his reactions, but not to completely comatose him, hence he must have gasped as his body hit the freezing water. He was too intoxicated to know or reason how to get out of the car, and as I said, the cold water killed him almost instantly by shutting off his air supply.'

So, no case to answer there. But if this was a professional killing then surely that was exactly what they would be expected to find – Collins's accidental death, Irene Ebury's death by natural causes, and Peter Ebury's respiratory failure. The hairs tingled on the back of his neck. He didn't like the thought of it one little bit. He'd dearly love to know if the Intelligence Directorate had someone in mind for these deaths. But even if they did, they wouldn't tell him; this thought fuelled his anger. He didn't like being kept in the dark, and he especially disliked not being trusted.

The day was drawing in as they headed back to the station. Horton felt restless and irritable. Maybe his mood rubbed off on Cantelli because he caught him glancing at his watch several times in an hour. Then Horton's mind rose above the fog of this blasted case to remember that Cantelli's father was being buried tomorrow. Feeling guilty that he had completely forgotten about it, he sent Cantelli home before he could get caught up with Uckfield's investigation late into the night. Cantelli slipped away without protest and a grateful nod.

Horton went in search of the officer who had arrested Farnsworth on the drink drive charge and found him in the canteen. Fetching a coffee, Horton pulled up a chair opposite PC Bateson, a broad-shouldered, redheaded man in his mid-forties.

'What was Farnsworth like last night when you brought him in?'

'Spitting blood and threatening to tell the newspapers what a useless bunch of idiots we were. Pity that second test was negative. We couldn't even charge him for using the mobile phone whilst driving because by the time we reached him he'd hung up. Not that it makes any difference now. I hear he's been found dead.'

'Yes. Did he mention anything about where he was going? Or about being late for an appointment?'

'No, but he kept looking at his watch. We said he could make a call, but he simply said, "I won't be here that long, officer." And the bugger wasn't.'

'Where did you pull him over?'

'Along Milton Road, just before the turn off into Velder Avenue.'

Which would have taken Farnsworth on to the dual carriageway heading north out of the city, and past both Salterns and Oldham's Wharfs. But perhaps Farnsworth hadn't intended turning into Velder Avenue. He could have been heading straight on which would have taken him past the prison and eventually out of town. He could have been visiting yet another one of his sexual conquests.

'Did he let you drive his car here?'

Bateson eyed him incredulously. 'He said he would rather take the chance on it being vandalized than let me or Harris in it. He left it in the pub car park.'

'Did anyone drop him back there?'

'We didn't. Someone might have done.'

'Call into the pub tonight, Bateson. Ask if anyone saw Farnsworth drive off. If so when and in what direction.'

Horton then checked with John Gatcombe, the custody clerk who had been on duty last night. Gatcombe confirmed what Bateson had said about Farnsworth's mood. 'No one arranged for him to be taken back to his car from here. I assumed he called a taxi on his mobile.'

Horton would get Walters on to that tomorrow morning. He pushed open the door to the incident suite and found Uckfield, Dennings and Trueman staring at the crime board as though it might reveal the answer to Farnsworth's death. All three were jacketless. Both Dennings and Uckfield were showing signs of fatigue and frustration: Dennings by the sweat patches under his arms and Uckfield by the deep scowl on his careworn craggy face. Trueman, though, looked as fresh as when he had started work some twelve hours ago. Horton suddenly became conscious that he hadn't changed back into his normal clothes. He'd completely forgotten that.

'Well?' Uckfield demanded.

Horton knew he was referring to Dr Clayton's findings.

Perching himself on the edge of a vacant desk, he quickly brought them up to speed with her findings and his investigations of the day without any mention of his diversion to the bed-and-breakfast hotel opposite the Rest Haven Nursing Home. He had half expected to see Lee here on some pretext or other, but then he surmised if Uckfield had been taken into the Intelligence Directorate's confidence, he could relay all this information to its boss, who in turn would inform Lee.

Uckfield listened impatiently with a grunt here and there and some rolling of his eyes, especially when Horton got to the part about Farnsworth's Narcissistic Personality Disorder. When Horton had finished, Uckfield summarized, 'So Jackson and Kirkwood are our strongest suspects.'

Horton nodded. 'Yes, with Ryan Oldham as an outside possibility.'

Uckfield crossed to the water cooler and wrenched a plastic

cup from the cone. Over his shoulder he said, 'Trueman, find out if any of our suspects are karate experts, and that includes Corinna Denton and Daisy Pemberton. Get a list of all the martial arts clubs in the city and cross-check their members with those of the sub-aqua club.'

Uckfield took his drink and crossed to the crime board. 'Nothing's shown up from the questioning at Oldham's Wharf so tomorrow, Dennings, take Marsden and another officer with you and get over to Farnsworth's house in Haslemere. Talk to the neighbours, and Deansworth estate agency. Find out what's the word on Farnsworth. Is there someone we don't know about? Horton, you interview Oldham.'

Horton didn't mention the funerals. He could fit Oldham in before going to Daniel Collins's cremation. Addressing Trueman, he said, 'Did you find out what Farnsworth did in the navy?'

'He went in a seaman and came out one. I haven't yet been able to get access to his full service record, but I'm working on it. He missed the Gulf War and the Falklands so there wasn't much to shout about. He was born and raised in Bognor. His parents are both dead and he was an only child.'

Had Farnsworth been spoilt rotten by his doting parents? Had they contributed to his Narcissist Personality Disorder without realizing it? wondered Horton. He wouldn't mind talking to some of Farnsworth's ex-shipmates to see what they had made of him. He wondered also if Farnsworth had learnt to dive in the navy. Not that it probably had any relevance.

He said, 'I could have a word with the police psychologist, see what he says about Farnsworth's NPD.'

Uckfield threw his crushed cup into the bin. 'If you think it will help.' Horton could tell by his tone that Uckfield was of the opinion it wouldn't.

Horton made his way back to the CID office feeling drained and dejected. His week off was looking more attractive by the minute. This case was beginning to get to him. Was it one case or three? According to Doctor Clayton it was one: Farnsworth's death. It was time to go home and hopefully sleep, but he knew his unanswered questions would conspire to keep him tossing and turning. He recalled that he had intended to drop into Jensen House to see if his old neighbour, Mrs Cobden, recognized Irene Ebury from the photograph taken from Peter's belongings. Even if she did though he wasn't sure where that would get him. Besides it hardly took priority now.

He drew up sharply at the door to the CID office. DC Lee was at his desk and it looked as though she was searching it. As though some instinct had alerted her, she glanced up and saw him. He gave her top marks for not starting guiltily. She simply straightened up and stared at him enquiringly as if she had been waiting for him.

'Looking for something?' he asked casually, though his guts were in a tight knot.

She didn't bat an eyelid and there wasn't the faintest sign of a guilty flush on her face. 'The case notes on the Peter Ebury robbery have just come in, guv. I was about to leave you a note.' She gestured to the manila folder in front of her on his desk. On it was stuck a blank yellow Post-it note.

He didn't believe her. Had she been skimming through Peter Ebury's file making sure it was all there or had she taken something from it? Though if she had extracted something he couldn't see where she could possibly have concealed it without it showing. His phone rang giving her the chance to slip out. It was Sergeant Elkins of the Marine Unit.

'Perry Jackson's boat is still at Hythe Marina and it hasn't been out for at least a month.'

So if he did kill his partner then he didn't use his own boat to ferry the body or to take Farnsworth to Oldham's Wharf. He watched Lee leave the CID office.

'I've checked with both Sparkes and Northney Marinas on Hayling Island,' Elkins continued. 'but nothing went out from there last night.'

'OK. Thanks.'

He rang off and glanced down at his desk. What had Lee been about to write on the Post-it note. Nothing, he guessed. It was just a ploy in case she got caught in his office. She must already have had access to the Peter Ebury file, so there would have been no need for her to take a sneaky look at it. And if it wasn't that, then what had she been hoping to find in his office?

He stiffened. There was one file that wasn't here but on his boat which had a connection with the Rest Haven or rather with Irene Ebury. The missing person's file on his mother. Could she have been interested in that? But there was so little information in it. Certainly nothing to worry the Intelligence Directorate, apart from its connection with Irene.

There was a tap on his door and he looked up to see Lee.

'I thought you'd gone home,' he said, surprised and annoyed.

'Just on my way, guv.' She hesitated. 'Are we still looking into the deaths of Irene and Peter Ebury? Only I could take a look at those statements from the home tomorrow morning, and see if there are any discrepancies. It could still tie in with Daniel's death. I could also check if Farnsworth had any connections with the Rest Haven.'

So it was the nursing home. And she had to come back to make sure he hadn't forgotten it.

He had to know why. 'Cantelli's already done that. There's no connection.' She didn't look disappointed or annoyed that he hadn't kept her informed, but then he hadn't expected her to show any emotion. 'There's something else though I'd like you to do. Interview Marion Keynes. Put her under pressure. I still think she stole Irene's belongings.' There was no hint in Lee's eyes that she knew otherwise. 'And get the addresses of a couple of the residents' relatives and talk to them. Do they have any concerns about the place? See what you can ferret out.'

'Yes, guv.' She made to leave but paused at the door. Turning back, she said, 'Are you going to Daniel's funeral tomorrow? I was wondering if I could come along. Two sets of eyes might be better than one.'

He held her gaze for a moment. All he could see was a genuine interest in following up a gut feeling. He said, 'I'll see you at the crematorium at ten thirty.'

FIFTEEN

Thursday, 8.45 a.m.

'Farnsworth was a pain in the arse,' Ryan Oldham said. Horton was sitting across Oldham's desk in the man's shambolic office. It was teeming with papers and littered with dirt and gravel. The rain beat against the roof of the Portakabin and the wind whistled through the thin walls, killing the meagre amount of heat that the narrow storage heaters were limping out. Oldham, wrapped in a giant waterproof windcheater and wearing Hunters so filthy that Horton could hardly see they were green, said, 'Farnsworth was a publicity-centred prick who didn't care who he upset or ruined just as long as it got his ugly mug in the newspapers. And if someone bumped him off then he had it coming to him. He cost me money, not to mention a lot of hassle and I can't say I'm crying buckets over the man's death.'

'You mean the exploitation of the seabed.'

Oldham snorted. It was like an elephant sneezing, thought Horton, except without the snot.

'Exploitation my arse! Did he live in a tent? No, the bugger lived in a ruddy great house built of bricks, and I bet his driveway was block-paved. Where the hell does he think the sand and gravel not to mention concrete come from to build that, the moon? If we don't dredge the seabed then we have to extract it from the land, but no doubt being a bloody diver that's what he would have preferred. And then we'd have all the NIMBYs on our backs, not to mention the tree huggers and planet-saving weirdos.' Leaning forward, Oldham continued, 'And don't let all that TV crap fool you about the bed of the Solent being one big archaeological find. OK, so there are wrecks there, but there is more rubbish than wrecks. There are bombs, armaments, munitions and God alone knows what else. The navy have dumped there for years, not to mention what the Luftwaffe and the Royal Air Force chucked out. And who cleans that up? Muggings here, that's who.'

Oldham stabbed his big chest so hard that Horton almost winced. He must be made of iron.

'It costs me a fortune, especially as I have to call in the bomb disposal squad and you lot every time a dredger returns with a bomb. And I have to close down operations, sometimes for hours. That's why I've had to go to the expense of building that bloody bomb shelter so the bloody things can be transported there and defused without causing too much disruption to my business. If my customers don't get their deliveries, they go elsewhere. Do I get compensation for that? Like buggery I do.'

Horton opened his mouth to speak, but Oldham was in full flow.

'Everything we do is above board. Always has been but Farnsworth wanted a story and the press lapped it up. Now the

man's dead it's started all over again. Have you seen those tossers
out there? You'd think this fucking awful weather would have
put them off, but no, there they are, huddled under umbrellas
with their tongues hanging out, their eyes popping and their
bloody cameras and Dictaphones stuck in your face every five
minutes. Can't you move them on?'

Horton had fought his way through them throwing 'no
comments' in the air like confetti at a wedding. 'We've got an
officer on the gate.'

'Oh, yeah, I forgot that,' Oldham replied facetiously. 'The
bastards want to know why Farnsworth was killed on my premises. Did it have anything to do with our former row? Were the
police investigating me? Jesus, as if it isn't bad enough losing
business because the prick decided to get himself killed on my
land, without being accused of bumping him off. Now you show
up with your great big fat feet pointing the finger at me.'

Horton excused the mixed metaphor. 'No one's pointing the
finger at you, Mr Oldham,' he said equably, and felt like adding
that he didn't have big flat feet. 'You're just helping us—'

Oldham's roar and the slamming of his hand upon his desk
made the whole building shake. 'Don't say with your inquiries.
That makes it sound like you've already made up your mind I
killed the slippery sod.'

'I was going to say by giving us useful background information,' Horton replied quietly. He felt there was something more
here to justify Oldham's fury.

Oldham lunged forward. Horton held his position and kept
his gaze firmly fixed on Oldham's face.

'I didn't want him dead. I just wanted him to bugger off and
pick on someone else.'

Horton said nothing.

After a moment Oldham sat back with a sigh that was like a
strong south-westerly but not so damp. He added, with all the
force of an announcement on cup final day at Pompey football
ground, 'Obviously he did pick on someone else only this time
he got more than he bargained for.'

'Any idea who?'

'No.'

Horton held Oldham's gaze and noted the intelligence in the
piercing blue-grey eyes. He wouldn't like to cross Ryan Oldham
either in business or personal life. He let the silence hang for a

moment, hearing the telephone ringing in the adjoining Portakabin and someone saying, 'The police are with him now. He's not in a very good mood, best tell him later.' Tell him what? Horton wondered. Whatever it was he hoped he'd be several miles away by then.

'Did Farnsworth ever come here, before his death, that is?'

'No.'

'Did you ever threaten him?'

'No.'

'Meet him?'

'Once and that was more than I could stomach. I was at a Chamber of Commerce lunch at the Queen's Hotel. I don't usually go to them, but this one I did, more's the pity. It was part of a marketing drive by some whiz-kid I engaged for six months. Waste of fucking time.'

'When was this?' Horton asked.

'Last August.'

He thought back to what Daisy had told him about Farnsworth's row with Oldham – that had been in August.

'Do you practise the martial arts, Mr Oldham? Karate, that kind of thing?'

Oldham stared at Horton as if he'd just announced he was going to take his clothes off and dance naked round the yard.

'Do I what?'

No, thought Horton, stupid question, but then it was his job to ask stupid questions as well as intelligent ones because sometimes the stupid ones got you the answers.

Oldham said, 'Look at the size of me. Do I need some namby-pamby oriental crap to fight my way out of trouble?'

Horton would hardly call it namby-pamby, but he took Oldham's point. This man would simply crush someone. And if he was going to kill, then he certainly wouldn't have done so in his own backyard and arranged the body so meticulously.

Horton held Oldham's hostile glare and said evenly, 'I need to eliminate you and then concentrate on finding who did kill him.'

'When you find him give him my regards.'

Horton kept his expression impassive. After a short pause, he added, 'What was the row with Farnsworth about? And don't tell me there was no row or that it was over raping the seabed because I won't believe you.' It was like playing a game of poker,

Horton thought. Oldham was eyeing him as though he was trying to judge whether he could bluff his way out of this.

After a moment Oldham sniffed and then thrust his sixteen-stone bulk across the desk. His face was so close to Horton that he could see every blemish and every line on it.

'If this goes any further than this room or reaches those pricks out there, you're dead meat, Horton, understand?'

'I'll overlook the fact that you've threatened a senior police officer. Go on.'

'The row was over that tosser's approaches towards my wife, Mavis. Yeah, the bastard made a play for her.'

'When? How?' Horton asked surprised. He had no idea what Mavis looked like, but he imagined someone so completely different to Daisy and Corinna that it was difficult for him to think that Farnsworth would have wasted so much as a winning smile on her. Then he silently scolded himself. He'd once admonished PC Johns for stereotyping people and jumping to conclusions based on his own prejudices and here he was doing the same.

'It was at that stupid Chamber of Commerce lunch that I told you about in August. Farnsworth showed up. Fuck knows why but he made a beeline for Mavis and started chatting her up.'

Horton didn't think Mavis would be very flattered to hear her husband say that. His eyes quickly searched Oldham's desk and cabinet tops, but there was no photograph of her, or anyone, only pictures of trucks.

'I thought, OK, it's only a lunch, let the bastard have his fun. Mavis could handle him. If it boosted her ego then no harm done, except I discovered he called her the next day and asked her to meet him. She told him to sod off, politely of course, but that didn't suit the scumbag. He kept on pestering her, Mavis told me. I phoned him and told him to piss off or I'd crush his balls. He got the message.'

And that must have been the telephone conversation that Daisy had overheard. He said, 'As a result of which Farnsworth said he would get even.'

'He started telling the press I was a profiteering capitalist bastard.'

'And did you threaten him again because of that? Did you arrange to meet him here on Tuesday night? Did you kill him?'

Oldham looked as if he was about to explode. His eyes were

hot with rage. Horton remained still and silent. Then after a moment the fire went out of him. Steadily he said, 'I didn't kill him and I didn't meet him here. Someone's used those press stories to dump his body in my yard to implicate me.'

'So who hates you enough to do that?'

'Hates me?' Oldham looked surprised, then scowled. 'I guess I've got a few enemies, but I doubt they'd go to the trouble of killing that jumped-up idiot just to get even with me.'

'Why not? It's losing you money, maybe that's what they wanted.'

Oldham hauled himself up, shaking his head. He reminded Horton of a cross between a bull mastiff and a St Bernard dog. 'The type of men I know who'd like to see me ruined wouldn't have the brains to work that out. They'd come armed with base-ball bats and smash the place up. I reckon your killer read that stuff in the paper and thought they'd sidetrack you lot into thinking I did it, just to waste your time, and I've already wasted enough of mine.' Oldham crossed to the door and flung it open.

Horton didn't always oblige but on this occasion he thought Oldham was correct. He *was* wasting his time here.

After fighting his way through the reporters, he climbed on the Harley, but instead of heading for the crematorium he turned left and followed the short road south towards the sailing centre.

Kicking down the stand, he gazed up at the modern glass building with its tower like a truncated lighthouse giving high visibility across all aspects of Langstone Harbour. Pity it had been dark when Farnsworth had been killed and no one here to witness it. But then that was why the killer had chosen such an isolated location late at night.

Stepping past the row of dinghies and canoes, he made for the shore, where he turned northwards and after fifty yards came to a steel-wired fence and a rusted sign that told him he was at Oldham's Wharf and he could go no further. The fence didn't go all the way down to the lowest tidemark and if he had been wearing waders maybe he could have squelched his way in the mud directly to the quayside. Though he wouldn't like to have tried it.

He squinted through the slanting rain at Langstone Harbour. On a high tide and with a good engine no one would have seen or heard their killer come here by boat. Oldham's security lights would also have been on to show the killer the way. There were no uniformed patrol officers or guard dogs, though the sign said there were. Dennings had confirmed that. And the killer knew this because he had either studied the place, visited it or worked there. Ian Keynes would know everything about Oldham's Wharf.

Horton returned to the sailing centre and after showing his warrant card retrieved a list of boat owners and members. Scanning it quickly he couldn't see Manners, Lester, Jackson, Kirkwood or Keynes on the list. He tucked it inside his jacket and headed for the crematorium.

It was the right sort of weather for a funeral, he thought, wet, windy and thoroughly depressing. The kind of day where you never got to switch off the lights in your house and the chill and damp seeped right through to your bones.

His mind returned to the case notes on Peter Ebury. Last night, over a hastily prepared meal, he had read them. Two things had jumped out at him. The first, why was the armoured vehicle with the store's takings in a country lane when Ebury and Mayfield had held it up? It was off the beaten track and not on the route they should have taken to their next collection. The driver had said that he wanted a pee, but there were plenty of other places to stop for that along the top of Portsdown Hill. And whoever had heard of a security guard stopping for a pee with a van load of money?

The second point was why had it been so easy for Peter to get caught? If he had been as clever and manipulative as the deputy governor of Kingston Prison had said, then why hadn't he figured out a better escape route?

Ebury had pleaded not guilty, a charge that could hardly stick when discovered with a car full of money. But Ebury's story had been that he and Mayfield had been in the process of stealing the car when the police arrived. They'd walked from a pub in the nearby village of Clanfield and, seeing the car abandoned in the lay-by on the A3 to London, intended to steal it to get back to Portsmouth. They claimed to have known nothing about the money until the police showed up. No one in any of the pubs could give them an alibi and Thomson, the other security guard, had recognized their voices. The gun was found near the lay-by with Ebury's prints on it and there was gun residue on his hands. Mayfield had confessed under questioning, and pleaded guilty. Only then had Ebury changed his plea to guilty. Case closed . . . except it left a bad taste in Horton's mouth.

He swung into the crematorium and found Lee waiting for him in her car.

'Marion Keynes swears blind she never stole Irene's belongings,' she said as Horton eased himself into the Ford.

'You believe her?'

Lee shrugged. 'She's definitely hiding something, and with a bit more pressure we could get to the truth.'

Which is what? thought Horton.

'Did you get anything from re-examining the statements?'

'I haven't had the chance to go through them yet.'

Was she lying? He thought so. He wouldn't mind betting that she had sat in her hotel bedroom late into the night analysing every word, but either she didn't want to be drawn to comment or had spotted something and wanted to check it out first.

'I'm going to the Rest Haven after this to get the names and addresses of some relatives,' she added.

Through the rain, Horton saw Gary Manners, the sub-aqua club secretary, climb out of his Jaguar and run towards the chapel. The hearse arrived and behind it a large black limousine carrying Mr and Mrs Collins. Horton pushed open the car door allowing a blast of wind and rain to hurl itself angrily at him.

'Leave speaking to the relatives for now. Call on all the pawn-brokers, antique and junk shops near to where Marion Keynes lives to see if any of Irene's jewellery has shown up. Cantelli put out a circular but there's been no response. Put some pressure on.' That would keep her busy for a while, he thought wryly.

'Couldn't DC Walters do that?'

Horton paused and eyed her coldly. 'I'm asking you to do it, Lee.'

Anger flashed for a moment in her dark eyes. Tough! If she wanted to be one of his team then she would act accordingly, he thought with satisfaction. Either that or tell him the truth. He pulled off his heavy leather jacket as they filed into the chapel.

Daisy Pemberton gave him a sad smile which made his heart skip half a beat. She looked even more attractive in black, with her beret perched at an angle on her dark hair. Seeing her reminded him that he hadn't contacted the police psychologist, but then he'd hardly had time for that.

He drew a scowl from Angela Northwood of the nursing home and a serious nod from Gary Manners, but there wasn't anyone else he knew or recognized, apart from the Collinses. He had wondered if Nathan Lester would show up, but there was no sign of him. Perhaps he couldn't leave his antiques shop, though Horton thought closing it for a couple of hours was hardly going to deprive the people of Portsmouth. And he had expected to see more people from the nursing home.

'Perhaps they're short-staffed,' Lee said, scouring the crowd of grieving friends and relatives as they filed out of the chapel. The service had been brief. The vicar had done his best to chart Daniel's short life, but Horton didn't think it had caught his personality as described to him by Daisy. None of his family and friends had spoken.

'Anyone here stir any thought processes, Lee?' he asked.

'No.'

But there was plenty to stir the emotions, he thought, glancing at Mr and Mrs Collins. The strain of their sorrow was etched on every pore of their haggard faces and the weight had fallen off them leaving them looking like a pair of walking skeletons. Whatever the outcome of their inquiries into Daniel's death, Horton hoped they'd reach a conclusion and one that wouldn't cause the Collinses any further sorrow, but he wouldn't bank on it.

'I'll have a word with Gary Manners. You get working on those junk shops and pawnbrokers.'

He watched Lee dash across the car park in the rain. Was she the only person here from the Intelligence Directorate or were her colleagues out there video-recording this crowd? He couldn't see anyone, but that didn't mean they weren't there.

'Sad occasion,' Gary Manners said solemnly after Horton nodded him a greeting. He watched as Daisy passed on her respects to the Collinses. Then she gave him a brief nod before turning towards the car park.

'Do you still believe Daniel's death was suspicious?' Manners continued. 'I guess you do otherwise you wouldn't be here. I can't think who would want to harm him. He was so quiet and ... well, nondescript. I don't mean that disrespectfully, but he's not the sort that gets himself killed.'

'Meaning Nick Farnsworth was.'

Manners eyed him carefully. Horton felt a frisson of excitement, sensing that Manners was making a rapid mental calculation about whether or not to reveal some information about Farnsworth. After a moment he said, 'If I'm honest, yes. Nick liked to live dangerously, especially where women were concerned.'

Horton had already gathered that. He wondered if Manners had suffered the same experience as Jason Kirkwood, but there was no bitterness in his tone or even a hint of jealousy.

'You think an angry husband or boyfriend killed Mr Farnsworth?'

'It's possible. He had a number of affairs.'

'He told you about them?'

Manners looked straight at Horton. 'Nick and I were in the navy together. We served on the same ship.'

Did you now! Horton surveyed Manners with interest, recalling Dr Clayton's words about certain personnel in the armed forces being trained to use karate. Manners looked a pretty fit bloke too.

'Nick couldn't help himself,' Manners continued. 'Sex was like a compulsion with him, or an illness depending on how you view it. He couldn't go without it. And he liked a conquest, the more difficult the better.'

Horton moved aside to let some of the mourners file past him. Soon the Collinses would be heading back for the wake. Manners' words made him think of Mavis Oldham. He guessed that the fact that she was married to a hard man like Ryan Oldham was the challenge rather than anything to do with the woman's charms, though it could be both.

'Are you married, sir?'

Manners, following Horton's reasoning, gave a twisted smile. 'Widowed, five years ago. And no, my wife didn't have an affair with Nick.'

Are you sure? thought Horton, holding his gaze.

'And before you ask I haven't got any daughters either.' Manners' expression was solemn and reflective when he added, 'I wasn't surprised Nick was picked for that television series; he was very charismatic.'

Could Manners have been jealous? He gave no sign of it. Horton was getting the impression though that Manners was edging towards telling him something important, only he wasn't quite sure how to say it. *OK, let's help him out.* 'Did you ever see him in a temper?'

'Nick didn't need to lose his temper. He could charm and joke his way out of problems.'

Evasive, but there was that slight hesitation and unease in Manner's demeanour. He needed more prompting. 'When he did lose his temper though, how did he behave?' *Now let's see what little secrets fly out.*

'If the person had really upset Nick, or hadn't let him get his way, or even made him look foolish, then he'd get his own back.'

Which tied in with what had happened to Ryan Oldham and what both Daisy and Jason Kirkwood had said about Farnsworth.

'How?'

'Whatever you valued Nick destroyed,' Manners said, now with an edge of bitterness in his voice.

At last. 'So what did he destroy of yours?'

Manners held his gaze. 'Let's walk to my car.'

Horton fell into step beside him. It was still raining, but Horton hardly noticed it and neither, he thought, did Manners. After a moment Manners resumed. 'We were both naval divers.'

Well, that answered one of Horton's questions. Only another hundred or so to go. 'What happened?'

'Nick and I were wreck-diving off Cornwall in 1994, not on navy time, but our own. Visibility was low and it was dark. We became separated. Unknown to Nick, or so I thought at the time, I got wedged in the wreck. I was running out of air. I didn't think I'd get out, but somehow I managed it. Nick had already begun his ascent to the surface. He said later that he thought I'd already gone up. Because I was short of air I ascended too quickly missing decompression stops. I was taken by the coastguard to hospital and then to the decompression chamber suffering from decompression illness. I didn't think it would have any long-term effects, and for many people it doesn't, but I was one of the unlucky ones. The whole incident had an adverse effect on me: nightmares, palpitations. I was eventually diagnosed with post-traumatic stress disorder, and along with that I ended up with ongoing pains in my joints and limbs. The navy said I had become a liability. I had to kiss goodbye to the Mine Warfare Clearance course that I was scheduled to undergo and Nick wasn't. I also had to kiss farewell to diving and the navy. The nearest I get to diving now is running the club and taking the boat out. Some people might say it's like rubbing salt into the wounds, but not for me. And if the navy taught me anything other than diving and discipline, it's good organizational skills. I'm second to none when it comes to health and safety. It's what I do for a living. I'm a health and safety inspector.'

'You're saying that Farnsworth knew you were trapped in that wreck and deliberately left you there?' Manners had just given himself the perfect motive for killing his old buddy.

'I didn't at the time, but years later, when he was drunk one night he let something slip. He said, "Pity your foot got wedged in that door." I never told him or anyone else that. So how did he know? He knew that being a diver and a naval one was the only thing I ever wanted to do. I was a better diver than him and destined for promotion. Nick couldn't stand that. He always had to be the best, and the person in the limelight.'

'So where were you between ten p.m. on Tuesday night and two a.m. Wednesday?'

'Oh, I realize I've just put myself in the frame for his death, but I didn't kill him. I was at home, alone. No alibi.'

'Have you ever been trained in or use karate?'

Manners' surprise at the question seemed genuine. 'I attended a course whilst in the navy, with Nick. Why do you want to know? Is that how he was killed?'

Horton remained silent.

Manners said, 'I see. Well, if you think I killed him, Inspector, then you are going to have to prove it.'

And that might not be so easy, Horton thought, watching Manners drive away. Was he capable of killing? Probably. And he hadn't denied it. Manners had access to a boat at the sub-aqua club and could have motored it to Oldham's Wharf where he had met Farnsworth, after they'd released him from the station. But why wait fifteen years to get his revenge? Had Farnsworth said something recently that had finally tipped Manners over the edge? It was possible.

He called Trueman, relayed his conversation with Manners and asked him to get a search warrant for Manners' apartment and the sub-aqua club. Then, glancing at his watch, he saw it was time to head back to Portsmouth and his second funeral of the day.

SIXTEEN

The cathedral car park was full, which didn't surprise him. Toni Cantelli had been a prominent and popular businessman in the city, owning two restaurants, which he'd handed over to his younger son, Tony, and his eldest daughter Isabella. Along with these there was a booming ice cream round, which Cantelli senior had started at the end of the war, and which had been the bedrock of his expansion.

Horton pulled in beside Dr Clayton's Mini Cooper. There was no sign of her. Perhaps she was already inside the cathedral where a crowd of people were huddled in the doorway, sheltering from the rain. He thought of Irene Ebury's funeral and that of her son, Peter – how many would attend that? Not many.

'I see you've come dressed for the part.'

He spun round to find Gaye Clayton behind him, standing under a large black umbrella. He'd only ever seen her dressed in her white coat, mortuary garb, or jeans and a sailing jacket. Now she was wearing black trousers with a short black raincoat, but it was the emerald scarf tied around her neck that drew his eyes to her small-featured, pale-skinned face, her short auburn hair and her green eyes which danced at him. He'd always thought her attractive, but now she looked positively stunning. And yet he found his mind veering towards Daisy Pemberton and cursed silently as he pushed thoughts of her away.

'It's black, isn't it?' he said, glancing down at his leather jacket, drawing a slight rise of her eyebrows.

'The emblem on it isn't.' She pointed at the red Harley Davidson logo.

'I don't think Mr Cantelli will care, Barney won't mind and God, if there is one, won't worry either, if that's the least of my sins.'

'And is it?'

She was teasing him but her face fell serious as the hearse pulled into the car park. 'I've got something to tell you, but later,' she hissed. He stared at her, frustrated at being kept waiting for news that might help him solve the case, but as the crowd around the entrance to the cathedral fell silent, all thoughts of Farnsworth, Daniel Collins and the Eburys evaporated.

Following the hearse were three black limousines: in the first Horton could see Barney, looking pale and drawn. His heart went out to him. Horton had no idea what it felt like to lose a father, never having had one, but he recalled the emotions he'd experienced when Bernard, his foster father had died, and understood something of how Cantelli must be feeling. He looked smaller and older than his brother Tony, who was three years his senior. With them were Barney's sisters: the dark-haired, olive-skinned and practical Isabella and the youngest, Marie. Horton hadn't seen her since she'd finished her postgraduate course in teacher training three years ago, but she hadn't changed much. At twenty-six she had been a raven-haired beauty and she was still a beauty. Beside her was Barney's mother; white-haired with a keen face, looking dignified yet solemn.

In the next car were Tony's wife, Emily, and his thirteen-year-old daughter, Michelle, and with them a young man of about twenty whom Horton recognized as Isabella's son, Johnny. Horton recalled the wild boy of sixteen who had got into trouble with the police after his father's death and how he had secured a place for him on the sailing trust. Now Johnny was skippering a rich man's yacht around the world. Horton was glad it had worked out for him.

In the third car was Charlotte, Barney's wife, wearing a wide-brimmed grey hat with a black felt band over her long dark hair, swept up, he noted, for the occasion. The sight of her always sent a warm glow through him. She was so different from Catherine both in looks and personality and yet to him Charlotte Cantelli personified everything a woman and mother should be and look like: warm, comforting, ample-proportioned, expansive and kind-hearted. A woman who had put her husband and children before her career, which if recalled had been nursing. OK, so the bra-waving feminist brigade would have him hanged, drawn and quartered for such outdated and male chauvinist thoughts, but he didn't care. Deep inside him he knew that Charlotte Cantelli represented something he'd never had, and which still caused an ache in the pit of his heart: a mother's warm and unquestioning love. Beside her were her five children: Ellen, Sadie, Marie and the twins, Joe and Molly.

As the cars drew to a halt in front of the church, Horton made to move forward when Gaye said, 'Here, take this.' She handed over the umbrella. 'You're taller than me and you're getting soaked.'

He held the umbrella aloft, wondering what it was she had to tell him. As the service progressed, Horton's thoughts flirted with the deaths of his final set of foster parents before turning to his mother. Was she dead? He had, of course, checked with the registrar, but there was no record of it. That didn't mean she wasn't dead, just that her body had either never been found or she'd changed her name because there was also no employment or NHS record for her. Had Irene Ebury known more about Jennifer's disappearance than she'd told the police? If so there was no way of knowing now.

He felt a sense of relief when the music finally played and they filed out. He nodded across to Barney, who gave a grim smile in return before climbing into the car. Horton had told Cantelli he wouldn't be attending the committal or the wake. Cantelli had understood.

As soon as the hearse pulled out of the car park, Horton turned to Gaye. 'So?'

'In my car.'

He folded himself into the Mini watching the rain stream down the window as people ran to their cars, doors slamming. One by one they pulled out of the car park, leaving his Harley and Gaye Clayton's Mini the only vehicles there.

'I took another look at the post-mortem report on Daniel Collins,' Gaye said. 'You seemed so certain that his death was suspicious that it bugged me. There is something—'

'What?' he asked eagerly with a quickening heartbeat.

'Take a look at these photographs taken before the autopsy.'

She reached over on to the back seat and retrieved a folder which she handed to him. He was staring at photographs of Daniel Collins on the mortuary slab. The final one was an enlarged picture of the back of Daniel's head.

'Three things,' she said, angling her body to face him. 'One, Daniel wasn't wearing a seat belt.'

Horton knew that from the firefighter's report. It hadn't properly registered with him when he'd read it earlier because that had been before he'd spoken to the people at the sub-aqua club and learnt more about Daniel's nature. Now it smacked him in the face. Why would a cautious man like Daniel not put on his seat belt? Because he was too drunk to bother was the obvious answer, but Horton didn't go for it.

Gaye continued, 'Two, there is a large contusion on his forehead consistent with bashing it against the windscreen in the crash.' She indicated the area on another of the photographs.

Horton couldn't see where she was leading him. There was nothing odd about either of these things.

'And three . . . go back to photograph number two.'

He duly did as she asked. He was once again looking at the back of Daniel Collins head and neck.

'Anything strike you?'

Horton peered at it. 'There's bruising on the neck.'

'Yes, which could be consistent with not wearing a seat belt and being thrown forward hitting his head against the windscreen, which didn't shatter, and then being thrown back to bash his head against the car headrest, maybe as a result of the impact of the car on the seabed.'

'So?' Horton looked puzzled.

'When did headrests make marks like that?' She pointed to the sides of Daniel's neck.

Horton was staring at what looked like blurs on the right and the left almost indistinguishable from the myriad of other bruising. He still couldn't see what she was driving at.

'I've enlarged them on the computer,' she added. And she handed him another image. 'It's quite clear that there are deeper marks either side of that general bruising.'

At last he got it! He was staring at the pressure marks of fingers. His heart was doing somersaults whilst his mind was racing with this new information. He had been right and so too had Mrs Collins.

'Someone pushed his head against the windscreen,' he cried triumphantly.

'Looks like it to me, which means he wasn't alone in that car. Daniel's death was not an accident, it was murder. I'll stake my reputation on that.'

And that was good enough for Horton. Now all Gaye Clayton had to do was find some evidence to say the same for Irene Ebury and her son, Peter.

'Is she sure?' asked Uckfield, later that evening after Horton had told him about Dr Clayton's findings.

Horton lifted his Coke and nodded at Uckfield's sceptical expression. They were sitting in a quiet corner of the bar of the Rudmore Cellars on the edge of the continental ferry port. After studying the photographs again that afternoon and running through his theory until he was happy with it, Horton had gone to Uckfield's office. But Uckfield had forestalled him by suggesting they talk over a swift half in a nearby pub. Horton had been surprised by the invitation. Once having a drink together after work would have been a regular occurrence, but since Horton's suspension on a suspected rape charge and Uckfield's promotion to superintendent, it had been rare. Uckfield's invitation now confirmed Horton's suspicions that Uckfield knew about the Intelligence Directorate's operation and he didn't want anyone else eavesdropping, such as DC Lee who had drawn a blank from her trawl of the antique shops and pawnbrokers close to where Marion Keynes lived. She appeared stoical about her exploits, but Horton could detect frustration simmering beneath the surface. Tomorrow she would start talking to the relatives of the residents of the Rest Haven.

Horton said, 'Certain. Daniel was plied with drink by his killer and then helped into his car—'

'Into the passenger seat?'

'Yes. The killer then drove the car southwards along the dual carriageway, on to the wharf and into the sea, knowing that it would be high tide and relying on the fact there would be very few people about that late on Christmas Eve.'

'He took a chance on not knocking himself out, or getting seriously injured going over like that?'

'He was wearing a seat belt and braced himself for the impact. He wasn't driving fast. He also had Daniel strapped in. Once underwater, our killer swops places with Daniel; a body is much lighter underwater, and more manoeuvrable.' Horton could see Uckfield eyeing him incredulously over the rim of his beer glass. 'It might have taken a bit of shoving and pushing, but it can be done.'

'Only if our killer has the lungs of a seal.'

'He was wearing an aqua lung.'

'Wouldn't Daniel Collins have thought it odd this bloke getting into his car wearing an aqua lung?' Uckfield said sarcastically.

'I expect Daniel was too drunk to notice or able to speak, but the killer wasn't wearing the aqua lung then. It was on the back seat of the car. And under his normal clothes the killer was wearing a dry suit. When the car hit the water, our killer holds his breath, releases the seat belt, reaches for his aqua lung and regulator and starts breathing. He then struggles into the apparatus knowing he has to act quickly in case anyone saw the car go into the sea. He swims out through the driver's window and around to the rear passenger side and into the car. That's what was bothering me about the photographs taken of the car after the incident, I knew there was something odd about it but couldn't work out what. All the windows were open. At first I thought, like Dr Clayton, it was because Daniel wanted some fresh air to help him sober up but it was because the killer needed access.'

Uckfield was shaking his head, but Horton could tell it was in amazement rather than disagreement. 'This is one hell of a crafty beggar we're up against.'

'Yes and a meticulous planner.' Horton thought of his conversation with Gary Manners. This fitted him perfectly. Hadn't he said that he was a whizz at organization and health and safety? And this needed a mind that would think through every implication and part of the plan to the last detail. The only flaw was Manners said he couldn't dive any more on account of his illness. But Horton only had his word for that.

He said, 'Our killer manoeuvres Daniel into the driver's seat. If he had left it there, he would have got away with it, but he doesn't know that Daniel Collins is dead, and maybe he's the kind that likes to be doubly-sure. So he thrusts Collins's head against the windscreen and back again to make sure the poor man won't regain consciousness. Then he swims off—'

'Where?'

Horton had been giving that considerable thought. 'There are a number of options. He has a boat nearby and is able to reach it. He climbs in, starts the motor and returns to either Eastney or Hayling Island to the south, where his car is parked. Alternatively, on the high tide, he takes the boat to Broadmarsh to the north and the public slipway there, where he hitches it up to his car and drives away.'

Uckfield sunk some more beer. 'I'll get some officers checking.'

Horton continued. 'Or he could have resurfaced further along the shore to the south where he comes up on the beach, changes into some clothes he's left there behind a bush on Milton

Common, and then walks away, returning later to collect his diving gear.'

'So we need to ask if anyone saw a man walking along the dual carriageway in either direction in the early hours of Christmas morning. I'll give a press conference tomorrow, and before you ask, yes, I told Madeleine that it was over between us.'

'How did she take it?'

'Threatened to make a noise. I told her that when it came to noise I could roar a hell of a lot louder than her. It seemed to shut her up. Pity really because I liked her and she was a right little—'

'There is another theory,' Horton interrupted, not wanting to hear about Uckfield's sexual prowess or Madeleine's come to that. 'Our killer took his boat northwards to the sailing centre, next to Oldham's Wharf, where he hitches it to a trailer on the back of his car and drives away, or it could still be there on the shoreline. The sailing centre's CCTV doesn't show any cars in the car park that night though.'

Horton could see Uckfield's mind ticking over. He added, 'I've run the details of Daniel Collins's method of death through the ACR and nothing like this shows up locally, though there have been one or two cases of bodies found in cars in other parts of the country. I've asked Trueman to look into them, but I don't think they're connected.'

'So who have we got in the frame for both Collins and Farnsworth's murders?' Uckfield asked sharply.

Horton sat forward. 'Gary Manners. He claims not to dive any more, has a phobia for it on account of the accident with Farnsworth, but we only have Manners' word for that. He says he acts as coxswain on the dives. Manners would have known about the row Farnsworth had with Oldham, so maybe he thought he could implicate Oldham in Farnsworth's death. It's also worth checking to see if Manners has ever visited Oldham's to carry out a health and safety inspection. Perhaps that's where he got the idea from. And he has good cause to hate Farnsworth on account of screwing up his career.' Horton briefly relayed the conversation he'd had with Manners at the crematorium.

'Manners could have lured Farnsworth to the sailing centre with the promise of some information or by threat. The uniformed patrol says they stopped Farnsworth as he was heading that way. Farnsworth was worried at the station in case he was going to be late for his appointment, but Manners hung on for him, perhaps he even saw DC Lee on the radio as we left the sub-aqua club, and guessed we might pull Farnsworth over. Under cover of darkness, Manners kills Farnsworth, then transports him in a boat to Oldham's Wharf where he manages to get Farnsworth ashore and throws him in the pit. He then arranges the body to look as though he'd fallen in.'

'Sounds good enough to me. What about Daniel Collins?'

'Manners knew Daniel Collins and had been diving with him on several occasions. Our only stumbling block there is why Manners would want Daniel Collins dead.'

And as far as Horton could see Manners had no connection with the Rest Haven Nursing Home.

'We'll ask him when we bring him in tomorrow morning, nice and early. Nothing like a dawn swoop to get them worried.' Uckfield grinned. 'Dennings can interview him.'

Uckfield must have seen that Horton looked about to protest because he quickly added, 'Manners has already spoken to you so a fresh face, and one as gruesome as Dennings', might frighten Manners into talking.' Uckfield drained his glass. 'Another?'

'No. I'm off home.'

'The boat, you mean?'

'Yes.' Horton stiffened at Uckfield's sneer.

'Why don't you get yourself a flat?'

'Why should I?'

'You're not still expecting to go back to live with Catherine, are you?'

Horton said nothing.

After a moment Uckfield added, 'Any more news from Catherine about Emma?'

'No.'

Uckfield hesitated and Horton thought here it comes – maybe this was the real reason we're here drinking like old buddies.

'Look, Andy, what's the sticking point between you and Catherine?'

So that was it? Horton curbed his anger at the thought that Catherine had gone blabbing to her friend Alison Uckfield and Alison had got her husband to do Catherine's dirty work. Once, and not so long ago, Uckfield had thought him capable of hitting Catherine because she had intimated to Alison Uckfield that's where her bruises came from, when it was overactive sex with that oaf she was dating.

Evenly he said, 'The sticking point, as you call it, Steve, is me wanting to spend time with my daughter. I don't think that's much to ask, and I don't mean for an hour every other Wednesday. I want something more permanent than that.'

'But how? In our job that's not always possible. Take this case, for example, or any serious crime. We don't keep office hours and neither do we work to any sodding European Time Directive. If we did the public would get less of us than they already do and the criminals would be laughing behind their murders, mugging and thefts. If you said that you could have Emma every weekend, or even every other weekend, how do you know you won't be called in to help in an investigation or be already deep into one?'

Horton felt panic and fury in equal measures. He knew Uckfield was right and it was what any courtroom judge would say. He was also angry that Uckfield was backing Catherine's point. He could just hear her saying: *talk some sense into him, Steve. He'll listen to you.*

Like hell he would! But he remained silent and stayed put because there was more to come, and Horton wanted to know what Uckfield was really driving at.

'I'll be honest with you,' Uckfield said, which rang alarm bells with Horton loud enough to make him deaf because in his experience that always heralded a lie. 'I want you on my team and Dennings off it. He's got the intelligence of a woodlouse and that's insulting the insects.'

Horton tried not to look shocked. Maybe this time Uckfield *was* being honest. He hadn't expected this. OK, so it was what he had long been hoping to hear. But why? And especially now? Was Dennings threatening to tell about Uckfield's peccadilloes? No, it had to be more than that.

'How are you going to do that, Steve?' Horton asked quietly, the deaths of Collins and Farnsworth sidelined for a moment.

Uckfield leaned across the low table. 'The Port Special Branch team has a vacancy. It's right up Dennings' street. National security, anti-terrorist role. I've told him that I'll back his application for a transfer, but the bugger's sticking. He won't be for long.'

Horton was beginning to get an uncomfortable feeling

about this. 'I can hardly see Dennings shining in an intelligence-gathering role.'

'So he hasn't got your brains, but basic surveillance, undercover work and pitching in with a bit of muscle when needed is what he does very well, and that's what they want. When I get him out I want you on my team, but I can't recommend you for it, and with a possible promotion, if I can't rely on you pulling your weight at all hours and at the drop of a hat. I have to justify it upwards.'

So that was it? Horton's stomach clenched. He felt his body go rigid with anger and he fought to control it. Steadily he said, 'Let me get this clear. I get to be on the major crime team, working with you as a DI—'

'Acting DCI,' corrected Uckfield.

'Acting DCI,' Horton stressed, 'If I give up my right to see Emma.'

'No, nothing like that,' Uckfield reassured hastily, sitting back, but Horton saw his eyes narrow perceptibly. 'You can still see your daughter. Of course you bloody can.'

'When?' Horton kept his voice even. He wanted to know the full facts of this deal and he wanted Uckfield to believe he was considering it.

'When it's convenient to both you and Catherine.'

Horton held Uckfield's stare. 'You mean give up my right of access to Emma and the hope that she can stay with me?'

'Andy, you know what our job's like. We don't work nine to five. You're a good officer. You've got a career ahead of you now all that rubbish about rape is over. Once Dennings is gone, you can step into his shoes. It would be great to have you back working with me. We make a good team, always did.' Uckfield smiled.

Horton thought it was like a poisonous snake telling him its bite wouldn't hurt a bit. He tossed back his Coke, and scraped back his chair. 'I'll think about it.'

'Great.' Uckfield beamed, then frowned. 'But not too long, eh? If I get shot of Dennings, I can't keep postponing his replacement for ever. We need to move swiftly.'

'Right.'

Outside Horton paused to put on his helmet and wait for his racing heart to settle down. Who had put Uckfield up to this? Was it really Catherine? DC Lee's face swam before his eyes and he stared at the dockside cranes beyond the pub. Did they really think they could silence him with threats? But silence him over what, for heaven's sake? He knew nothing. No, this had to be Catherine.

Horton swung the Harley round and slowly made his way on to the motorway slip road where he waited on the hard shoulder. Uckfield was a long time coming out. Perhaps he'd gone for a slash. It was a good five minutes before he appeared. Had he stayed for another drink? Perhaps he'd called Catherine.

Horton moved off before Uckfield reached him. If he sacrificed his right for regular access to Emma would Uckfield really make him acting DCI on his team? He did work late. He would like to have said it was because he had nothing to go home for, but even during his marriage he had worked long hours. And when undercover in Specialist Investigations he'd be gone for days. Catherine was using it as one of the examples of his unreasonable behaviour and grounds for divorce. She was right. He had often wondered if marriage and a police career were compatible, and thought probably not given the high number of divorces. Maybe with the Alison Uckfields of this world, not ambitious, content to wrap her life around her children, church and friends, it didn't matter. But Catherine had been and still was, as ambitious as him. He hadn't been there to share the childcare. That had been left to his mother-in-law and the nursery. With Emma now at school it must be easier for Catherine, but not that easy.

He didn't like to admit it but Uckfield had a point. What would happen when a big case came along and he wanted to be a part of it – correction – he felt compelled to be part of it. It was what he loved. But he loved Emma too.

He thrust it out of his mind and concentrated on the rain-drenched road until he reached the marina. After his run he still felt pent up. He made himself something to eat whilst worrying away at what Uckfield had said. Was his proposal genuine? Or was it some kind of test to see if he went blabbing to Dennings?

He had no answers and was unlikely to get them. He knew he wouldn't sleep well. There was too much swirling around in his head: along with Collins, Farnsworth and Dennings there was Uckfield's ultimatum. He felt tense and irritable. It was like that sensation just before a storm. Some people experienced headaches and migraine, but with him it was a tightness across

his chest and a heightened alertness, as if his whole body was
being put in a state of readiness. For what, he had no idea, but
sooner or later something was going to break. He only hoped it
wasn't him.

SEVENTEEN

Friday, 7.35 a.m.

'Y ou're early,' Horton said, finding Cantelli already in the
CID office the next morning.
     Horton had dropped into the major crime suite on his
way through the station and had learnt from Trueman that Gary
Manners had been brought in at six a.m., and he'd requested a
solicitor before being interviewed. Manners was no fool. If he
was their killer, then, like the man had said, they were going to
have to prove it. There'd be no confession there. Trueman also
said that the search warrants for Manners' apartment and the
sub-aqua club would be through later that day.
     'Couldn't sleep,' Cantelli said.
     Snap, thought Horton. He didn't need to ask what had
disturbed Cantelli's dreams. Activity would help. It always
worked with him, though he knew that it merely postponed the
problems and didn't solve them. But he didn't want to think
about Emma and that job offer of Uckfield's now. He had a
murderer to catch.
     Yesterday DC Marsden had returned from Haslemere with the
news that Farnsworth had been a highly successful estate agent
and had made a mint of money in the London commuter belt in
a rising property market. Farnsworth was, Marsden had quoted
from his sources, articulate, had lots of nervous energy and people
took to him. He was able to fool most of the people most of the
time. Horton guessed that fitted the profile of a narcissistic
personality disorder. Dennings reported that no will had been
found in Farnsworth's house and there was nothing to throw any
light on who had killed him and why.
     The contents of his house were being searched and his personal
papers had been bagged up and Trueman's team were going

through them and looking into Farnsworth's finances, which on first glance looked very healthy indeed. DC Marsden had the task of tracking down and interviewing Farnsworth's previous girlfriends, which, Horton thought, might take some time.

By the time he'd brought Cantelli up to date with the events of the previous day, Walters had arrived. He detailed him to find Chalky White, one of their more useful informers, and get him asking around the pubs and clubs to see if Marion or Ian Keynes had been trying to pass off stolen goods.

Horton handed the case notes on the armed robbery to Cantelli. 'Read through that, Barney, and see if it tallies with your memory. Is there anything missing or does anything strike you as unusual?'

Cantelli took the file. 'About Farnsworth's death – don't laugh at this, but it was something that Johnny, my nephew, said to me yesterday about treasure hunting.'

'You mean as in chests with gold sovereigns?' Horton teased.

'Not quite.' Cantelli smiled.

That was better. Horton was glad to see a spark of life back in the sergeant's dark eyes.

'Johnny says that diving is highly competitive,' continued Cantelli. 'And when it comes to wreck hunting there's big money to be made. Not only in discovering a long-lost wreck but also in the selling of antiquities.'

Horton thought back to his conversation with Ryan Oldham who had claimed the Solent was littered with rubbish and wrecks. Cantelli's theory might not be so far-fetched at that. Discovering something like the *Mary Rose,* Henry the Eighth's Tudor warship, would make someone's name in marine archaeological circles, which Farnsworth would have loved.

'Go on.'

'Say Daniel Collins discovers a wreck whilst out diving with Nathan Lester and Gary Manners. They're sworn to secrecy until they can confirm its significance and rightfully claim it, but Lester blabs to Farnsworth. Farnsworth approaches Manners and wants to muscle in on the act. But Manners hates Farnsworth on account of the accident years ago. And Manners wants the glory and fame for himself so he starts killing off his rivals, first Daniel Collins and then Nick Farnsworth.'

'Which means that Lester is his next victim, or would have been if we didn't have Manners here. Get Lester's home address. If Manners is our killer, then Lester will feel very relieved when he knows we've got him in for questioning, so relieved that he might tell us everything.'

Horton rang through the information to Uckfield, explaining Cantelli's theory, which drew a snort of disbelief, but Horton knew he'd put it to Manners. As he rang off another thought occurred to Horton. To Cantelli he said, 'Lester could have told Perry Jackson about the wreck. Maybe he wanted to take the credit for it.'

'Would he have killed Daniel Collins though?'

Horton considered the fact. He couldn't see Jackson swimming in and out of car windows, but he might have got Lester to do his dirty work for him. 'Let's ask him.'

'And this?' Cantelli indicated Ebury's file.

'Read it later.'

Cantelli pushed it in the drawer of his desk and hurried after Horton.

Fifteen minutes later Jackson opened the door of his hotel bedroom with a pained look on his face. 'What is it now?' he snapped, grudgingly letting them in.

'Packing, sir?' asked Cantelli, nodding at the holdall on the bed.

'I think that's what it's called, Sergeant,' Jackson replied with heavy sarcasm. 'I refuse to be kept a prisoner here any longer.'

'We asked to be notified when you left the hotel.'

'I haven't *left*. I am in the *process* of leaving,' Jackson said pedantically, stepping around Cantelli as he carried his clothes from the hotel wardrobe to the holdall. 'I am not a criminal and neither will I be treated like one.'

That remains to be seen, thought Horton. He said, 'When did you first meet Daniel Collins?'

'Who?'

Jackson didn't even pause in his packing. He was very good if he was lying.

Sternly Horton said, 'Mr Jackson, will you stop that and answer our questions, otherwise we'll have no option but to take you to the station.'

Jackson pulled up abruptly. 'You can't do that!'

'We can. So put down those socks and let's see if we can get this cleared up.'

Jackson glared at Horton before capitulating with a great deal of huffing and puffing. 'Well?' he demanded belligerently, glancing at his watch with the air of a man who has two minutes to spare and has started counting.

'Daniel Collins?' repeated Horton, folding himself into one of the armchairs opposite the bed whilst Cantelli sat in the other one. Horton looked pointedly at Jackson, who after a moment sat down heavily on the bed with a deep scowl.

'I've never heard of him.'

Horton decided to help him out. 'He used to dive with Nathan Lester. Didn't Lester mention him?'

'No.'

Maybe Jackson was a good liar. Horton said, 'How did you feel when Nick was asked to give the keynote address at the international conference this June?'

Jackson looked surprised, was that at the change of subject or that Horton knew about the conference?

'What's this got to do with Nick's death?'

'I think we'd get through this interview much quicker if only one of us asks the questions.'

'I didn't *feel* anything. If Nick wanted to give the talk, then fine.'

'You weren't jealous?'

'Why should I be? I don't like that sort of thing.'

Oh, yeah, thought Horton, pull the other one.

'What sort of thing *do* you like, sir?' asked Cantelli.

Jackson swivelled his gaze. 'Diving, researching and writing. I don't spout humorous anecdotes or embellish fact with fiction. I am writing a book about my exploits on the wreck series based on facts, not the silly schoolboy pranks and adventures that Nick liked to conjure up. And if you don't mind –' he glanced pointedly at his watch – 'I'm having lunch with my editor in London, and I have a train to catch.'

And if Collins had discovered an important wreck, wouldn't that make a nice bit of publicity for Jackson's book, not to mention perhaps a completely new commission?

'What will happen to the series now?' asked Horton.

'It will carry on as usual.'

'It can hardly do that with Nicholas Farnsworth dead,' Horton said, trying to goad Jackson into displaying some kind of emotion for his partner's death. He might just have well not bothered.

Jackson rolled his eyes and sighed. 'I meant the programme will continue.'

'With another diver?' Horton recalled that Kirkwood had said the series had been the brainchild of Perry Jackson, who had sold it to the production company, so he must have a say over his diving companion.

'Yes. I've already spoken to him. And he's a much better choice than Nick.'

That was quick work, thought Horton. Too bloody quick for his liking. He guessed production companies had a schedule to keep, especially if they were tied to a strict filming timetable, but Nick Farnsworth hadn't even been buried yet. Perhaps TV companies had understudies like the theatre did. He really didn't know much about them. 'How is he a better choice?'

'He'll give the series a more serious tone. Nick was always looking to sensationalize the programme, and his vanity was huge. He wanted to be a star. We're not the stars, I used to tell him, the wrecks we find and their history are the real stars, but Nick couldn't see that. I want to make the series more educational; something that is sadly lacking in our dire culture of dreadful reality television shows. The public need to be aware that we have a duty to protect our underwater heritage, and who better to dive with me and take over from Nick than Nathan Lester.'

Horton just about hid his surprise. Cantelli's pencil hovered for a moment over his notebook. Horton just couldn't see the little squirrel-faced man with the nine o'clock shadow and oily skin being a substitute for the tall, good-looking, charismatic Farnsworth. And Horton didn't think the viewers would go for it either. He doubted Cantelli's daughter, Marie, would be quite so thrilled if her dad came home with Lester's signed photograph.

Had Jackson chosen Lester because he would make Jackson look more attractive and dashing? Perhaps Jackson had got sick of being the boring one and wanted to have a go at being enig- matic. Had these two men been plotting this when Horton had visited them after Nick's death? Perhaps they had colluded in killing both Collins and Farnsworth. Lester now seemed to have a very good motive for wanting Farnsworth out of the way.

Jackson rose. 'Now if you've finished . . .'

I haven't even begun, thought Horton.

'Where were you on Christmas Eve night?' Horton asked sharply.

Jackson hovered above the bed and then sat down again with a heavy sigh. 'At home.'

'Alone?'

There was some hesitation before Jackson answered, 'No.'

So truth won out. Horton noted a slight flush under Jackson's dusky skin.

'Now, let me guess. You were with Nicholas Farnsworth's ex-wife, Annette Hill.'

'So what if I was?' Jackson leapt up furious.

Horton eyed him steadily. Jackson picked up a tie from the bed and began to run it through his hands.

'Did Farnsworth know about your affair with his ex-wife?'

'They divorced years ago,' Jackson snarled. 'And I don't see that it has anything to do with the investigation.'

'Why didn't you choose her as your diving partner?' Cantelli asked.

'Because she hates publicity. She prefers to lecture.'

'When did you meet her?' Horton this time.

'About a year ago. I was asked to give a lecture at Bournemouth University on the work I'd done on The Kravel Project. It's an early sixteenth-century wreck in the Baltic. I was working with a team from Southampton University, surveying and recording it. Annette and I hit it off immediately.'

'I didn't think you liked giving talks.'

'I don't, but I made an exception for Annette. She's very well respected in underwater archaeological circles. I've read her books on wrecks . . .'

Something clicked in Horton's mind: *A. Hill.* 'Is that Dr A.W. Hill?'

'Yes.' Jackson looked shocked. 'You've read Annette's books?'

'I've seen them.' And he had, in Daniel Collins's lair, only he hadn't made the connection until now. 'Go on.'

Jackson looked as though he wanted to ask more questions about his girlfriend's books, and then decided against it. Perhaps, Horton thought, it was his cold stare that put him off, either that or the fact that he was running out of time to catch his train because Jackson looked at his watch again before saying, 'Nick hated her being so well known. Jealous, of course. She's an expert, like me. We both have Masters in marine archaeology and Annette has a PhD. We've worked extensively on wrecks around the world, whereas Nick was just an estate agent with an interest in diving.'

Blimey, this man's ego was as big as Farnsworth's, thought Horton. No wonder they clashed. 'If you despised Farnsworth that much, and you have a say in who co-presents with you, why didn't you sack him?'

For the first time during the interview Jackson looked uncomfortable. 'He was good for the ratings.'

Maybe, but there seemed more to it than that. Horton recalled what had happened to Ryan Oldham and Gary Manners. Jackson knew about Farnsworth's ways of getting even with those who thwarted him and Horton could see that Jackson's Achilles heel was his reputation. Farnsworth would have found a way to ruin Jackson and Jackson knew it. What a relief Farnsworth's death must have been to him. The case for Jackson being their killer, possibly in league with Lester, was beginning to build, especially if you put it with Cantelli's theory about a wreck.

Cantelli said, 'How did Farnsworth take your affair with his wife?'

'Ex-wife,' Jackson sniped. 'As I keep saying, he couldn't care less. By then he'd moved on. There were several affairs before Farnsworth took up with Corinna. I told Corinna she was a fool to give up Jason for Nick, but she wouldn't listen.'

'Why didn't you go to the Caribbean with Ms Hill?' Cantelli again.

'Dr Hill,' corrected Jackson. 'Because I was committed to the programme. Now, if you don't mind . . .'

Horton rose. Taking his cue, Cantelli did the same, slowly putting away his notebook. 'We'll need to talk to you again, sir.'

'Then you'll do so in the presence of my solicitor,' said Jackson.

'Of course,' Cantelli continued cheerfully, as they headed towards the door.

On the threshold, Horton turned. 'When will you be back from London, sir?'

'Late this afternoon. Why?'

'We'll let you know when we need you at the station.' He made it sound like a threat and a forgone conclusion, which was his intention.

Jackson slammed the door on them. Horton hoped that he wouldn't do a disappearing act. Horton had already made one mistake by not taking those threatening telephone calls seriously, although that seemed to have little relevance now to their case. But he didn't want to give Uckfield or Superintendent Reine the slightest cause to ball him out.

He said as much to Cantelli as they took the stairs to the ground floor.

'Jackson's a stuffed shirt but my money's on Nathan Lester,' Cantelli answered. 'He gets Farnsworth's job and the wreck, and he dived with Daniel Collins.'

Yes, thought Horton, and not only that but Lester was small and wiry – the ideal build to climb in and out of car windows.

EIGHTEEN

'Are you thinking what I'm thinking?' Cantelli said, peering through the grilled windows of Lester's antiques shop some minutes later.

'Antiques and antiquities,' Horton answered, though antiques was a kind word for the junk he could see in the gloom beyond the grill. The room was crammed with heavy old furniture and bric-a-brac rather than valuable memorabilia from sunken wrecks.

The door was locked and the closed sign displayed. Getting no response from Lester's house, a neighbour had directed them to the shop, which was situated in one of the less fashionable shopping areas of the city, on a busy road running from east to west and not far from the cemetery opposite Mr and Mrs Collins's house. Lester's Emporium was sandwiched between a cheap and grubby café and a Chinese takeaway, and shared the street with a charity shop, a newsagent, a pub and a betting shop. Starring in a television programme was a long way from this and Horton reckoned that Lester must have thought his ship had come in.

'Let's try Fort Cumberland. He might be in the marine archae-ological offices.' And if he wasn't then Horton would instruct Uniform to force an entry into Lester's home. After all he might be lying ill inside.

There was no car outside the marine archaeological office, but Horton recalled that Lester rode a bicycle. That wasn't here either, and it hadn't been in the forecourt of Lester's terraced house or in the narrow hallway when he'd looked through the letter box.

Cantelli rattled the door but it refused to budge. Peering through the grimy window to its left, Horton saw only a deserted, darkened office. Climbing back in the car, they headed for the main building a few hundred yards further along the road towards the centre of the Fort.

Before Horton could push open the door to the reception area, a slight man with a haggard expression and tired eyes, wearing an anorak over a uniform and carrying a plastic sandwich box stepped out. Horton recognized him instantly as Mr Kingsway from the Rest Haven Nursing Home.

'How's your mother? Has she mentioned the intruder again?' asked Horton, after the usual preliminary greetings were over.

Kingsway looked sheepish. 'I made a bit of a fool of myself, didn't I? But she was so adamant. I called in yesterday to check she was OK and she muttered something about it, but I managed to divert her by talking about the past. That's not difficult,' he added sadly. 'It's where they all live.'

He left a short pause before adding more brightly, 'Anyway, I'd better be going. Need my beauty sleep. I've been on since nine.'

Horton watched him climb into a silver saloon car, sensing that he'd just heard something important but couldn't quite grasp what it was. Never mind, he hoped it would come to him later.

The receptionist told them that no one had seen Nathan Lester since Wednesday. She handed over the key and they made their way back to the marine archaeological offices. Cantelli flicked on the lights in the outer office and began mooching around the desks, whilst Horton headed for the inner office where he'd previously interviewed Jackson. There was no sign of Lester and nothing that Horton could see to tell them where he was.

After dropping the keys back to reception, Horton said, 'Let's check the sub-aqua club.'

The gates to the car park were locked and bolted, so Lester couldn't be there either.

'He's probably away on an antique-hunting expedition,' Cantelli said.

It was possible and perhaps, thought Horton, his neighbouring shopkeepers could tell them where Lester was and when they'd last seen him.

The consensus was they had no idea and didn't much care either. Not that he was unpopular, just that he kept himself to himself. Stuck up was one woman's rather uncharitable opinion, but then she was voluble about anything and everything. And she didn't have a kind word to say about anyone, least of all the police. The shop was hardly ever open, and she, like the other shopkeepers, reckoned that Lester did most of his business on the Internet and through word of mouth. The last sighting of him was late Thursday afternoon about four p.m.

'I don't much care for this "word of mouth" stuff,' Cantelli said, stretching the seat belt across him. 'It sounds like he's passing off stolen goods, after buying them in dodgy pubs and backstreet alleys. I think we'll take a good look around Lester's Aladdin's cave. I'll get a warrant.'

'Good idea. And whilst you're looking, you might see if Irene Ebury's stuff has turned up there. I got Lee to check the shops and pawnbrokers in the area where Keynes lives, but not in the area where she works, and the Rest Haven isn't far from here. She could have heard about Lester from Daniel Collins and thought Lester was worth approaching.'

'Unless Daniel stole them and sold them to Lester.'

Horton didn't much like the sound of that. For Mr and Mrs Collins's sake he hoped that wasn't so. But it hadn't escaped his notice that Daniel lived almost on Lester's doorstep. In fact a few streets away. The sooner they got hold of Lester the better. He'd try one more avenue before busting into Lester's home.

Returning to the Queen's Hotel, Horton found Corinna Denton and Jason Kirkwood together in Kirkwood's bedroom but there was no sign of Lester. And neither, they both claimed, had he been in touch with either of them.

Cantelli said, 'Has Mr Lester made any suggestions about where you should dive for this series?'

Horton knew where Cantelli's questions were leading. He was probing a link with the discovery of a wreck.

'Not to me,' Kirkwood said, shuffling some papers around on the bed where both he and Corinna were perched. She'd been crying and clearly had had little sleep. Wearing her customary black she had a large jumper stretched over her knees which she hugged to her chin.

'Have you changed your diving location at all in the last couple of months?' Cantelli persisted.

Corinna looked up and with a puzzled frown said, 'Nick did mention something about switching locations.'

Kirkwood started surprised. 'That's news to me. When?'

'Monday.

Horton glanced at Cantelli. 'Where did he suggest you dive?'

'I'll show you on the chart.'

She shifted position and shuffled down the bed. Leaning towards Horton she stabbed at a spot that was just off the eastern tip of the Isle of Wight, not far out of Bembridge Harbour. Kirkwood leaned over to see where it was, whilst Cantelli too craned his neck.

'Why there?' asked Kirkwood.

'Nick didn't say.'

Maybe it had been a whim, or could Cantelli be right, wondered Horton, and that somewhere in that region lay an important hitherto undiscovered wreck?

He left Corinna and Kirkwood with instructions to contact him the moment they heard from Nathan Lester and radioed for Uniform assistance to break into Lester's house. Twenty minutes later he was pacing the small living room, puzzled and irritated. Lester wasn't here and there were no signs he'd left in a hurry.

'His passport's still here,' Cantelli said, delving into a drawer in a heavy old bookcase and pulling out a small maroon document.

The house was crammed with antique furniture, which seemed completely out of place in the tiny rooms they'd swiftly searched. Horton had put one officer outside the front door to stop anyone from entering, while another was asking the neighbours for their opinions and last sightings of Nathan Lester.

'He's not travelled far,' Cantelli added, flicking through the passport.

Horton examined a small octagonal mahogany table in the corner by a door that led into a small conservatory. 'I'm no antiques expert, but I'd say there's some good stuff here, better than in his junk shop. He's just got no taste when it comes to placing things in their correct stetting, or in decorating,' he said, staring at the faded wallpaper that didn't look as though it had been changed since 1970. Keep it long enough, he thought, and it would come back in fashion. The house was grubby, uncared for and overfull. It smelt as though it had never been aired and looked as though it had never been dusted.

'He likes his books,' Cantelli said, craning his neck to read the spines of those in the bookcase. 'Lots on diving, marine life, and antiques. Some first editions here too,' he added, picking one out and opening it in a cloud of dust that made him sneeze.

There were also books lining the stairs and more in each of the three bedrooms, along with antique glass, more furniture and china. This place, thought Horton, was like an antiques shop. Several clocks scattered around the house suddenly burst into life.

'Blimey, I wouldn't like to sleep with that lot chiming all the quarter hours,' Cantelli cried, glancing at his own watch. 'They're slow. It's half past one. I wondered why my stomach was beginning to make strange noises.'

'Contact the art and antiques squad when you get back to the station, after you've grabbed some lunch,' Horton said pointedly. 'I want someone logging this lot to check if any of it has been stolen.'

He walked through to the kitchen. His shoes stuck to the grime on the cracked linoleum and he screwed up his face with disgust at the dirt and fat-encrusted kitchen work surfaces, littered with crockery, some used and some untouched and clearly an over-spill of a job lot brought from the house of a deceased person. What Lester couldn't fit in the emporium he obviously tried to squeeze in here.

How could Jackson have given someone who lived like this the position of co-presenter? Horton thought, amazed. It just didn't ring true. Jackson must be mad. Either that or Jackson had been blackmailed into appointing Lester. Maybe Lester *had* killed Daniel Collins under Jackson's instructions and threatened to go to the police unless Jackson gave him the job.

Horton flicked opened the waste bin, glad he was wearing his latex gloves. He didn't like to think what he might catch otherwise. There were the remains of a couple of ready meals inside. The bread was beginning to go off in the bread bin, but the cupboards were fairly well stocked with food. It didn't look as though Lester had fled. If he had, then he must have gone by taxi or train, seeing as he didn't have a car.

He heard Cantelli give a surprised whistle and hurried back to the living room to find him waving a wodge of bank statements. 'There's some serious money here, Andy.'

'Coming in or going out?'

'Both. I haven't looked through them all and they're not in any order, but, according to this one in 2004, Lester had over thirty thousand pounds in his bank account. I wonder how much he's got now. I can't find a recent statement, but it's probably here somewhere.'

'And judging by this –' Horton waved his arm around the room – 'and his mouldy shop, I'd say not a great deal. There are no empty bottles lying around, so it doesn't look as if he's a drinker but maybe he gambles.'

'Not in the betting shop near his emporium. I asked the manager. He said Lester had never been in. Perhaps he gambles on the Internet.'

There was no sign of a computer, but then Horton thought they might have missed it amongst all the furniture. Lester could have used a computer in his shop or the one in the marine archaeological offices. But that was all speculation.

'Bag up all the personal documents you can find, Barney.' He'd get DC Lee to sift through it, which would keep her occupied for several hours, he thought, wondering where she was. He hadn't heard from her or seen her this morning.

'Don't we need a search warrant?'

'Lester's life might be in danger. This could help us to find him.'

Cantelli eyed him sceptically.

Horton added, 'But you'd better apply for one anyway.' And then they could really tear this place to pieces.

Horton had reached the door when Cantelli called him back. He was holding a photograph album.

'This will make your heart sing.'

Horton found himself looking at several photographs of Nick Farnsworth with Nathan Lester in naval uniform on-board ship. In a couple of them Farnsworth had his arm loosely round Lester's shoulder. In others Lester was just standing close by with an enraptured expression on his squirrel-like features. Horton slipped one out of its plastic holder and flicked it over. Obligingly Lester had written the date on the back: June 1995. That was after Gary Manners' diving accident and could have been after he had left the navy.

Horton rang through to the station and asked Trueman to tell Uckfield about Lester and then to find out more about his navy record. Had Farnsworth wrecked Lester's career as well as

Manners'? Had the two of them conspired to get even with Farnsworth? If so why had it taken them so many years?

Outside Horton spoke to PC Allen and discovered that Lester was rarely seen, never heard and no one knew anything about him. It was par for the course. He was about to call the arts and antiques squad when his phone rang. It was Dr Clayton.

'Something you might find interesting,' she announced brusquely.

He was surprised to hear anger in her voice. In the short space of time he'd known her, since August, he'd only seen her lose her temper once and that was over remarks made about her competence by DI Dennings. What or who had upset her now? It surely couldn't be Dennings. But then the DI had a knack of rubbing everyone up the wrong way, including his boss, it seemed.

'Like you, Inspector, I don't like coincidences and I particularly don't like being told what I should find before all the tests have been completed.'

Ah! So that was it. But test results on which body? One of the Eburys? It had to be. His heart went into overdrive.

He opened the car door and slid into the passenger seat as Cantelli emerged from Lester's house carrying a large plastic bag full of papers and the photograph album. Barney stopped to talk to the PC at the door.

Stiffly Gaye continued. 'I sent Peter Ebury's blood for analysis, as you well know. Twenty minutes ago I enquired about the results to be told they weren't ready. I said, "What the hell are you doing, recycling them for Dracula?" I was fobbed off with some pathetic excuse about being short-staffed and equipment breaking down. Three minutes ago I got a phone call from a smooth-talking, grovelling bastard who said the blood analysis need not concern me. Me! Did you hear that, Horton?'

Oh, yes, he heard it. He could have punched the air with glee. Instead he threw Cantelli a smile and got raised eyebrows in return. Hadn't he known it? This confirmed his suspicions. If Peter Ebury's death was down to natural causes then he was Clark Gable.

NINETEEN

'I had to let Manners go. His lawyer kept bleating on about releasing him or charging him, and what the hell evidence do I have?' Uckfield exploded, shovelling a large portion of steak and kidney pie into his mouth. 'The bastard was like a fucking iceberg sitting there, staring at me, his mouth shut tighter than a duck's arse. And it'll take more than dynamite to blow him out of the water.'

Horton had to agree. He bit into his ham baguette in the almost empty canteen. The lunchtime rush hour had been and gone. It was just after three. Horton had said nothing about Peter Ebury's blood test. Miraculously, Gaye had told him that she'd taken a second blood sample at the time of the post-mortem, which she would analyse once everyone had left the lab.

Lee had returned shortly after Horton. She'd been interviewing some of the relatives of residents of the Rest Haven, and, according to her, no one really knew Daniel Collins and no one had seen or heard him talk about Nicholas Farnsworth. None of the relatives had any complaints to make about the staff. Dead end.

After updating her on the events of the morning, Horton had set her to work sifting through Lester's bank statements, wondering when she would slip out and let her boss in the Intelligence Directorate know of this new development. Trueman had put out an alert for Lester, but so far no one seemed to have seen him at any of the city's three main railway stations, and neither had he caught any of the ferries across to the Isle of Wight, Gosport or Hayling Island. But it was too early to say with any real certainty that he had left the area.

Cantelli had resumed his studies of the case notes on the Peter Ebury armed robbery. Dr Clayton's news confirmed Horton's view that Peter had been silenced, and so too he reckoned had Irene. The key to their deaths had to be the armed robbery eight years ago. And he wouldn't mind betting it was that that the Intelligence Directorate was investigating. Had there been a master criminal behind it? Someone that Peter Ebury could identify. But if that were so then why wait until now to kill Peter? Horton said nothing to Lee about this and told Cantelli not to let on what he was doing if he could help it.

Uckfield's voice broke through Horton's thoughts. 'Do you think there's any truth in this wreck theory of Cantelli's?'

Horton brought his mind back to the present. 'Why would Farnsworth want to change the dive location if there wasn't?'

'Are there any wrecks in that area?'

'I could check it out with the university tomorrow.' Then he remembered that it was Saturday, there wouldn't be anyone to ask. And he was meant to be on leave.

'Well, I don't fancy sending the divers out into the Solent on a wild treasure hunt. It could take them forever and cost a fortune. And it's not coming out of my budget.'

It occurred to Horton that there was somewhere else they could check for details of wrecks, the marine archaeological offices. He remembered Lester indicating the computer and saying they were building a database of wrecks and other significant finds. But maybe this was one find that he and his fellow conspirators didn't want logged.

Uckfield cleaned his plate with a piece of bread. 'Haven't we got anything else?'

Horton heard the note of desperation and knew it was because Uckfield wanted to crack this case before the Intelligence Directorate. Horton didn't blame him for that. He felt the same way.

'Unless the search teams and Forensic come up with something we're down to probing backgrounds. But Manners isn't our only suspect. Jackson has plenty of motives for wanting his co-presenter out of the way, but as to killing Daniel Collins . . . he claims not to know him.'

'He could be lying.'

'If he isn't, then why kill Collins unless it *is* over the discovery of a wreck? And that goes for Manners too. Why would *he* kill Daniel Collins?'

'Because he didn't like the colour of his eyes?' Uckfield said. Behind the flippancy Horton knew was frustration.

'Manners freely admits to practising martial arts several years ago but not recently,' Horton continued. 'And Sergeant Trueman can't find any record of Jackson belonging to a martial arts club. He did however spend some time in the Far East, and has written a book about diving in South East Asia so maybe he picked it up then.' Though Horton had difficulty imagining the rather pompous Jackson kung-fuing.

Uckfield gulped back his coffee. 'We'll bring him in tomorrow.'

Which meant that Horton would have to leave this case to Dennings, something he didn't much care for – that was always assuming Jackson would return from London. He didn't think he would run away though. A man with his superiority complex couldn't possibly contemplate the police being cleverer than him. And that was another reason why Horton was warming towards Jackson as their killer. These murders had been meticulously planned and inventive.

'Trueman's also checked to see if Lester was or is a member of a martial arts club. No joy. Then there's Farnsworth's missing fingers.' Horton hadn't lost sight of that, though he'd not got around to asking the university forensic psychologist about it. Now it was too late. It would have to wait until Monday and for someone else to do it, unless he asked Daisy Pemberton. He felt a small tremor of excitement at the prospect of seeing her again, which he quickly quashed. He didn't care for her knack of reading him or the thought that she might be able to penetrate the dark recesses of his soul.

He said, 'Collins's body wasn't mutilated and neither was he killed by a karate blow. The methods of death are completely different. And as far as we can ascertain Collins didn't know Farnsworth.'

'Jesus! It's like the magic bloody roundabout.'

Horton couldn't help agreeing. His head too was beginning to spin with it all. 'If their deaths are unrelated, we're looking for two killers.'

'And the Chief Constable is looking for a result,' Uckfield replied, scraping back his chair. 'So I suggest we get back to work and find one.'

Horton watched Uckfield march away. Why couldn't they locate Nathan Lester? Where the devil was the man? Dead? Had Manners killed him before they'd pulled him in? Or had Jackson dispensed with Lester after promising him a place on the television programme. A promise granted under duress and the threat of blackmail.

And what significance did those missing fingers have? Marsden had so far drawn a blank in Haslemere trying to find some of

Farnsworth's ex-lovers, which Horton thought rather surprising. He was convinced there must be many littered about. Maybe they just didn't want to be involved and were keeping quiet. There was one person though who had got closer to Farnsworth than anyone else and he didn't mean Corinna Denton.

He tossed back the remainder of his coffee which had gone cold and rose. Despite his personal misgivings he reckoned it was time to talk to Daisy Pemberton.

'How well do you know Nathan Lester?' he asked, taking a seat in the main cabin. The wind was rising and he could feel the boat gently rocking.

Sliding in beside him so that she was facing him diagonally across the tables, she eyed him, clearly curious at the question. 'Only through the sub-aqua club, why?'

He tried hard not to be influenced by the smell of her perfume or the allure of those eyes.

'We're trying to find him,' he said more tersely that he should have. 'Do you know where he might be? He's not at home, in his shop or at the marine archaeological offices . . .'

'And he's not at the sub-aqua club otherwise your officers would have found him. I saw them earlier and spoke to Gary. He says you think he killed Nick and Daniel. You're wrong, of course.'

He felt a stab of annoyance at her arrogance, but took great care not to show it.

Leaning forward and gazing steadily at him, she said, 'Gary Manners is the most honest and reliable person I know.'

'Those qualities don't preclude him from committing murder,' he said evenly, but he was irritated by her supreme confidence.

'He isn't your killer.'

'Farnsworth destroyed his career.' He saw the merest flicker of surprise on her face. So lover boy hadn't told her that then, but then he wouldn't have done. It would have shown him up in a bad light. 'Farnsworth left Manners trapped in a wreck. Manners could have died. As a result his navy and diving career were finished.'

She sat back and eyed him closely. After a moment she nodded. 'OK, you win on that one. I didn't know. *But* I still say Gary is not your killer. And I don't know where Nathan is. You surely can't suspect him? He worshipped the ground Nick walked on.'

'Maybe he got jealous.'

'Of me?' she scoffed, wide-eyed.

'Or Corinna Denton.'

But Daisy was shaking her head. 'Nathan didn't operate like that. He wasn't homosexual and neither was Nick, or even bisexual. You can take my word for that.'

Horton wished he didn't have to. He didn't care for the image of her with Farnsworth. And maybe she saw that because he had the feeling she was teasing, or was that tormenting him with it.

'That doesn't mean to say that he wasn't infatuated with Farnsworth.'

She thought for a moment, then nodded. 'I guess he was judging from the few times I saw them together, but I still don't have him profiled as a killer.'

Despite his irritation with her he found himself interested to hear her views. After all, that was what he was here for. 'Why not?' he asked.

'Because from the little I know about Nick's death, and from what you told me about Daniel's – if the two are linked – then they have been committed by someone of above average intelligence, and socially able. Someone who is creative and rational and that isn't Nathan Lester. From what I've seen of Nathan Lester and Nick separately and interacting, Nick made Lester feel more secure, powerful and influential. He wouldn't kill the man who gave him status. *If* he did, and it's a big if, then he would have done so in a moment of madness. It would have been completely unplanned, messy and he'd have left a trail to his front door. In fact I think he would have confessed to it and wanted to be punished. I see even less reason for Lester to want to kill Daniel Collins.'

Horton agreed up to a point. To his mind, though, they didn't know nearly enough about Lester's background – or Farnsworth's come to that. And if Lester had killed Farnsworth and Collins on someone's instructions and had then wanted to confess he would have been too much of a risk to let live.

He said, 'Are you saying that Nick Farnsworth used Nathan Lester the same way he used and manipulated women to get what he wanted?' Ah, she didn't much care for that, he thought, watching her shift and run her hand through her hair. And if that were true then what did Nathan Lester have that Farnsworth wanted? Was hero-worship enough? He guessed for Farnsworth it probably was.

'I think Nick had grown tired of Nathan,' she said, scotching that idea. 'The last couple of times I saw them together, in early December, Nick barely spoke to him and when he did he wasn't very nice. And if you think that's even more reason for Nathan to want Nick dead, then I can see your reasoning, but I just can't see him killing the man he lived for a kind word from.'

Horton wasn't as convinced as she was about that, but it did explain why Lester had been so upset on hearing about Farnsworth's death. But why would he take his hero's place on the television programme, and so rapidly? That smacked of an element of calculation to Horton, especially as he had found Lester in a meeting with Jackson the morning of Farnsworth's death. How many other times had they met to perhaps plan Farnsworth's death? Lester might be very clever at creating a profile of himself designed to fool people. If he was, then it extended to his chaotic house and junk shop. But then, as he'd already considered, Jackson could be the planner and Nathan his executioner.

'Daniel Collins went diving with Nathan Lester over the summer months until September. Did he or Farnsworth ever mention discovering a wreck?'

She shook her head, looking baffled. 'No.'

That didn't mean to say they hadn't. He doubted if Farnsworth would have told her anyway.

'Do you have the details of Farnsworth's previous girlfriends?'

'A couple. Would you like their addresses?' She powered up her computer. 'Nick went out with Rosemary Taylor for three years. The poor woman. But she's happily married now to a garage mechanic and lives in Brighton. The one before me was Stephanie Wilson. Nick was with her for a year. She's living in Spain with her parents. They emigrated there four years ago. I can't see either of them killing Nick.'

Horton tossed up whether to tell her about Nick Farnsworth's missing fingers. Deciding he had nothing to lose by doing so, he asked, 'Do you know why someone would want to cut off three fingers of Mr Farnsworth's left hand?'

She eyed him sharply, then sat back with a thoughtful look on her urchin face. He could see her weighing up this new information, her mind trying to fit it into what she knew about the people surrounding Farnsworth and those who had known him.

'And Daniel Collins?'

'Fingers all accounted for.'

'You think it could be a husband or boyfriend seeking revenge?'

He shrugged. He didn't know what to think any more. As Uckfield had said, they seemed to be going round in circles.

'I suppose it's possible,' she said after a moment, but reluctantly. 'Was Nick battered or disfigured in any other way?'

'No.'

'So why cut off his fingers?' she muttered to herself. 'Was it after death?'

'Yes.'

'So cutting off a dead man's fingers . . .' she mused. Then suddenly she was sitting bolt upright, her skin flushed, eyes shining. 'Of course!'

'What is it?' he asked, his own excitement rising as she tapped into her computer.

'Hang on.'

He did with little patience.

'There.' She swivelled the screen to face him. For a spilt second he was bemused by what he saw, thick fleshy tube-like masses of white and orange clinging to rocks, some kind of coral, and then into his mind flashed the photograph on the wall of Daniel's study.

Daisy said, '*Alcyonium digitatum*, better known as Dead Man's Fingers. And you can find it just off Bembridge on the Isle of Wight. I've dived there many times both with Nick and with Daniel.'

And Farnsworth had wanted to change the location of the dive for the series to that area. He must have found a wreck there, or nearby, or one of the others had – Manners, Collins or Lester – and one of them had told Farnsworth about it. Cantelli had been right. This was about discovering an important wreck.

'Do you have the exact location?' he asked.

Once again she tapped into her computer. 'Give me your e-mail address and I'll send it across to you.'

He obliged. Perhaps now it was time to call out the police divers. And time to talk to Manners again and bring Jackson in.

After thanking Daisy, he returned to the station. Hurrying to CID he was surprised to see it deserted. Where the blazes was everyone? Then he saw that it was just after six thirty. Walters must have gone home and so too must have Cantelli; his jacket wasn't on the hook behind the door.

He made for his office to check that the e-mails Daisy had sent over had come through but paused to stop at Lee's desk. On it were Lester's bank statements. She'd got them into some kind of order with the most recent on top. He quickly flicked through them. There were large gaps but one two years ago showed Lester to have a considerable amount of money. Slowly it had dwindled until the latest statement he was looking at, dated last August, showed Lester to be in the red to the tune of a thousand pounds. So what had he spent it on?

Rummaging further on Lee's desk he found her notes. Lester had paid a six-year lease on the shop a year ago, which had taken a chunk out of his finances. He'd also put a deposit on his house, which he had purchased at the same time. Horton guessed that Lester's shop had been haemorrhaging money.

He sat back deep in thought. Where had Lester got his money from in the first place? Had a relative died and left him a legacy? Or perhaps it was his gratuity from leaving the navy or his savings.

Snatching up the phone, Horton called the major-incident suite and got Trueman.

'Walters and Lee are here helping to man the phones,' Trueman said. 'They haven't stopped ringing since the super-intendent's press call asking for witnesses who might have seen a man on the dual carriageway on Christmas Eve. You wouldn't have thought there would have been that many people out, but I think the whole of Portsmouth must have been wandering up and down that road.'

Horton wondered how DC Lee was liking her stint at manning the phones – not much, he guessed.

'We've not had a chance to get much on Nathan Lester,' Trueman added. 'Except that he's single and lived in Bordon before moving to Portsmouth two years ago. He left the navy in 2004 and started his antiques business here in 2007. There's no record of any employment between those years and Lester wasn't claiming benefit.'

Bordon was a growing town which had sprung up from the army based there. It was twenty-six miles from Portsmouth and thirteen miles from Haslemere, where Farnsworth had lived and worked. Horton wondered if Lester had made contact with Farnsworth when he had been working in Haslemere. Daisy had said that Farnsworth was sick of Nathan following him round like a pet dog, so Horton guessed that it was likely. He also wondered what Lester had done during those three years.

He'd like to find out, but as he crossed his office and viewed the pile of paper on his desk, he knew that he had run out of time to work on this case. He hated leaving unfinished business, a decided drawback in his job – half the cases they handled were unfinished. He'd have to leave the Collins and Farnsworth murders to others. And what about the deaths of the Eburys? What would DC Lee do about that in his absence? he wondered as he clicked open his e-mails, thinking that perhaps he could come in over the weekend. But Uckfield had made it clear last night that he couldn't expect to have regular and prolonged access to Emma if he was working all the hours God sent. If he wanted Emma, then he had to change his working habits, simple as that. And if he wanted that place on the major crime team, with the chance of promotion, he'd have to give up the idea of regular access to Emma. There was no contest.

His phone rang. He was surprised to hear Charlotte's voice.

'Is Barney there, Andy?'

'No. I thought he'd gone home.'

'He was here earlier. He left two hours ago. He promised he'd get back in time for Molly's dance concert, and he's not answering his mobile.'

Something evil crept into the office. Horton felt his stomach go into spasm. It was as if the air quivered with danger and that feeling of a thunderstorm approaching was back with a vengeance.

'Is anything wrong?'

He'd not spoken and yet Charlotte had sensed something in his silence.

'He's probably out on an interview,' he said, hoping the enforced lightness of his tone deceived her. He was eager to get her off the phone and start his enquiries about Cantelli, but she forestalled him.

'Barney seemed very excited about something. He was in the attic looking out his old notebooks; you know, the unofficial ones a lot of police officers keep.'

Horton's pulse began to race. Rapidly his mind made the connections. Cantelli had found some anomaly in the Peter Ebury case notes and had rushed home to check his notes. But why hadn't he returned here? Cantelli must have wanted to check something out.

After trying to reassure Charlotte, which he thought he failed miserably at doing, he rang off and hurried to Cantelli's desk. There was no message on it, but the Peter Ebury file had gone. He called Cantelli's mobile, but just as Charlotte had said all he got was the answer phone. He left a message and then rang through to the front desk.

'Did Sergeant Cantelli say where he was going when he logged out?'

'Home. I asked if he had started working part-time.'

Horton rose and began to pace his office, his mind whirling. After a couple of minutes the space seemed too small to contain him and his anxieties. He'd worked with Cantelli on and off for most of his police career. He was more than a colleague – more than a friend; he was the older brother that Horton had never had. And Horton could *feel* something was wrong. It simply wasn't like Cantelli not to check in or at least tell him what he was following up.

He swept up his jacket and helmet and swiftly marched down the corridor towards the exit. Any faster and he'd have to break into a run. But valiantly he fought to control his fear and urged himself to think calmly and rationally. Panicking wouldn't find Cantelli and besides, he tried to reassure himself, the sergeant could still stroll into the station chewing his gum with that grin on his face. *Then why didn't he believe that.*

At the rear entrance he took a surreptitious deep breath and stopped long enough to call the desk and tell them to phone him on his mobile the moment Cantelli showed up. Then he rang Trueman again.

'If Cantelli phones in or turns up get him to call me.'

Horton should have known that a good officer like Trueman would instantly pick up the concern his voice. 'Anything wrong?'

'I don't know.' He relayed what Charlotte had told him.

'Want me to put a call out for him?'

'No, leave it for now. I'll find him.'

'Andy . . . call in and let me know what's happening.'

Horton heard his warning and unease. 'OK. Don't say anything to Uckfield yet. Is DC Lee still there?'

'Yes. But hold on . . .'

There was short pause. Then Trueman came back on the line. 'She's just gone in with the super. What's going on, Andy?'

'What do you mean?'

'Well, clearly she's not who she says she is.'

Horton took a breath. 'She's Intelligence Directorate.'

Trueman sniffed. 'I guessed she was one of the funny buggers.'

'How?' Horton asked sharply.

'Because she asked too many intelligent questions. And she's very curious about you.'

'What did you tell her?'

'What do you think?'

'Thanks.' Horton signed off. Now all he had to do was find Cantelli.

TWENTY

Horton made for the sea. It was the only place where he could really think straight. At Old Portsmouth he climbed the ancient walls until he was staring over the battlements across the narrow harbour entrance. There was a stiff moist breeze. He hoped it might help to clear his addled brain. Below him, in the dark, the sea looked like black treacle slurping on to the pebbled beach. With the lights of Gosport to his right, he put himself in Cantelli's shoes. Where the hell had he gone? What was he up to?

His mobile rang. At last. It must be Cantelli. But it wasn't.

'Peter Ebury's blood test,' Dr Clayton announced. 'I found traces of heroin and I can tell you quite categorically that there were no signs in the autopsy of him taking or injecting heroin or any other substance, which means he must have taken it orally.'

Or someone pushed it in his mouth, Horton thought, with a shudder and a rush of adrenalin as he recalled the fight Ebury had had with the prisoner, Ludlow.

'It wouldn't have been a large quantity,' Gaye continued, 'but if it was raw it would have affected the respiratory system enough to kill him, which only a blood analysis will reveal.'

And Horton guessed that the Intelligence Directorate and the prison authorities had been hoping to keep that quiet. No wonder Geoff Welton, the governor, had looked so ill. He must have known that Peter Ebury's death was not a natural one, and heroin smuggling inside a prison was the end of the line as far as his career went.

'Has Cantelli contacted you?'

'No.' She sounded surprised.

'You've not told him or anyone else this?' he asked keenly.

'No. Why? What's wrong? Is Cantelli OK?'

He heard the concern in her voice. 'I hope so,' he said anxiously, but he didn't know.

He rang off promising to keep her posted and then called Trueman.

'Phone the prison and ask if Cantelli's been there, or is still there. Call me back.'

Trueman obeyed without a murmur, as Horton knew he would. While he waited, the anxious knot in his gut tightened. He made his way back to the Harley, his mind jumping about like a cart-load of mischievous monkeys. Peter Ebury had been murdered inside prison. So had Irene also been killed? He wouldn't mind betting so, though proving it would be nigh on impossible. The question was why kill them? And had Cantelli found the key to that secret? Had Irene said something at the time of her son's arrest or at the trial that had alerted Cantelli? But Cantelli hadn't recalled her even though he had a memory like an elephant. Or had Peter Ebury said something about his mother back then that, when Cantelli checked his notebooks, still puzzled him?

His phone rang as he reached the Harley and he snatched it up before it could ring twice.

'Cantelli was at the prison,' Trueman said. 'He spoke to Anston, the deputy governor, and Ludlow, the prisoner who attacked Peter Ebury and left just over an hour ago.'

'Did he say where he was going?'

'No.'

Horton cursed. 'Did Anston say what Cantelli wanted?'

'Only that Cantelli knew that the fight had something to do with Ebury's mother. But whatever it was, Ludlow was too scared to confirm or deny it.'

Horton had been half right. And that meant there was only one other place Cantelli could be – the Rest Haven Nursing Home.

He headed along the seafront with Steven Kingsway's words, spoken earlier that morning, ringing in his ears: *they all live in the past*. And it was Irene's past that was the key to unlocking her and her son's deaths. Where had she been and what had she been doing from 1963 to 1973 when she had returned to Portsmouth pregnant with Peter? Could Peter Ebury have been fathered by someone wanted by the police? Had Irene been paid off when she became pregnant or had she been running scared when she returned to Portsmouth in 1973? If so she'd had ample time to betray someone powerful, so if his theory was correct, Peter's father hadn't known about his son's existence until quite recently. Irene had kept that secret safe for many years until someone in the Rest Haven had heard her talking about it and this time had believed her. Could that someone have been Daniel Collins? If so, that meant their wreck theory was shot to pieces, or at least as far as Daniel Collins's death was concerned. And that meant that Farnsworth could have been killed by Gary Manners for revenge or Perry Jackson because he was sick of his co-presenter.

He pulled up outside the Rest Haven and scanned the street. If Cantelli was here then where was his car? Perhaps he'd only just missed him, he thought hopefully, pressing the bell. Cantelli could already be heading for home.

He was shown into the manager's room, where he was surprised to see Marion Keynes. Her face registered shock before she frowned with displeasure and irritation.

'Feeling better?' he said with heavy sarcasm.

'What do you want?'

Information, he thought, but asked, 'Has Sergeant Cantelli been here?'

'No.'

She looked as though she was telling the truth, and she had no reason to lie. His concern deepened. Perhaps Cantelli had forgotten to switch on his mobile phone. He'd try him again at home after he'd got what he wanted here. Trying hard to subdue his worries about Cantelli and not quite succeeding, he said, 'Irene Ebury – what did she talk about?'

Keynes looked surprised and irritated. 'I told you it was just ramblings.'

'Find someone who knows,' he said sharply. 'And preferably someone who has worked here since Irene was admitted.'

'You can't be serious.' She obviously saw that he was because she huffed for a while, then finally heaved herself up. Squeezing past him, she snarled, 'I'll fetch Cheryl.'

While he waited, Horton took the opportunity to have a quick poke around the office. There was little of any importance on the desk. He tried the filing cabinet. It should have been locked, but it wasn't. He slid open the drawer and flicked through the folders until he came to 'E'. Irene's file had gone. Horton wasn't really surprised. Either Angela Northwood, the daytime manager, had already archived it, or Lee or one of her colleagues, had got hold of it.

He straightened up at the sound of footsteps, and not having time to return to his seat, he took the one Marion Keynes had vacated. Cheryl breezed in.

'You wanted to see me,' she said, smiling at him.

He liked her immediately. There was warmth in her sparkling brown eyes and a love of life in the laughter lines on her middle-aged face. He waved her into the seat opposite.

'Tell me everything you can about Irene Ebury.'

She smiled sadly for a moment and looked reflective. Horton could see it was no act. He waited for her to ask why he wanted to know, but she didn't.

'I remember when she first came. Poor Irene. She didn't want to be here. She was aggressive and abusive and very adamant that there was nothing wrong with her. She was afraid. I could see that immediately. And who wouldn't be? She was ill and alone.'

Cheryl's words pulled him up with a guilty jolt. He cursed himself for not having spoken to her before. But he had seen Irene as a puzzle to be solved, a key to his mother's disappearance, an old woman with dementia. He hadn't seen the person, the woman, the real Irene Ebury and that was his downfall. In those few sentences uttered by Cheryl, and by her sympathetic expression, Irene had suddenly become a living, breathing person. He knew it was why he'd had so much trouble with this case. Like many before him, he had dismissed the residents as not 'real' people, God help him. He thought of Mrs Kingsway and her claims of an intruder. Something had sparked that idea in her mind. It must have been based on the truth, but was that in the past or more recent?

'I wouldn't have said that Irene was in an advanced state of vascular dementia then,' Cheryl continued. 'And she could have lived with someone, or even on her own with care, for a while, but she would have deteriorated within a year or so and she certainly did, especially when her son was refused his appeal. She had very lucid moments, when she would tell me that Peter was innocent. Oh, she admitted he'd committed crimes in the past, but she didn't believe he could have killed that security guard. She was convinced he would be released. When he wasn't, she went downhill quite quickly. It was as if what little light there was inside her, which her dementia hadn't already extinguished, finally went out. Then she had a couple of small strokes.'

Horton assimilated what she was saying. On what grounds had Peter Ebury appealed? He'd been caught red-handed.

He said, 'I read somewhere that dementia patients often regress to a part of their past life. Not only in speech but also often in behaviour. How did Irene behave?'

Cheryl smiled. 'She was back at the catwalk, pretending to be a model.'

'She was Miss Southsea in 1957.'

'So she said. I think she must also have worked in a night-club or casino, because she always wanted to serve the drinks and she loved her cards. She would get quite agitated if we wouldn't give her a pack, she kept shuffling them.'

'Did she ever mention anyone from her past?'

'Just the famous people she'd met.'

Which could have been true, Horton thought, if she had worked in a club in London. 'Anyone in particular?'

'Frank Sinatra.'

Horton smiled with Cheryl. Marion Keynes had also mentioned him. He'd rule that out. 'Do you think you could write down the names for me, as and when you remember them? Any names that you can recall, whether famous or not.'

'DC Lee has already asked me to do that.'

He hid his surprise and cursed silently. 'When?'

'Yesterday.'

So she must have returned here last night because Cheryl wouldn't have been on duty until after six thirty.

He said, 'I'd like you to give the list to me.' But you're on holiday, said his small voice. He ignored it.

'Did anyone visit Irene over the years?'

'No.'

'Did you see her belongings?'

Cheryl looked confused at the question. Horton elaborated. 'Letters, photographs?'

'Oh. Yes. She had a couple of photographs of her son when he was a little boy. He was very good-looking. Fair, with bright blue eyes.'

'Any others?'

Cheryl thought hard. 'It's years since I've seen them, but, yes, there were others. Irene was in a swimsuit on holiday abroad.'

'How do you know it was abroad?'

'Well, it didn't look like Bognor.' She smiled. 'The sea was too blue. Irene must have been in her early thirties. She was beside a swimming pool at a villa and there were a number of people in the picture, but I can't remember what they looked like. Apart from that I don't remember seeing any other photos and there were no letters.'

The door opened and Marion Keynes glowered at him. 'I need Cheryl to help get our residents to bed. Mrs Kingsway's being difficult again.'

'Does she still think she saw an intruder in her bedroom?' Horton addressed Cheryl.

'I'm afraid so. It's why she doesn't want to go to bed. She's frightened that he'll come back and kill her.'

'There was no intruder,' Marion Keynes declared hotly.

Horton said, 'Then why say it?' He turned to Cheryl. 'She couldn't have seen Dr Eastwood because I believe you took Mrs Kingsway from the room before he arrived.'

'Yes. And she was sound asleep when Marion called me into the room.'

He rose, feeling frustrated. He was on the Intelligence Directorate's track, but how far behind them he didn't know. And he'd got no nearer to finding Cantelli.

'I'll show you out,' Cheryl said.

In the corridor Horton could hear an old lady protesting very loudly and forcefully and another person trying to reassure her without success.

'Mrs Kingsway,' Cheryl explained, with an anxious glance at Horton before hurrying to the aid of her colleague, leaving Horton to follow her into the residents' lounge.

Mrs Kingsway was a small and very frail elderly lady and clearly distressed. She was waving her arms about and shouting. Horton couldn't make out what she was saying. She wouldn't let Cheryl or the slight, fair-haired girl in her late twenties touch her. The television was blaring out, ironically he noticed, with a repeat of the *Diving in Devon* series and there was Nicholas Farnsworth's handsome face glistening with seawater, whilst behind him was the squat, sturdy and studious Jackson.

'It's her favourite programme,' Cheryl tossed over her shoulder at Horton. 'She can't bear it if it's not on the television. We've got a recording of it which we play, but we can't have it on twenty-four hours a day. Now, Marjorie, you're quite safe. No one's going to hurt you.'

Cheryl gently took her arm, but Marjorie Kingsway pulled away from her and at the same time managed to slip out of the sleeve of her cardigan.

Horton stared at an ugly purple stain on the top of Mrs Kingsway's frail arm. If he wasn't mistaken, then it was a bruise.

Following his gaze, Cheryl said, 'Elderly people's skin is very fragile. Mrs Kingsway's had quite a few falls lately.'

But a fall doesn't look like that, thought Horton, staring at what had clearly been inflicted by a hand. He could see where a thumb had pressed into the vulnerable paper-thin skin. He wouldn't mind betting she had a matching one on the other arm. It looked as though someone had grabbed her forcibly. Was it the intruder she had told her son about or Marion Keynes perhaps? Maybe Angela Northwood? But it could be any member of staff, though he felt sure it hadn't been Cheryl.

Mrs Kingsway glanced at Horton, then sat down heavily on one of the upright chairs placed around the wall and stared at the television screen.

He asked the other care assistant to leave them for a moment, which she did with a curious backward glance. Turning to Cheryl, Horton said, 'I want you to call a doctor to examine her, but not Dr Eastwood.'

'You can't think any of us have harmed her?' Cheryl cried, horrified.

'Someone has.'

Cheryl looked worried. 'She's got a bruise on the other arm in the same place.'

As he'd guessed. 'Why didn't you report it?'

'I did, to the agency nurse, when I came on duty Monday night. I assumed she'd left a note or told Angela in the morning.'

'The bruises weren't there Sunday night?'

'No.'

And Marion Keynes was off sick then, so she couldn't be

responsible for them. It could be this agency nurse, he supposed, or had the bruises been inflicted during Monday? He recalled Angela Northwood's harassed expression, but somehow he couldn't see her forcibly grabbing the old lady.

His phone rang. Hoping and praying it was Cantelli, he stepped into the hall to answer it. Again he was disappointed. It was Chalky White.

'Don't know if this is important, Mr Horton, but you said you wanted to know if Ian Keynes or his misses were passing off stuff.'

'What have you got?' Horton snapped impatiently.

'Ian Keynes was talking to some bloke in the gents' toilet of the Black Swan about an hour ago. I was in one of the traps and heard them. I peered over the top of the door, nearly broke my bleeding neck getting down off the pan.'

'For heaven's sake get on with it.'

'Keynes gave this bloke a piece of paper and said, "Here's what you want. Take that to any chemist and you'll get your tablets." This bloke gave him a wodge of money, couldn't see how much, but it looked like a bloody expensive prescription to me. Cheaper to get it on the NHS I would have thought.'

'Not the tablets he wanted I expect,' Horton said, ringing off after telling Chalky White he'd done his bit.

Certain pieces of the puzzle were finally dropping into place: Dr Eastwood's hostility when he and Cantelli had interviewed him in his consulting room; that photograph on Marion Keynes' mantelpiece of Ian Keynes in diving gear; Eastwood's eagerness to respond to an out of hours call taken on his mobile phone so early in the morning – and it wasn't out of duty to his patients.

Returning to Cheryl, he found Mrs Kingsway flinging her arms about.

'She thinks she's swimming,' Cheryl explained. 'She says she used to have a lovely big house in the country, in Surrey, with a swimming pool, but I don't think it's true, after all she wouldn't have been moved here by social services if she had had that much money. And her son's never mentioned it or so the daytime staff have told me. He's worked abroad for years. We didn't even know he existed until early December when he showed up here. I guess they didn't get on. Now he visits her regularly. Shame it's too late for her to recognize him. She does give him a hard time. She thinks more of that diver on the television than she does her poor son.'

Cheryl gazed sadly at the programme where Farnsworth's handsome smiling face filled the screen.

Several thoughts flashed through Horton's mind, but one shone brighter than the others. God, what an idiot he'd been! The outraged son, the alleged intruder story, the bruises on the old lady's arms . . . No one had spoken to Mrs Kingsway to get her version of the intruder story and even if they had done, she could have claimed that her son was the intruder because in her mind he was a stranger.

What kind of man could hurt his mother like that? Horton wondered. An evil bastard, came the answer, and one angry and frustrated because of his mother's continual rejection. Those bruises clearly weren't the first if Cheryl was to be believed, and he had no reason to doubt her. He hurried down the corridor to Marion Keynes' office.

'I thought you'd gone.' She looked up, annoyed.

'I want to see Mrs Kingsway's personal file, now,' he snapped.

'It's confidential.'

He leant over the desk, thrusting his face close to hers, and in a low voice said, 'A doctor will be here soon to examine the bruises on Mrs Kingsway's arms and unless you give me her file, I will arrest you for assault.'

'That's a lie. You can't do that!'

He held her gaze. Her indignation was genuine. There was, however, the matter of the prescriptions and Dr Eastwood.

'Then let's try something that's closer to the truth,' he said, easing back and sitting down opposite her. 'Whose idea was it to kill Daniel Collins, yours or your husband's?'

'You're mad!'

She didn't look frightened and neither did she look smug, simply amazed.

Undeterred he continued. 'Daniel discovered that you and Dr Eastwood are working a prescription scam. Eastwood writes false prescriptions using the names of the residents, which you or your husband then sell. Did you get Eastwood to willingly participate or have you got something on him?'

Marion Keynes glared at him, but he detected a slight shift in her body language that told him he was right.

'Perhaps he just wanted to supplement his income. After all

doctors aren't that well paid,' he continued with heavy sarcasm. 'Or had Dr Eastwood made a mistake somewhere along the line, or eased a difficult or troublesome patient to his or her death and you discovered it. In return for your silence and understanding you forced him to co-operate?'

Alarm and fear crossed her flabby face. At last he'd got to the truth. So that was how it had started. Christ, what a pair! If Cantelli had been here he'd have exploded. But Cantelli wasn't here.

Clearly Marion Keynes wasn't going to confess yet.

'I believe the prescriptions are for a range of powerful anti-depressants and painkillers. There's a growing market for them, particularly amongst the young,' said Horton. 'They are addicts, just like those addicted to heroin and crack cocaine, and supplying them is a serious crime. Did you want to say something?'

She'd opened her mouth to speak, perhaps to protest or explain, but she snapped it shut again and continue to glare at him through eyes like slits in a battlement.

'If they can't get the quantities they need from their GP, or the Internet, they buy prescriptions on the black market. Daniel discovered your secret and threatened to tell in return for money. You or rather your husband killed him.' He rose. 'Marion Keynes, I am arresting you for the murder of—'

'No, wait.'

Horton eyed her closely, but he didn't resume his seat.

'All right. I admit to the prescription fraud and selling the drugs, but I haven't the faintest idea what you're talking about with Daniel. He died in a car accident. We haven't killed anyone,' she insisted. 'That's the truth.'

He wasn't sure if Marion Keynes would know the truth if it jumped out and bit her.

'Then give me Mrs Kingsway's file.'

She rose and wrenched open the filing cabinet. After a moment she handed it across to him and he slipped it inside his jacket.

'About the prescriptions . . .'

At the door he turned and said, 'I think you'd better find yourself a very good lawyer.'

The fear on her face was a reward in itself. Outside he rang Trueman and told him to get a unit over to the Rest Haven and to Marion Keynes' home immediately. Then, wondering if Marion

might already be warning her husband, he asked Trueman to put
out a call for Ian Keynes' arrest. He briefly told him what had
happened and asked him to alert the Prescription Fraud Team
and arrest Dr Eastwood. If they trod on the Intelligence
Directorate's toes then tough.

'Any sign of Nathan Lester?'

'No.'

'What about Barney?' Horton felt his heart knock against his
ribs.

'He's not phoned in and I've been trying his mobile every ten
minutes.'

Horton swore and asked to speak to Lee.

'Where's Sergeant Cantelli?' he rapped when she came on the
line.

'I don't know—'

'Cut the crap, Lee. This is no time to play silly buggers. He
went to the prison to find out something about Peter Ebury and
he got it. So where have you got him?'

Silence. He could almost hear her mind racing. What was she
going to do: tell him he was barking mad or admit it?

'I'll call you back.'

Under the glow of the street lamp, Horton quickly skimmed
the contents of Marjorie Kingsway's file. It hardly seemed worth
taking as there was so little information in it. Mrs Kingsway had
been moved into the Rest Haven by social services a year ago
from another nursing home on the seafront, which Horton knew
to be rather an expensive one, and much more exclusive that the
Rest Haven. He guessed her money had run out. Nursing care
for the elderly and sick wasn't free in England. Where had
Marjorie lived before the expensive nursing home on the seafront?
Trueman would find out, of course. So what now? Hang around
and wait for Trueman to come back?

Where could Cantelli be? Horton shivered and it wasn't from
the cold. He couldn't shake off his feeling of dread and the
thought that something might have happened to him.

The door of the Rest Haven opened and Marion Keynes scut-
tled out. Too late to make her escape, he thought with grim
satisfaction, as the patrol car sped round the corner. He watched
the panic cross her face. Then her body slumped. She glared
at him as he instructed PC Seaton to take her away. He ought
to go back inside and explain to Cheryl what had happened,

but he detailed PC Allen to do that. Trueman would handle the rest.

But he couldn't just hang around. He had to do something. It was time to confront Kingsway. He'd be at work. Action would help him to stop worrying about Cantelli. But as Horton climbed on the Harley and headed for Fort Cumberland, he knew that nothing on earth would prevent him from doing that.

TWENTY-ONE

The daytime security officer let him through the entry gates.

He was too early to speak to Steven Kingsway, he was informed. He wouldn't be on duty for another twenty minutes. Horton felt irritated by the delay. Perhaps it would be better to leave this to Uniform. They could bring Kingsway in and someone else could question him about his assault on his mother. But Horton didn't want to hand this over.

'Has Mr Kingsway worked here long?' he asked.

'Three weeks and that's three too long if you ask me. Good job he's on nights and I don't have to work with him. Thinks he's God's gift to the world that one.'

Horton was surprised to learn Kingsway had only been working there a short time, though he shouldn't have been after what Cheryl had told him.

'Where did he work before?'

'Oil rigs. Earning a fortune, so he says, risking his life to give us all our central heating and petrol for our cars. To hear him talk, you'd have thought he was the only bugger in the world bringing oil out. Says he was a skilled man, an engineer. If he was, then what's he doing guarding a load of old artefacts in an ancient monument?'

The job went some way to explaining Kingsway's absence, but even oil-rig workers got time off, Horton thought. Why had Kingsway suddenly developed a conscience about his mother? Perhaps he'd had no choice but to return home. He could have been made redundant or been sacked.

'Do you want to wait for him?' asked the guard. 'He shouldn't be long.'

Horton hesitated for a fraction before declining. He was too impatient and anxious to hang around here, twiddling his thumbs and listening to the security man talking. He could use the time more productively, he thought, by having a quick poke around the marine archaeological offices. There might be something there that could tell him where Nathan Lester had gone and why Farnsworth had been killed. Daniel Collins, too, if Marion Keynes were to be believed. He wondered if Cantelli had been right all along with his wreck theory.

Collecting the key, Horton left the Harley outside the main office and jogged to the marine archaeological offices. The salty wind tore and bit into him whilst the thin slanting rain seemed to cut right through his leathers. With relief he unlocked the door and stepped inside the musty smelling room. The security light outside illuminated it enough for him to see that it was exactly as it had been earlier that day when he'd last been here with Cantelli. Instinctively he reached for his mobile to check it was on, though he knew it was. He wondered if he could have missed a call or message, but no, the screen was blank.

Increasingly troubled by Cantelli's continuing silence, he poked around the desks with no idea of what he was hoping to find. There certainly wasn't any mention of a wreck found near Dead Man's Fingers off the Isle of Wight. For a moment he stared at the three computer screens wondering if it was worth switching one on, but then decided it would serve no purpose and headed swiftly for the inner office where he'd previously interviewed Jackson. Again there was no change and certainly no sign of Nathan Lester. Had he really expected to see him here? He didn't know. Maybe he had hoped, but the shabby room was empty except for books and documents spilling out of every orifice and littered on every surface. He felt disheartened and eaten up with anxiety. Why didn't Lee ring him? Surely she'd had time to clear things with her boss. Cantelli must be with them. If he wasn't . . .

His phone rang. It was Lee.

'My boss is on his way to the station. But I can tell you that none of us have seen Sergeant Cantelli since he left the prison this afternoon.'

Horton stiffened with fury. 'You had him followed.'

'No. Mr Anston, the deputy governor, called us to say that Sergeant Cantelli had been making inquiries about Peter Ebury. Before we could pick up Cantelli's trail, he'd vanished. We don't know where he is.'

Horton's blood turned to ice. 'Then you'd better find him,' he said harshly. 'Ask your contacts. And interview that bloody prisoner.'

He was about to ring off when she said: 'We would if we could.'

Horton tensed. His heart jumped several beats.

'He was found with a plastic bag over his head ten minutes ago.'

Horton cursed loudly and vehemently, whilst his heart sank to the depths of his being. He felt sick inside.

'Where are you, Inspector?' Her voice came from somewhere distant.

'Find Cantelli,' he shouted and punched the line dead. He felt like hurling the bloody thing across the room and with it everyone in the Intelligence Directorate. They'd screwed up. They had to find Cantelli because if they didn't or if . . . he didn't even want to think about it. It made him ill. Where could Cantelli be? Who had got hold of him?

He cursed again. He would collect the Harley and head back. He'd call Uniform to bring Kingsway in. His heart wasn't in this investigation any more. His mind was in turmoil. He couldn't think of anything but Cantelli. What had he discovered from that prisoner? Who else had been watching the prison? He knew he couldn't stay here a moment longer. Even if he had to question every prisoner and screw in Kingston nick, or walk the streets to find just one person who had seen Barney, then he'd do it and for as long as it took.

Swiftly he crossed to the door, but froze at the sound of a car pulling up outside. A door slammed. He waited for the door to open, but it didn't happen. Puzzled, he gazed out of the small window to his right. The rain had stopped for a brief moment, and behind scudding clouds, the moon made a brief appearance. In the glare of the security light he saw a silver saloon. He recognized it as Kingsway's. The man was nowhere in sight though. Was he here to do his security rounds? Horton dashed a glance at his watch. No, he'd only been inside ten minutes. Kingsway was due on duty in about five minutes' time. He must have stopped off here before checking into the main building. Yes, there he was, emerging from somewhere on Horton's far right-hand side, and he was wheeling a platform trolley.

Horton made to leave when something forestalled him. He couldn't say what exactly, but his instincts were telling him to stay put. He watched as Kingsway opened the boot of his car. After a couple of seconds he emerged with a grunt before man-handling something very heavy, judging by the growling and groaning he was doing, on to the trolley. It looked like a roll of carpet. Horton's first thoughts were that Kingsway was illegally dumping household rubbish before his copper's brain jolted into gear. No carpet was that heavy surely. His flesh crawled, as his eyes narrowed into the night to focus on the shape. He stiffened. If he wasn't mistaken it was a body. He couldn't see whose, but his first thoughts were of Nathan Lester. Why would Kingsway want to kill Lester though? The only reason he could think of was that it had to be something to do with Farnsworth. And now, at last, he quickly put the facts together. Kingsway wasn't only guilty of striking his mother, but of killing the person she was fixated on: Farnsworth.

He peered into the night as Kingsway manoeuvred the trolley. In so doing he pushed it past the window. There, at the end of the rug, was an opening and in the glimpse of moonlight Horton saw . . . He froze. His heart stopped. Jesus! No! It couldn't be. There was a mass of black curly hair. It wasn't Nathan Lester. It was Barney. Kingsway had killed Barney Cantelli.

Without thinking, Horton wrenched open the door and in a blind rage rushed across to Kingsway. He'd kill the bastard for this. Kingsway turned. Saw him. And before Horton knew it, Kingsway swivelled round, kicked out and struck Horton in the midriff. Horton doubled over as the breath was sucked from his body and pain shot through him. The ground came up to greet his bleary-eyed vision. Before he could even think of moving or breathing, something cut through the back of his neck, the shock seemed to slice his body like a meat cleaver. There was an acute flash of pain. And then absolutely nothing.

TWENTY-TWO

He was no longer in the car park. He knew that immediately by the darkness pressing on his eyeballs, the stench, and the filthy water in his face. His neck was as sore as hell and his hands and feet were tied, but he was alive. He didn't know about Cantelli. Fear gripped him as he recalled the body being hauled out of Kingsway's car. His heart was so heavy with sorrow that he could hardly breathe. Charlotte. Barney's five kids. He shivered uncontrollably. If he had a choice he'd rather be dead if it meant Cantelli could live.

It was an effort to move, the pain of his loss was almost too much to bear, but he forced himself into an upright position. Was there still hope that Barney might be alive? He had to cling on to that.

He tried to focus his eyes. It was pitch black. He could see nothing. His senses told him though that he was underground. And his reasoning, which was slowly surfacing through his throbbing head and the pain of his sorrow, said that he must be in one of the tunnels under the Fort Cumberland earth mounds. He dug his nails into his palms and felt the sweat trickle down his back. The tunnel was pressing down on him. His stomach heaved. His heart raced. He could hear his breathing coming in gasps. Air. He had to get air. But there wasn't any. He struggled to rise, but his bonds were too tight and limiting. Desperately he tried to fight off the rising attack of claustrophobia.

Calm, keep calm. Think rationally. Think of Cantelli, he might still be alive and if he is, then he needs your help to get out of here. What use are you to him as a quivering heap? Charlotte is relying on you. Barney could be in here somewhere within reach.

He emptied his lungs slowly. It did the trick. He wasn't sure how long it took, but gradually his heart rate settled down, though not to normal. This wasn't bloody normal. There was a noise to the right of him. Sharply he brought his head round, then wished he hadn't when a shaft of pain shot through him almost making him lose consciousness. A shape loomed out of the darkness.

'Let's see you, Kingsway,' he shouted, though his throat was dry and his voice hoarse.

A powerful torch swung full beam on Horton. He blinked and tried to snatch his head away from the glare, but it wouldn't go.

'You shouldn't have attacked me,' came the voice from the darkness. 'I'm sorry you've been involved.'

'What do you want? Forgiveness?' Horton snarled, but he recognized the whining tone of self-justification that was so familiar to him when hearing a confession to a crime.

The beam swung away and Horton watched Kingsway settle himself opposite, on the trolley that had brought him and Cantelli here. He quickly scanned the area and picked out the slumped body of Cantelli about nine feet from him. His heart plummeted to the depths of his being.

'Is he dead?' he asked in a flat resigned voice.

'He might be now.'

Horton clenched his fists and tried to leap up, but once again he was defeated by his bonds. He fell back deflated, but anger stirred within him, fuelling his determination to get out of here alive and feed Kingsway to the seagulls. He told himself there was still a chance that Cantelli was alive. Kingsway had said 'now' which meant he hadn't killed Cantelli outright. Horton clung to that hope. It was all he had. And it meant he had to find a way to overpower Kingsway or persuade him to give himself up.

'Why make things worse for yourself, Kingsway? Let us both go and I'll see that you get a fair trial. With a good solicitor you might not get long.'

But Kingsway didn't hear him. Almost regretfully he said, 'If she hadn't let that grinning idiot of a diver fool her, then none of this would have happened.'

Horton quickly saw the way Kingsway's mind was working. Here was a man seeking to apportion blame for his own crimes and shortcomings. Something Horton guessed Kingsway had done for most of his life. Nothing would ever be his fault. Perhaps if he appeared to understand and empathize with him, he could eventually talk his way out of this. But what had Farnsworth done to an old lady like Marjorie Kingsway? Sex wasn't the motive for his actions and neither was it love or success, but it could have been power and the type of power that came from exerting influence over a vulnerable person to give Farnsworth the money and possessions he craved.

Now, putting everything he had seen and learnt over the last few days together, Horton saw clearly what must have happened and he was beginning to understand where Nathan Lester fitted into this. He recalled Cheryl's words: *she used to have a lovely big house in the country, in Surrey, with a swimming pool . . .* And Haslemere, where Farnsworth had worked as an estate agent, was in Surrey.

'Did Farnsworth undervalue your mother's house?' he asked, making an effort to keep his tone mater-of-fact.

'Yes. He got Lester to pose as the buyer and then they sold it on for a big profit, which they split between them.'

That explained the thirty thousand pounds in Lester's bank account. Marjorie Kingsway probably wasn't their first victim or their last. How many others had they swindled? wondered Horton.

Kingsway said, 'And before that Farnsworth got Lester into my mother's house to value the antiques. He said they were worthless and then sold them for their proper value.'

That fitted too. Although Horton hadn't seen the items in Lester's shop close up, he'd seen enough in the man's house to know that some of it was valuable. He said, 'How do you know this?'

'Lester told me before he died.'

Horton took a breath. He was facing a man who had killed twice – Farnsworth and Lester – three times if Cantelli was dead. Horton took a deep breath and tried to still his pounding heart. It would be four if he couldn't find a way out of this.

Kingsway was clearly unbalanced and probably psychotic. Horton reckoned the only way to deal with him was to feign sympathy and understanding. Hostility would only make Kingsway clam up, or worse strike him unconscious and then leave him here to die. The thought didn't bear thinking about, so he shoved it aside and said, 'Where's Lester?'

'In here somewhere, along with his bicycle.'

Horton suppressed a shudder. He recalled the small, squirrel-faced man. He had been a criminal, yes, but Horton knew that it was because of Farnsworth's manipulative charm that Lester had committed the crimes against Marjorie Kingsway.

Kingsway continued. 'I phoned him on Thursday night and told him that I'd discovered an important wreck off the Isle of Wight. I knew he wouldn't be able to resist it just like Farnsworth couldn't. I met Lester here and gave him a swift karate blow to the throat, like I did with Farnsworth, and Lester was dead. I'd learnt how to dive and practised the martial arts when I was in the army.'

Horton guessed that Farnsworth's diving gloves and fins had also ended up in here. It would have been easy for Kingsway to have carried them over from Farnsworth's car which Kingsway had left parked in Southsea Marina opposite.

'But Daniel was different. I was sorry I had to kill him.'

Horton stared at Kingsway and suddenly saw that for once Marion Keynes had been telling the truth when she said that neither she nor her husband had killed Daniel Collins. The distraught features of Mr and Mrs Collins flashed through Horton's mind. Oh, he'd like to bring Kingsway to justice for their sake, though he knew it wouldn't alleviate the pain of their loss.

'He saw you hit your mother,' Horton said, realizing what must have happened.

'I just pushed her and she fell over. It was an accident.'

Horton didn't believe that for one moment. Or that it had been the only attack.

'I was upset because she kept whining on and on about how I wasn't her son,' Kingsway said. 'Daniel was there when it happened and he threatened to report me. I had to find a way to silence him. I knew he was crazy about diving, because he'd told me on one of my visits to the home. An idea suddenly came to me. I decided to play on the fact that my stupid mother thought Nick was her son. I spun Daniel a story that she was right. I told him that Nick was my half-brother and that we'd been estranged for years, but I was in the process of making it up with Nick. I promised I could get Daniel a place on the programme if he kept quiet. The stupid man nearly wet his pants.'

Horton's fists clenched behind him, angry at Kingsway's cruelty, but also at Daniel Collins's stupidity.

'On Christmas Eve I told Daniel I'd arranged a meeting with Farnsworth at the sailing centre,' Kingsway continued. 'I clocked in here, but no one knows whether I'm working or not, so I slipped out and drove there and met Daniel in the car park. I poured drink down his throat, he wasn't very strong, and I knew how to handle him. Then I put him in his car and drove it off Salterns Wharf . . .'

'Where you then slipped on the aqua lung and manoeuvred Daniel into the driving seat.'

Kingsway nodded. 'I couldn't take the chance that he might spoil everything.'

Kingsway rose. The torchlight swept away from Horton plunging him into darkness. He willed himself not to think of being underground. Then Kingsway put the light back on himself. Horton saw him run a tongue over his lips. Perhaps this tunnel was getting to him. Kingsway was a diver, he could tolerate the dark but being in the depths of the sea was very different from being under tons of earth.

'When did you decide to kill Farnsworth?' Horton asked, straining for any sound from Cantelli and hearing none.

'When I found my mother left in that dump to rot.'

But Horton knew Kingsway's anger and desire for revenge wasn't fuelled by his feelings for his mother. He hadn't been near her for years. No, he reckoned that Kingsway's sense of outrage had been driven by the fact that he'd come home broke, expecting to feed off his mother's money, and had discovered that not only had that gone, but so too had his inheritance.

'She never thought I was good enough,' Kingsway said, almost eager for Horton to understand. 'My father died when I was ten. He'd worked in London. He was a financial genius. I don't think she minded him dying. In fact it probably suited her. She was a frigid, hard cow. And she couldn't stand the sight of me. She packed me off to boarding school when I was four and didn't even want me home for the holidays. I spent them pushed between relatives, who didn't much like me either. She didn't care that I loathed that school.'

Oh, yes. Horton could see how Kingsway laid the blame for all his misfortunes on his childhood and predominantly his mother. Time was short. He had to do something. But what? Anything was preferable to being entombed. God, that word! It made him almost sick with fear. He shifted position and forced himself to concentrate on Kingsway.

'When I went into the army as an ordinary rank and diver she refused to have anything to do with me. Now do you blame me for not keeping in touch?'

Horton nodded as if he understood. His mouth was dry, his palms damp, his brain a whirl of thoughts. If only he could move, but he was tied up like a parcel.

'I owed her nothing. But she owed me. It was my money and I deserved it for all I'd suffered. It was a shock seeing her like that, dribbling and old, with her mind gone. She didn't know who I was. That didn't bother me much. I thought, OK, so she's got her punishment, but there should still be some money around. I couldn't work out how she had ended up in a place like that, when she could have afforded private nursing care. Angela Northwood told me that my mother had been moved into the Rest Haven from a more expensive retirement home because her medical condition had deteriorated and her money had run out. That didn't make sense to me. I began to make enquiries. Then I saw her watching that TV diving programme. Daniel Collins was in the room. Mum pointed at Farnsworth, got excited, and pushed me away. She babbled on about Nick being her son, not me.'

So Kingsway had been rejected again. 'Is that when you decided on revenge?' asked Horton.

'She deserved it,' Kingsway said with bitterness.

'And you discovered what Farnsworth had done to her.'

Kingsway leaned forward and said eagerly, 'I was justified in killing him and Lester. You can hardly blame me after what they did.'

What Farnsworth and Lester had done was criminal and they had deserved to be punished for preying on a feeble elderly lady, but Kingsway hadn't killed them out of love for his mother, but out of hatred of her. Even if he had killed out of love, it still wouldn't have justified his actions, but Horton knew that nothing would ever convince Kingsway of that.

Kingsway fell silent as though exhausted by his confession. Horton could hear the wind moaning through the tunnel, the scurrying rats and the dripping water, but then came another sound and one he hadn't noticed before. He struggled to identify it. It sounded like soft chirping noises, but not from any bird he'd ever heard. Had Kingsway heard it? Apparently not, he thought, dashing a glance at him. His expression showed he was deep in the past. His body was slumped almost as though it was drained of energy. He'd made his confession and lived through the emotions of the past few days and perhaps even his childhood. Soon Kingsway would leave. And he and Cantelli would be alone.

Horton tensed. Through the helter-skelter thoughts in his mind, suddenly and forcibly a memory struck him. He'd been in one of these tunnels with Emma. The guide had said something and Emma had shuddered and drawn closer to him. What was it? Horton knew it was important. Then it came to him. He'd talked about a rare bat roosting in the underground tunnels; he'd even mentioned its name – the long-eared grey bat. Could the noise of chittering be these bats? Even if it were, how could it help him and Barney? He glanced across at the inert bundle and with a heavy heart wondered if he was already too late. Then he heard another noise that sounded very much like a groan. His heart lifted. Dare he hope? Was it possible that Barney was still alive? Had he imagined that sound or merely wished it?

Anxiously he dashed a glance at Kingsway, praying he'd heard nothing. There was no sign that he had. If Barney was regaining consciousness, then Horton willed him to do it silently. He had to distract Kingsway's attention and the way to do that was to keep him talking.

'How did you kill Farnsworth, Steven?'

The use of Kingsway's first name and the gentleness of Horton's voice prodded Kingsway out of his reverie.

Pulling himself up, he said, 'I'd already found out that Nathan Lester kept an antiques shop. I followed him a few times and discovered his interest in diving and that he often visited the marine archaeological offices. I called into the main reception and asked if they had any vacancies. They were desperate for a night-time security officer. I'd lost my job on the oil rigs. They made me redundant.'

By the shiftiness in Kingsway's eyes, Horton doubted if that was the truth. More likely he'd been sacked for some misdemeanour. His employment record would be an interesting one to view, if Horton got the chance, and he might just get that if the plan that was taking shape in his mind came off.

'Go on,' he encouraged, shifting a couple of inches closer to Kingsway. He seemed not to notice.

'I was just working out how to get Farnsworth here, when I read that article in the newspaper on Monday afternoon, about the anonymous telephone calls. It said that Farnsworth was staying in the Queen's Hotel.'

So Horton hadn't been that far wrong; Farnsworth's publicity prank had helped to sign his death warrant.

'I drove to the Queen's Hotel on Tuesday and managed to

waylay him,' Kingsway continued. 'He thought I wanted his autograph, but I told him that I'd found a wreck out by Dead Man's Fingers. I promised to tell him exactly where it was if he met me on Tuesday evening in front of the sailing centre. I said we had to be careful because I didn't want anyone else knowing about it. Farnsworth was late, but I waited. When he arrived I knocked him out, but I didn't kill him, not then. I stripped him naked and put him in one of the boats on the shore along with his diving suit, which he kept in the back of his car. I took the boat round to Oldham's Wharf. When Farnsworth came round I forced him, with the threat that I'd cut off his balls, to get into his diving gear. He tried to charm his way out, but he did as I asked. I told him why he had to die. He said he'd pay the money back but I didn't believe him. I struck a karate blow across his throat.'

'And you used the loader shovel truck to tip him into the pit where you laid him out.'

'Yes. I threw his fingers, the knife and his mobile phone into the sea on the way back to the sailing centre.'

'Why Oldham's Wharf, Steven?'

'I'd heard about Farnsworth's altercation with Oldham and thought it might implicate him and throw the scent off me.'

'One thing puzzles me,' Horton said, easing his position and shuffling another few inches closer to Kingsway. 'Was it you who broke into Oldham's and moved that truck on Sunday night or early hours of Monday morning?'

Soon it would be time to strike. Horton prepared himself. His senses were stretched to breaking point. He knew that his timing had to be perfect. Cock this up and it would be the end for him and Barney. There was nothing to tell him when the exact time would be right to strike, only his instinct.

'Yes. I wanted to check I could get into the yard—'

Horton opened his mouth and roared as loud as he could.

Kingsway shot up startled, the torchlight flew around the cavern as Horton bellowed. His lungs were fit to bursting point. He had to be right. He steeled himself for the moment when the torch would come crashing down on his skull, or the karate chop would silence him forever.

Then suddenly they were all around them: bats with huge wings diving and squealing Horton ducked down instinctively, but they weren't interested in him. Startled by the bright light that Kingsway was now waving about madly, they flapped against him causing him to screech and wave his arms around, the light was spinning like something in a disco and startling the bats even further.

The inert bundle to the left of Horton leapt up, grabbed Kingsway round the ankles and brought him crashing to the ground with a great cry of pain. The torch rolled out of Kingsway's grasp. Horton pulled himself up, jumped forward and sat down heavily on the man's arse. Cantelli wrenched Kingsway's arms behind his back, reached into his pocket and snapped the cuffs on. Then he picked up the torch.

'Had a nice nap?' Horton said with evident relief as Cantelli loosened his bonds.

'I was in the middle of this wonderful dream with Ingrid Bergman.'

Kingsway groaned. The bats retreated. Horton handed the rope that had bound him, over to Cantelli. 'Tie his ankles, Barney, otherwise with his bloody kung fu we might get a bellyful.'

'Tell me about it,' Cantelli said feelingly. 'Only it wasn't in the belly. Not sure I'll be able to sing bass for a while.'

Horton gave a grim smile. Christ, it was good to have him back.

'I hope Charlotte doesn't want any more children. We might have to adopt.'

'What happened? Let's get him on this trolley that he's so bloody fond of. And we'll push him out.'

'It was just one of those things,' Cantelli replied, standing up with a groan and a hand on his back as Kingsway lay on the trolley. 'I'd left the prison and was heading up Lake Road, past the diving shop, when I saw Kingsway come out. I thought diver – Daniel Collins, Nicolas Farnsworth . . . I know a lot of people dive, but I was curious so I darted into the shop.'

They began to push the trolley towards the exit. Soon, Horton thought with relief, he'd feel the damp wind on his face.

'Kingsway had been a regular customer since the beginning of December. He told the owner that he'd served in the army as a diver and had dived all over the world. I asked if Nathan Lester was a customer, and he was. I thought there might be a connection, or Kingsway could tell me where Lester was. I had Kingsway's address because I'd got it from his car registration plate. You know what I'm like with car registrations; it's a bit of an obsession of mine.'

Horton knew all too well. This time it had nearly cost Cantelli his life.

'I thought I'd call on Kingsway on the way back to the station. He obviously thought I'd twigged whatever it was he was up to, kicked me in the goolies and then did the old karate chop on the back of my neck. Good job I didn't get the karate chop on the throat like Farnsworth otherwise I'd be brown bread.'

'How much of his story did you hear?'

'From the bit about him losing his job on the oil rigs.'

Horton told him the rest, and about Marion and Ian Keynes; by the time he'd finished they'd reached the entrance. Kingsway was awake and groaning.

'What did you find out about Peter Ebury?' asked Horton, sucking in the air and thinking that the biting wind had never felt better or the sea smelt sweeter.

'He was set up for that robbery. Oh, he did it all right, no question about that, but he did it with someone's blessing or so Ludlow, the prisoner he fought with on the day he died, told me. The man was shit scared. He asked me for protection. I told Anston.'

And Anston had passed that on to DC Lee. But it was too late. Ludlow knew what fate was in store for him or his family.

Cantelli said, 'I knew my notes didn't tally with those official case notes. Peter was too cocky. I'd written that down when I arrested him. He said, "I've got powerful friends, they'll take care of me." Someone had told Peter they'd make sure he would get off. Only he didn't because this person wanted Peter Ebury safely locked away, and his mother to keep her mouth shut otherwise her son would die. I guess he said the same to Peter; that his mother would die if he so much as whispered a name.'

'And when Peter learns that his mother is dead, he goes to the governor with his information and a request that he be given protection.'

'I guess so.'

The only problem with that, Horton thought, was it didn't tie in with the Intelligence Directorate's surveillance on the Rest Haven which began on 29 December, two days before Irene died.

Cantelli said, 'When I confronted Ludlow with this, he admitted that he'd been told to silence Peter Ebury.'

Horton said, 'Irene tried to keep quiet, but when her mind

began going back to the good old days, then the fires in her flat started.'

'Deliberate?'

'Probably, and that was what Lee was trying to discover when she visited social services. Whoever was threatening Irene decided it might be best to put her away somewhere where everyone thought she was senile anyway and take no notice of her. They must have known she had the beginnings of dementia, which means that someone was keeping a close eye on her.'

'Who do you reckon it is?'

'No idea, but Buckland, the ex-copper, probably knew, which was why Peter Ebury was told to kill him and make it look like a robbery. Peter was their hit man and their fall guy. That's my theory anyway.' And Horton thought it might also be Lee's.

Cantelli looked worried. 'There is something else. I searched Buckland's flat with DCI Crampton, but I got called away. He claimed he didn't find anything, but I'd jotted down that he seemed excited about something. Two days later his boy got run over and Crampton went on compassionate leave. As I said, Jempson took over, but we'd already charged Ebury and Mayfield, and the case was sewn up. When Crampton came back to work, he was different. Quieter, edgy. Everyone put it down to his being upset about his boy. But I'm not so sure now. I think he might have found something in Buckland's flat and someone didn't want him to expose what it was.'

Horton felt sorry for Crampton if this was the truth, and angry that a good police officer could have been threatened into silence. Did Lee and her boss know this? If not should he say anything? He looked at Cantelli. If he did it would mean dragging him into it and he didn't want to put Cantelli or his family at risk.

'We'll leave that to Lee and her colleagues.'

Cantelli looked about to protest, then must have read something in Horton's expression because he nodded solemnly and said, 'If you say so, Andy.'

There was a short pause, pregnant with all their unspoken thoughts about extortion, blackmail, and cover-ups, before Horton nodded at the recumbent figure of Steven Kingsway. 'You'd better formally charge him.'

'He's your collar.'

'No, he's yours. You earned it. Get a patrol car here to collect him. And call Charlotte.'

Stepping aside Horton rang Uckfield.

'Where the fuck are you?'

'That's no way to greet an old friend. I'm fine and so is Sergeant Cantelli. Thanks for asking.'

Uckfield grunted, as Horton continued. 'We're at Fort Cumberland, and Cantelli has arrested Steven Kingsway for the murder of Daniel Collins, Nicholas Farnsworth and Nathan Lester.'

'Who the hell is Kingsway?' Uckfield cried in exasperation.

'It's a long story, but DC Lee might be able to tell you.' Horton rang off. To Kingsway he said, 'Hope you like prison food.'

Kingsway made no reply.

Stretching his hands into Kingsway's pockets, Horton retrieved the keys to the security gates, and ran down to let the patrol car inside. Returning, he said to Cantelli, 'How's Charlotte?'

'Angry and relieved. Thanks, Andy.'

'What for?' Horton exchanged a smile with Cantelli. He felt tired now that the adrenalin surge was easing off. He was also heartily thankful. He couldn't imagine a world without Barney Cantelli.

'Aren't you coming?' Cantelli said, climbing into the back of the patrol car. Kingsway was sandwiched between him and a uniformed officer.

'No, there's something I've got to do first.'

TWENTY-THREE

Horton collected the Harley and rode across to the marina. There was still a great deal unexplained, such as who had stolen Irene Ebury's belongings? Who had Peter Ebury threatened to expose? And how much did the Intelligence Directorate know about his mother? Did she figure in their investigations?

He stared down at the boats. There was a light shining in the cabin on Daisy's boat. He thought of that determined chin, the neat little figure and her quick incisive brain. It would be nice to have some female company and to talk over some aspects of the case. He was certain Daisy would find Steven Kingsway fascinating. Then he reminded himself that while Daisy was a psychologist, she was not the police one. *And* he didn't fancy being analysed. He couldn't divulge the details of the case anyway; it could hinder Kingsway's trial.

A car pulled in behind him. A door slammed, footsteps, then someone was standing beside him. He turned to find a tall, slender man in his early fifties with silver hair and keen grey eyes, wearing an expensive raincoat over an immaculately tailored suit.

'Detective Chief Superintendent Jack Sawyer,' he introduced in a voice as smooth as chocolate but not so appealing. He flourished a warrant card which Horton barely glanced at. He didn't need to read it to know that this was the head of the Intelligence Directorate. His eyes travelled to the car where DC Lee was sitting in the front passenger seat. In the rear was a man in his early forties with close-cropped brown hair, wearing a green waxed jacket and an inscrutable expression.

'How much do you know?' asked Sawyer. His attitude was polite but restrained.

'Not as much as you, sir,' replied Horton, which won him a smile of sorts.

'We still don't know who Peter Ebury was protecting. Have you any idea?'

'Me? Why should I know?' It was evident to Horton that Sawyer knew about his mother having worked with Irene Ebury. Again he wondered how much more Sawyer knew about Jennifer Horton and her disappearance. He desperately wanted to ask, but knew he couldn't because even if he kept his expression void and his voice bland, a sharp-eyed man like Sawyer would see the pain inside him. And he didn't want anyone to know how much it hurt. Betraying vulnerability led to exploitation. He'd learnt that the hard way in his youth. He said, 'Pity the prisoner who attacked Peter Ebury is dead. He could have told you.'

'Yes, and if Sergeant Cantelli hadn't paid him a visit he might still be alive.'

'You should have spoken to him sooner instead of hanging on our coat-tails.' Horton knew that the Intelligence Directorate had specialist teams focusing on prison intelligence. They'd probably been monitoring Peter Ebury for months, years even.

Horton asked, 'Did Mayfield, Peter's accomplice, know that the armed robbery was a put-up job?'

'I don't think so. He was rather simple and worshipped the ground Peter Ebury walked on.'

Horton knew that; Cantelli had told him. He wondered now if Mayfield had died of natural causes, or whether he too had been eliminated.

He said, 'It would have been simpler to have killed Buckland without setting up the armed robbery and then disposed of Peter.'

'Not for Zeus.'

'Who?' Horton asked surprised, racking his brains trying to recall the name before swiftly realizing it was a code name. His theory had been right then. This Zeus was the master criminal who the Intelligence Directorate were after, and he had a connection with Irene Ebury and her son Peter. And what about Jennifer? Had she known this Zeus? Horton scrutinized Sawyer for some sign that perhaps she had, but Sawyer's expression was giving nothing away.

'We call him Zeus because he wields his thunderbolts to control his family of crooks,' Sawyer said.

'Didn't do classics at my comprehensive school,' Horton said cynically.

'Zeus wanted Peter out of the way, but he also wanted him alive.'

'Because Peter was one of his troublesome sons, as a result of his affair with Irene Ebury.'

'I thought you didn't do classics.'

'I'm a detective. I worked it out. So Zeus offered Peter a big pay-off, a good solicitor and a reprieve on appeal if he proved his worth and shot Buckland. Only Peter didn't get what he was promised. When he didn't, Irene Ebury started threatening to talk about the good old days, so her flat was set on fire a couple of times, but she managed to escape unhurt. It was probably only a warning to them both anyway. If Zeus had wanted her dead there would have been no escaping. Peter was told that Zeus would leave Irene alone if he kept his mouth shut and served his time like a good boy. If he didn't, then they'd kill him and his mother.'

Sawyer said nothing, but Horton knew he was right. 'And then Irene conveniently got dementia and was pushed into a rest home.' Horton watched Lee climb out of the car. 'But what Zeus didn't realize was that as the dementia progresses the patient begins to remember more of the past, not less of it. Not that it really mattered because everyone dismissed what Irene was saying anyway. So who did you have in the Rest Haven listening to her rambles?'

Lee answered. 'Claire Butler. She's a DC. We pulled her out on the third of January, two days after Irene died. There didn't seem much point in her staying on.'

And that was what Angela Northwood had meant when she had said she was a care assistant down: *wretched woman didn't show up for work yesterday or today and there's no word from her.*

'And you were just calling off your surveillance on the fifth of January when Cantelli and I arrived. What alerted you to staging the surveillance in the first place, Inspector Lee? It is inspector, isn't it?

'Yes.'

She gave him a hesitant smile, which he didn't return. It wasn't her fault, he told himself. She was just doing her job, but he didn't like being deceived.

She said, 'When Peter's mother went into the nursing home, Peter kept quiet for a couple of years working out how he could expose Zeus and still live to tell the tale. Of course we knew nothing about Zeus then . . .'

'And do you now?'

Sawyer answered. 'We're a couple of steps further forward, thanks to Peter.'

Horton knew that Sawyer wouldn't say anything more, but whatever this Zeus had done, and still did, it had to be a serious international crime, and a sophisticated large-scale one for the Intelligence Directorate to be involved.

Lee said, 'Early in December Peter was told that his mother was getting worse. That it wouldn't be long before she died.'

'Who told him that?' Horton asked sharply. That certainly wasn't what Angela Northwood had said and though Dr Clayton had said Irene had clogged lungs and arteries, death hadn't been imminent.

As if he'd never spoken, Lee said, 'Peter thought that now might be the time to put his plan into action.'

'I bet he did,' Horton muttered, 'with a little prompting from you.'

'On the twenty-first of December Peter asked to see the governor. He told Geoff Welton that he knew someone the police would dearly love to get their hands on and he was prepared to tell them who it was in return for a new identity, money and a fresh start overseas. Geoff Welton had been primed that this might happen one day. He contacted us immediately. We arranged, through Mr Welton, a visitor to talk to Ebury in the governor's office where Ebury was brought after trashing his cell. There we did a deal with Ebury, but he wasn't going to tell us Zeus's identity until we had given him a new identity and a fresh start overseas.'

Would they have gone so far as letting out a man convicted of murder? wondered Horton. He reckoned so. 'You strung Ebury along.'

Sawyer answered. 'For a while, yes. We told him we were arranging it and we put a surveillance operation on his mother and DC Butler into the home.'

Then the light dawned on Horton. He tensed with anger and swivelled his hard gaze between them. 'Then you let the word out that Peter was ready to talk. Just so you could see who showed up at the nursing home, only when he did, you cocked it up. You missed him. Where was your precious DC Butler? On the day shift, I guess. And you had no one on night duty except you, Inspector Lee, and waxed-jacket over there.'

Silence. Horton knew that these two were never going to admit failure. He felt angry for Irene Ebury. She hadn't deserved to be used as bait. He knew the stakes were high and that to catch scum you had to think and sometimes act like scum, but Inspector Lee had fallen down on her job. And he could see that she knew it.

Stiffly Horton continued. 'When the staff were drinking to celebrate New Year's Eve, one of Zeus's operatives entered the Rest Haven from the back gardens on to the flat-roof kitchen extension and in through the landing window, the only one in the house that isn't double-glazed. Then all he had to do was climb the remaining stairs, dart into Irene's room and kill her.'

'There's no evidence of that,' Lee snapped. 'Irene Ebury died of natural causes.'

'Like Peter Ebury, supposedly,' scoffed Horton. 'She could have been injected with air, or she awoke and was frightened to death. Maybe Mrs Kingsway really did see someone, and her son used it as a reason to disguise his own bullying of his frail elderly mother.'

It also meant that the intruder had known the layout of the

Rest Haven and where Irene Ebury had slept so he must have visited there, perhaps posing as a workman or relative. On New Year's Eve he had taken advantage of the fact that the staff would be drinking to slip in and kill Irene.

'Did you know about the prescription fraud?' he asked and saw that they did. 'You thought Daniel Collins was involved in that, and that his death was just an unfortunate accident until his mother refused to believe it. Then you wondered if he had been Zeus's eyes and ears all the time. The surveillance had been called off, but by working with me, Inspector Lee, you could follow up that lead. Well, Daniel Collins was killed by Steven Kingsway.' And he told them of Kingsway's confession. Neither Lee nor Sawyer showed any emotion or reaction. He finished by asking who had stolen Irene's belongings.

Inspector Lee answered. 'There was nothing in them. DC Butler had already been through them, but we didn't take them.'

So Irene's killer had probably seen how lax Marion Keynes was in keeping her office locked, or he'd managed to take impressions of the keys to the basement.

'And there was no photograph or mention of your mother,' Sawyer said.

Horton tensed. He wondered how long they had known about Irene's link with his mother. He wasn't going to ask though and give them the satisfaction of seeing his curiosity. He also wondered if Sawyer was telling the truth. He wouldn't put it past him to lie.

Coldly he said, 'You told Peter Ebury about his mother's death on New Year's Day. He knew he was next. He was relying on you to get him out, but again you were too late.'

And Sawyer didn't much like him saying that. Well, tough. Horton guessed that Sawyer had taken Peter Ebury's belongings from the prison and had left only those two photographs, which he had deemed to have no significance, and no chance of leading Horton to Zeus.

'Have you found the social worker who helped Irene to move?' he asked. 'Naomi Bennett.'

Lee threw a glance at Sawyer, who nodded. 'She says Irene took what few letters and photographs she had with her. The rest of her furniture went to a second-hand dealer.'

He didn't believe it. 'How did Peter find out who his father was?'

Sawyer said, 'He says his mother finally told him.'

Maybe she did, Horton thought, but he couldn't believe a word these two told him. 'Haven't you traced Irene's whereabouts during those missing years – 1963 to 1973?'

Surely that would reveal Zeus's identity. Maybe it had, but the Intelligence Directorate, and whatever other agency they were working in co-operation with, didn't have enough evidence to bring him in and certainly not to convict him.

'We're working on it.' Sawyer smiled, but his eyes were as hard as marbles.

'So what happens now?'

'We carry on. And you can help. We know that Irene Ebury worked with your mother in the casino and that your mother disappeared in November 1978. Zeus could be responsible for that.'

'I doubt that. Irene knew this man before then. She returned to Portsmouth when she was pregnant with Peter.'

'She could still have confided in Jennifer.'

She could have done, but Horton fervently hoped not. Now he knew the reason why Inspector Lee had been assigned to his team and DCI Bliss seconded elsewhere. When Lee had seen him arrive at the Rest Haven, and when word had got back to Sawyer that he had been to the prison enquiring about Peter Ebury's death, Sawyer thought that Horton might lead him to Zeus, or at the least uncover some fresh information. Bliss had wanted him to drop the case, but Sawyer didn't and he needed someone on the inside. Horton wondered how much Superintendent Reine and Uckfield had been told.

Sawyer continued, confirming Horton's thoughts. 'The fact that your mother disappeared makes us think she knew something about Zeus. If he knows that you're alive and making inquiries, then you might help flush him out.'

Horton laughed mirthlessly. 'And be killed in the process? No, thanks.'

Sawyer remained silent. Horton stared across the marina. He knew what was being left unspoken, which was if he helped then he might discover what had really happened to his mother on that November day in 1978. If this Zeus was ruthless enough to kill, or have someone kill Irene and her son, Peter, and no doubt many others, then Horton knew he wouldn't think twice about threatening to kill him and even killing Emma. His stomach tightened. The world felt bleak and hostile.

Sawyer said, 'You would be posted to our team as a DCI.'

Horton's eyes swivelled to Lee. He didn't think she'd like that much, but again her expression gave nothing away. He turned back to face Sawyer. First Uckfield had promised him acting DCI on his team and now this. But Uckfield had made promises before and hadn't kept them and Uckfield's promise came with the condition that he give up fighting for regular access to Emma. Now Sawyer was offering him a higher prize and his conditions meant he could lose his life and possibly Emma's into the bargain.

In the silence came the whistle of the cold wind through the halyards. Whatever the prize and the promise it was something he could never accept. Emma's safety meant the world to him. If his mother had known Zeus, and had been going to meet him on the day she disappeared, then there was no doubt in his mind what had happened to her.

'My mother's dead,' he said. 'And my daughter's alive. I'd like to keep it that way.'

Sawyer swiftly turned and climbed into the car. Lee followed him without a backward glance. Horton watched the car until the tail lights disappeared. He climbed on his Harley. He'd be glad to get back to the station, and some kind of sanity, even if it did mean listening to DC Walters grumbling and Steven Kingsway's twisted reasoning behind him killing three people. But there was somewhere he had to go first and two people he had to see.

He swung off the seafront and headed for Bristol Road to tell Mr and Mrs Collins they'd been right about their son Daniel.